The String Games

Shelagh

The String Games

Gail Aldwin

All best
Gail Aldwin .

Victorina Press
www.victorinapress.com

The String Games
© Gail Aldwin

First published in the United Kingdom (2019) by
Victorina Press
Adderley Lodge Farm,
Adderley Road,
Market Drayton, TF9 3ST,
England

Typesetting and Layout: Heidi Hurst
Cover Art and Design: © Fiona Zechmeister
Photograph of author: ©Peter Roe

British Library Cataloguing in Publication Data
A catalogue record for this book is available from the British Library.

ISBN: 978-1-9996195-1-0 (paperback)

Typeset in 11pt Adobe Garamond Pro
Printed and Bound in the UK by 4edge Limited.

For Shirley, Fran and John

An idea strikes. Imogen turns around on the stairs to hurry back, but strangers stand like prongs. She battles to reach the office where her time is spent jostling for projects and promotions. As she sprints to her desk, heads turn but Imogen ignores her colleagues. Her fingers slip on the keyboard and she has to retype the password. Breath churns from deep in her lungs and her heart beats like a hammer. Why didn't she think of this before? She turns the screen, not wanting anyone to see what she's doing. It's a private matter. While she waits for the browser to load, she glances through the rain-stained window to the Thames. Water rucked like a crinkled cloth brings to mind a recurring image from her childhood. A little boy with wet hair shivers, wearing only his trunks. She wants to reach for him, press her arms around his shoulders, draw him into a hug. A big sister should keep her brother safe.

Typing his name will bring up the usual lilac lettering that tells Imogen she's used the same search term time and again. Her stomach knots like a ball of string. Determined to continue, she enters the name of the girl she used to be into the search bar: Nim Mashard. Clasping her hands, she waits to see whether this will locate new information about Josh's case.

PART ONE

Cat's Cradle
Thirteen years earlier

Nim peeled the glossy cover of the road atlas from her legs and shoved the book into the door pocket. Winding the window handle, she made the glass disappear into the panel and gusts of air pummelled her ears, drowning Josh's chatter from the back seat. Beside the road, puffs of dust turned the colours grimy. Trees were limp under the sun and yellowing banks of grass needed a good cut. There weren't any pavements in this part of France, so a man with caramel skin dragged his box on wheels at the roadside. His springy hair was layered with a scattering of dirt. Lifting his hand to wave, he stepped into the path of the car and Mum swerved, making the tyres shriek and sending Nim jolting forward. The engine spluttered and stopped, leaving the car pointing at some bushes.

'Bloody idiot.' Mum sank her head to the steering wheel. 'Thank Christ I missed him.'

Nim moved her seat belt to stop it digging into her shoulder.

'All his stuff's gone in the road.' Josh could see everything from his booster seat. 'Let's go and help.'

'You stay here.' Mum yanked her door open and left it hanging like a broken wing. She bent to pick up packages that had skidded towards the car.

Josh scrambled across the front seats and leaned out for a better view. 'I think they're football shirts. See, the man's folding a red one.'

'Wait,' said Nim, but Josh jumped out of the car and darted to grab one of the shirts that had ripped from its packaging. He held it against his chest, but the hem came down so far it looked more like a dress.

'Get back in the car,' Mum yelled, making Nim glad she had stayed put.

'It's a bit big for me,' said Josh.

Mum snatched the football shirt. 'Do as you're told, Josh.'

As soon as Mum turned, Josh dashed to pick up another shirt, but this time he took steady steps towards the man and offered it to him like a gift. The man grunted and piled the last of the shirts Mum had collected into the ripped cardboard box and secured the lot with an elastic snake. Mum mumbled something Nim couldn't hear and she gave Josh a push, sending him in the direction of the car.

'I want a football shirt.' Josh squeezed through the front seats back to his place.

'You know what Mum says: askers don't get.'

'But he's got loads.'

'Doesn't mean one of them is for you. Keep quiet now, Mum's on her way.'

Mum flopped into the driver's seat like she was made of rubber. The fob on the key chain clunked as she turned the engine on. 'That was a close call.'

'Is the man okay?' asked Nim.

'Of course he is,' said Mum.

They followed faded signs that showed the words Le

Camping, and Nim realised they must be very close. After passing another bundle of trees and a rock the size of a dog's kennel, there came a sign that pointed left. The car wriggled along a drive and went past a picnic area where families sat in the shade. Nim stretched her neck to gawp at the old men who were chucking silver balls onto the ground.

'What are they doing?' asked Nim.

'It's called boules,' said Mum. 'Strange sort of game, but that's the French for you.'

Mum tugged the wheel and drew the car to a stop in front of a shop. She put her hands behind her head and opened her mouth so wide Nim could see a flash of metal fillings. It wasn't polite to yawn without covering your mouth, but the rules didn't always apply to adults.

'Would you believe it?' said Mum. 'Non-stop talking all the way here and Josh has finally nodded off.'

Nim turned to see her brother slumped against the window, his white-blond curls wet around his forehead. 'He's dead to the world.' Nim reached for his shorts and gave them a tug. Josh's head flopped to the side and his Thomas the Tank Engine fell from his lap.

'Let him sleep,' said Mum. 'I'll get the keys.'

Mum walked to a door labelled La Reception du Camping. Understanding the language was going to be easy. After the summer holidays, Nim would have proper lessons taught by a lady called Madame. That was one of the good things about going into Year Six at Whitlock Primary, and with Josh starting in Reception, she'd be able to keep an eye on him at playtime.

A ripping noise came from the back seat and Nim hoped the pong wouldn't carry. When the boys at school farted everyone thought it was funny, but Josh wasn't being rude; farting in his sleep didn't count. As the fumes hit, Nim crinkled her nose and grappled with the door to escape into the fresh air. She knew it wasn't a good idea to leave Josh on his own, but a few minutes wouldn't matter. Wandering over to where the road bent, she counted the caravans lined up in a row. There were twelve in the first section. Most were pea-coloured, with large windows to the front. She didn't know how much room there was inside, but staying in one might be a bit of a squash when Dee and Ella arrived.

Footsteps on the decking alerted Nim that Mum was on her way back and so she scrambled into the car. Kicking a half empty bottle of water between her feet, Nim pretended she'd been sat there all along. Mum lobbed a carrier bag onto the back seat.

'I've got some milk and some bread so we won't starve. One afternoon we can come down to the shop and buy ice creams.'

'That's a good idea,' said Nim.

Mum jangled the set of keys she'd collected and tossed them to Nim. 'And now for a tour of the campsite.'

Number fifty-six, or cinquante-six as Mum kept saying, was at the top of the hill. It didn't look special but when Mum parked the car she rubbed her hands together. 'Let's wake up Josh and get inside.'

The caravan was dark with the curtains drawn, but Nim could make out a table and found her way to a sofa shaped like the letter 'C'. Mum slid the folding doors along their tracks to find the bedrooms and opened the windows to get rid of the stuffy air.

'Where's my bed?' asked Josh.

'You're sharing a room with Nim and Ella. It's this way.'

Squeezing into the tiny space, Josh pointed to the bunk that crossed above the other beds. 'I want to sleep up there.'

'I suppose that's okay. So long as you lie still and don't bring the whole contraption down.'

'Cool.' Josh grabbed the ladder and clambered up the rungs. 'I expose this is the best place to sleep.'

Mum made her eyes go wide. 'You *suppose* right.'

'Can't I have a go, Mum?' asked Nim.

'The twin beds are for you and Ella.'

It wasn't fair but Nim knew better than to argue. 'Alright, then.'

'Who's Ella?' Josh lay on the mattress and chewed his thumb.

'Doh!' Nim curled her fingers and knocked her knuckles lightly against Josh's forehead. 'She's Dee's daughter. She wants to be a ballerina. And you must remember Dee.'

'Dee-dee, wee-wee,' said Josh.

'Mais oui,' said Mum. 'Oui means "yes" in French.'

'That's funny,' Josh giggled.

'We're going to have a great time,' said Mum.

'Why can't Dad come on holiday with us?' asked Josh.

'Let's not go over that again. We're collecting Dee and Ella from the airport in the morning. We'll have loads of fun. You wait and see.' Mum turned her back and left the room. She wasn't exactly angry but it was easy to tell she didn't want to talk about Dad.

'It'll be okay, Josh.' Nim tightened the muscles in her forehead, thinking of the best advice to offer. 'We're at Dad's for the weekend, soon as we get home.'

'But I wish Dad was here.' Josh held his legs in the air like a worn-out puppy.

'I know.' Nim gave his tummy a pat. 'So do I.'

'I need Blankey,' said Josh.

The yellow blanket always made Josh feel better and he spent hours stroking the silky edge. 'You wait here. I'll get it.'

The boot of the car was open and inside was a huge empty space because Mum had already lugged the bags into the caravan. Nim hunted about the back seat where Josh's toys were stashed. She found a couple of engines and slung his yellow blanket over her arm. Sticking out from under the passenger seat was the special zipped carrying case that held her scooter. Nim had sneaked it into the car when Mum wasn't looking and now she was having a job getting it out. It was always difficult trying not to show she preferred one birthday present over another. She'd worn the denim jacket Mum had bought on her tenth birthday a few times. The shoulders were embroidered with golden buttercups, but one go in the washing machine and the blue dye had leaked, turning the flowers green. The jacket wasn't so lovely after that, but the scooter Dad had given her remained special and shiny. He often said he couldn't afford much, not with paying the mortgage and finding rent for his flat, but he did his best.

Nim tried to disguise the scooter case by draping Josh's blanket over it, but Mum with her eagle eyes spotted it as soon as Nim stepped into the caravan.

'I told you not to bring that thing,' Mum snapped, the lines on her forehead turning sharp. 'Shove it under the steps and don't let me see you playing with it.'

The airport at Rodez had huge windows instead of brick walls. Dodging around the counters, Nim saw onto the runway where there were two aeroplanes. Over the loud speakers, an announcement gabbled and Nim didn't understand what the lady was saying. When the words came in English, they didn't make sense either.

'What does that mean?' asked Nim.

'It means Dee and Ella will be here soon,' said Mum. 'Let's go outside and watch the plane come in.'

Standing beside the fence, Josh pressed his face against the diamond wires and managed to stick his nose right through the gap. Mum was busy staring up at the clouds. At first the aeroplane seemed small enough to fit inside a Christmas cracker, but then it got closer and more real. When the wheels stuck out it was ready to land, and it bounced on the runway before stopping in the distance.

'It'll take a while to taxi back,' said Mum.

'I want to go in a taxi,' said Josh.

'No. I mean. It just takes time for the plane to get back.'

'Oh.' Josh screwed up his face and pushed his nose and his lips against the chain fence.

Mum grabbed Josh's shoulder and pulled him away from the fence. There were marks like ruler lines across his face.

'You're filthy. When will you ever learn?' Mum found a bottle of water in her bag but instead of taking a drink, she wet a tissue and rubbed Josh's face.

'That hurts,' Josh complained.

'What a dirty face!' Mum threw the tattered paper onto the ground. 'We'll have to find the toilets. You need a good scrub.'

'I don't want to go,' said Josh.

'Yes you do,' said Mum. 'I won't have you embarrassing me.'

After a going-over with soap and water in the ladies, Josh waited beside the dryers, his hands in his pockets, as if the whirr from the machines could hide him. Even with his chin pointed towards the floor, his red-raw face still showed.

Turning towards the mirror, Nim straightened her fringe so it lay flat against her forehead. The hazel flashes in her blue eyes were just like Dad's and a pleasing tingle ran through her bones at the thought. If only she wasn't stuck with a mole on her cheek. Pressing her finger over the mark, she stared at the face that would look much better without it. Mum said that a beauty mark confirmed she was pretty, but the girls at school made jokes about the bug squashed on her face.

Jets of air spouted from the air conditioning units, making it cool on the concourse. Mum took a path through the crowds and the children followed. They stopped beside a group of men who held bits of paper with names written in capital letters, like ROTH and WEBER.

'What are they doing?' Josh was brave asking a question, testing out whether Mum had forgiven him.

'They're drivers waiting to collect their passengers.' Mum's voice had returned to normal.

12

'We should've made a sign for Dee and Ella,' said Nim.

'There's no need. We'll recognise them straight away.'

'I won't,' said Josh.

He was risking it again but Mum didn't hear. She was too busy looking around, and the pointed heels on her sandals made her extra tall. Whenever the sliding doors separated, Mum gripped her hands together like she was praying. Then, as the people traipsed through and melted into the crowd, Mum turned her head from side to side again.

You couldn't miss Dee when she finally arrived. What a bloody dress! Nim allowed the thought to spin around her head. So long as she didn't actually say the words, Mum couldn't tell her off. She could've said blood-red dress instead but that wouldn't be the same. Nim made her lips turn upwards in one of her special smiles, the sort she used when she was pleased with herself. The trouble with making jokes inside her head was that no one knew she was being funny. Not that it mattered with what happened next. Dee fell out of the line and headed straight for Mum. She flung her arms out wide and Mum disappeared into the hug. A lady with a trolley almost ran into them because they were blocking the way.

'Attention!' The lady's voice was sharp.

'Sorry.' Mum stepped aside to make some room but she continued to hold Dee's hand and their arms were like a skipping rope ready to turn.

The lady tutted and pressed her lips together as if she'd zipped them shut. She moved the trolley backwards before turning it around.

'She's being rude.' Ella slid between the mums and pointed her toes like she was about to do a ballet turn.

'Take no notice,' said Dee. 'Silly old moo.'

'Shush,' said Mum. 'The children are listening.'

'Cool,' said Dee. 'Give us a high five, Josh.'

Josh slapped Dee's palm. 'How old are you?' he asked.

'Be quiet, Josh. You're not supposed to ask questions like that,' said Nim.

'I'm four years old and tall for my age,' said Josh. 'I expose you're surprised.'

Dee made her eyebrows wiggle like worms.

'Josh supposes he looks older,' Mum explained.

'Got ya.' Dee made a clicking noise from the side of her mouth. 'I've got a few years on you.'

'My mum's thirty-five,' said Josh.

'And I'm six.' Ella wasn't going to be left out.

'Now we've got that sorted, let's find the car,' said Mum.

Dee lifted the bag with straps onto her shoulder and released the handle on the suitcase to pull it. While the others took the steps, Nim walked with Dee down the ramp. It must have been hard going for Dee. Her face turned to the colour of squashed raspberries as she humped the luggage.

'Can I help?' Nim wanted to have a go with the suitcase on wheels.

'That's kind of you.' Dee passed the handle over and they walked together. 'I can see we're going to get along just fine.'

Dee dumped her stuff in the mums' room and dug through the suitcase to find Ella's swimming costume along with her own. Like the little children, Nim was lathered with sunscreen and she wore her swimsuit under her shorts. In her backpack, she carried the picnic blanket. Mum had the towels, and Ella sulked until all three Barbies were packed inside her purple patent satchel. What a gorgeous bag! Nim would have loved one of those but knew she'd have to be ever so good before Mum would buy a bag like that. Clever old Josh understood there'd be fresh sticks at the river and he agreed to leave the pile he'd collected by the door without fussing like Ella. Mum unfolded a map of the campsite. 'Shall we go by the road or trek across the campsite and through the fields?'

'Let's take the short cut,' said Dee. 'I'm always up for an adventure.'

They set off, Mum wearing a hat with a floppy brim that sent a shadow across her nose. It was easy going until the path turned uphill as they walked beyond the campsite. Dee's panting gave a rhythm, and Nim tried not to notice but Josh kept squiggling his eyebrows and staring in Dee's direction.

'Give us a minute.' Dee sank into the shade beside some bracken.

'Let's admire the scenery.' Mum twirled in a circle. There wasn't much to see, but clumps of clouds like shaggy sheep danced across the blue. 'That was tough going.'

'Not for me.' Josh ran to the bank and back.

'I'll sit for a bit.' Dee pulled a small bottle of water from the pocket of her rucksack. She took a few glugs then offered it around but no one else was thirsty.

'We need to follow the fence alongside that field,' said Mum.

'Thank God it's downhill from here.'

'Isn't it pretty?' said Mum. 'The way the ground and the sky meet. It's like a wavy line running across a flag.'

'Good job the finish line is in sight,' said Dee.

'It's hot.' Mum fanned her face.

'Why are we waiting?' Josh took Thomas the Tank Engine from his pocket and made his arm into a train track, running the engine along it.

Ella pulled the fuzzy heads off stems of grass. 'Mummy's ready.'

'Okay, okay.' Dee lurched to a standing position. 'Let's get moving.'

'Wait a minute. That field has livestock in it. I think there might be bullocks,' said Mum.

'Great,' said Dee. 'I'm the one wearing red. They'll make straight for me and I'll have to dive out of the way like a Spanish matador or risk being gored.'

'What are you talking about?' asked Josh.

'I wonder whether we should carry on walking or go back for the car,' said Mum.

'It can only be a bit further,' said Nim.

'Don't worry about me, Jenny. I'm fine now I've had a rest.'

16

'Dee go first,' said Josh.

'You want me to be a decoy so the bulls don't chase you.' Dee pointed her fingers like horns and held them on either side of her head. She scraped the ground as if her sandals had become hooves. All the time, she kept her eyes fixed on Josh.

'Yikes.' Josh hid behind Mum.

'There's no escape.' Dee tore after him, dashing around Mum like she was a swinging pole until they all collapsed. It was strange to see Mum messing around, and Nim couldn't help but join in the laughter. Dee's hooting was so loud even the herd turned to stare.

'Now they're looking at us,' said Ella.

'But they're not moving,' said Dee. 'This is our chance.'

The race through the field brought them to a five-bar gate. Josh climbed to the top while Nim and Ella stepped on for a ride. It was Dee who released the gate and, with an extra push, they went in a semicircle until the metal *donged* against a stone.

'That was fun,' said Josh. 'Let's do it again.'

'Don't be silly,' said Mum.

'Perhaps on the way back,' said Dee.

They continued along a chalky path which wound through some trees. It was good to be in the shade for a minute, sunlight speckling the ground. Nim walked the long way around a tangle of nettles, and as she jerked Josh away from a possible sting, she stumbled and fell.

'Ouch.' Nim gripped her knee not wanting to see the damage, but a slippery feeling told her there was blood. 'It hurts.'

'How d'you manage that?' Mum turned out her bag and

found a tissue. The others crowded around her like a rubber ring.

'Let me see.' Dee waved her bottle of water. 'This'll douse any germs. You'll be right in no time.'

'I don't want to look,' said Nim.

Dee prised away Nim's hand. Instead of watching what was going to happen next, Nim concentrated on a stone stuck into the path. The smooth white shape made it look like an egg. She felt dribbles of water running down her leg and Mum mopped up.

'Pity I don't have a plaster,' said Mum.

Nim inspected the graze. Red pinpricks marked an oval shape the size of a grape. 'It could be worse.'

'That's the spirit.' Dee held Nim's elbow, helping her up. 'Best let the air get to it.'

Nim tested the strength in her leg by taking a couple of small steps. 'It's still bleeding.'

Mum dabbed the tissue over again. 'Stop moaning. There's hardly a drop.'

'Can we go now?' said Josh.

Holding her leg straight, Nim hobbled and the others slowed their pace so that Nim could keep up. Ella buzzed around Dee, pestering for attention. Mum would've barked a warning or done a backwards count from five if Josh was being a nuisance.

Where the path widened, there was a view of the river. It rippled downstream, but some of the water curled off into a pool where the surface was flat and reflected the trees. At one side, rocks were stacked together like building blocks, and further along reeds spiked the air. A girl paddled knee-deep, holding a fishing net and swinging a bucket in her hand.

Nim watched the girl stagger out of the water and make for a picnic table where her parents sat. The mother's voice trumpeted a welcome as the girl took her place and the dad ripped lids from the food containers, ready for lunch.

'There's organisation for you. Trust a French family to show us up as shambolic.' Mum swung the beach bag onto the ground.

'This is a reconnaissance visit,' said Dee. 'We'll be more sorted next time.'

'Are we going to come again?' Nim crossed her fingers behind her back.

'That's more than likely. It's perfect. Just right for sunbathing.' Mum kicked off her flip-flops and buried her toes in the sand.

'C'est magnifique,' said Dee.

'Is this the seaside?' said Josh.

'There's water but there aren't any waves,' said Mum.

'That's because we're at a river,' said Nim.

'Isn't it nice? They've made it like a special beach for us,' said Mum.

'We need our buckets and spades,' said Josh.

'Next time,' said Mum.

Dee spread the blanket half in sunshine and half in shade. The adults lay down next to each other and there was a bit of space for Nim at the edge. She wished the mums would shove over and give her a bit more room but they were already shoulder-to-shoulder. If she said anything Mum would only get cross. Josh sat on the sand in his trunks with his legs turned out like fins.

'Dig-dig-dig.' He shovelled a hole. 'This quarry is big-big-big for Thomas to chug-chug-chug all the way round.

That's right. Go-go-go on the track.'

'What's he wittering about?' mumbled Dee.

'Don't ask me,' said Mum.

'He's made a circuit for his train.' Nim didn't need to look to see what he was doing but the tassels on the blanket were itching through her costume, so she sat up.

'I made a wonderful landscrape,' said Josh.

'Yeah,' said Nim.

Ella arranged her Barbies so that they were stretched out like the mums for sunbathing. She was fussing with their hair and taking off their shoes. Nim was bored with nothing to do.

'Can I go and have a look at the rocks over there?' she asked.

'Stay put with us.' Mum had her eyes closed and was talking into the air.

'She'll be fine, Jenny.' Dee turned onto her side and gave Nim a wink. 'She's a sensible girl. She won't go far.'

'Okay,' said Mum. 'So long as you stay close to base.'

Nim sprang to her feet. 'Thanks.'

'You have a good time,' said Dee.

The rocks were flat and dented in places. She planted her sweaty hand against the side. Grains spotted her palm but her handprint vanished in seconds. She tried again, wanting to leave a mark, but again her print disappeared. Nim blew away her breath, wishing she could ride on the great gush from her lungs. Instead, she found a secret staircase to climb. Stretching her arms and balancing on her good knee, she made her way to the highest point. Nim pressed her cheek against the rock. The stone was cold. Turning, she studied the tree and the branches that stretched around her. The tree murmured and waved its curly leaves. It was an oak; she knew this from the leaf collection at school. Around the branch nearest to the rocks was a rope which was wound like spaghetti over a fork into a neat bundle. It was strange seeing it there, as if the wood needed holding together.

Through a crack between the rocks, she watched Josh. He used a stick to make marks on the ground, and Ella had her Barbies doing the splits. Now stripped off, Mum wore a bikini, and she rolled onto her stomach so that Dee could put on sunscreen. It wasn't like the slap-dash the children suffered in a lathering. Dee gave sweeping strokes along Mum's spine, then she pressed her fingers in circles around her hips, making Mum spread her toes. A funny feeling crept into Nim's tummy like she'd swallowed a spider and it was making a web in there. It was wrong to spy, but Mum and Dee knew each other from way back and Nim wondered what it was like to have Dee as an old friend. Nim had always wanted a best friend, but she'd never behave like that.

When Nim returned to base, Dee was wearing a swimming costume. It was the sort of blue on the Union Jack. The skin on Dee's shoulders bulged over the straps and her arm wobbled when she lifted it to point.

'Let's go to the far side of that tree. It's the best place for a swim,' said Dee.

'Cool,' said Josh. 'Come on, Mum.'

Mum shook her head. 'You go ahead and have fun with Dee.'

'But I want you to join in.'

'No way,' said Mum. 'I don't like getting wet.'

Nim got to her feet. 'Just five minutes, Mum?'

'What d'you think you're doing?' Mum slapped Nim's

ankle. 'You're standing in my sun. Off you go with Dee and give me some peace.'

Nim rubbed the sore skin. There was no need for Mum to be nasty, especially as Nim already had a bad knee. She watched Dee set off, dragging the inflatable crocodile that had taken all Dee's breath to blow up. Ella did a pirouette. Nim wished she could do turns like that, but then Ella twirled and collapsed into a sit-down strike. Nim galloped to catch up.

'Mummy, lift.' Ella shot her arms in the air like she was so keen to answer a question she used both hands.

'I'm not picking you up, Ella. You're too old and too heavy for lifting,' said Dee.

'Not too old.' Ella pushed out her bottom lip but left her arms waving.

'Look at Josh. He's younger than you and he's made it to the edge of the water.'

Josh turned when he heard his name and stamped his feet in a warrior dance. His chest and legs were a milky strip divided by his blue trunks. He stretched one leg over the water, about to step in. Nim's heart leapt. It wasn't right. She should be first in the river. She was the one who knew about swimming. As if she were in the running races on Sports Day Nim shot forward, but her legs went bandy as she ploughed through the sand. When she caught up with Josh, he was ankle deep. Nim hopped in beside him and her feet sank. The oozy riverbed slurped her toes as if it were going to drag her into the freezing depths. She gave a shiver and looked into the water where the shaggy slime on the rocks waggled.

'Be careful getting in,' she called to Dee. 'It's cold and slippy.'

'How cold?' Making a splash, Dee stepped into the water and gave a yelp. 'That's freezing!' Dee's swimming costume was see-through around her middle and her belly button was a coin among the blubber. She might be whale-sized but she was fun, too. With the water sloshing their calves, they waited for Ella.

'Are you a good swimmer, Nim?' asked Dee.

'I go to classes every week and sometimes I do synchro.'

'Synchro?'

'Synchronised swimming.'

'Oh.' Dee clapped her forehead with the flat of her hand as if she were trying to wake up her brain. 'Those long legs make you just right for that sort of activity.'

'Thanks.' Nim smiled at the compliment. It was strange getting used to Dee; she didn't act like other adults.

Nim took Josh's hand and for once he didn't pull away. When Ella dashed into the water, they all moved further along the river. With the water reaching to the top of Josh's trunks, Nim knew they'd gone far enough.

'We'd better stop here – any further and we'll be out of our depths,' said Nim.

'Very sensible,' said Dee. 'You must get that from your mother.'

Dee gave a smile and a wink at the same time and Nim's blood ran warmer.

'As you're the expert at swimming, Nim, you'd better take control of this crocodile.' Dee landed the inflatable on the water and grabbed the head to stop it floating away.

'I go first.' Josh pushed Nim so that she stumbled and he grabbed the crocodile's head. 'He's called Crocshanks and he's mine.'

'He's not yours, Josh. You've got to share,' said Nim.

'You give me a hand, Nim,' said Dee. 'Hold the tail while the little children have a ride.' Dee gripped the snout for Josh to swing his leg over and he squeezed the rubber until the crocodile's eyes were about to pop.

'Try not to do that, Josh. You'll let out the air and we'll have a soggy croc,' said Dee.

'Soggy croc.' He wriggled and managed to sit up.

'Your turn next.' Dee dumped Ella behind Josh and she clung onto his shoulders. 'Mind how you go.'

The little children rolled off the crocodile, splashing into the water. As soon as Josh came to the surface, he dived back on, trying to keep his place at the front. Ella wasn't interested in another go now that she was spitting water, and she pulled Dee's arm, trying to drag her to the shore.

'Nim needs her turn.' Dee shook free from Ella's grip and Nim did a leapfrog onto the crocodile's back. Its tail flipped into the air but Nim held tight. Josh kept his head above water and they paddled in the shallows. Josh's foot bashed against Nim's ankle, time and time again. It didn't really hurt but she got the message: he wanted to play on his own. That was typical of Josh. He wanted Crocshanks to himself. It wasn't worth arguing – adults usually took Josh's side and she didn't want Dee to choose between them. Slipping away, Nim swam to the side and hid beside some reeds. Josh might miss her now she was gone.

Watching from her hiding place, it took Josh a long time to notice anything was different. When Crocshanks became grounded, Josh gave a land-ahoy cry and shook his fist in the air.

'That's all very well, Josh. But what have you done with

Nim?' Dee spoke in an extra loud voice.

'She goed back.' Josh pointed in the direction of the camp where Mum was sunbathing.

'I can't see her.' Dee held her hand to her forehead, shading her eyes.

'Must be.' Josh wasn't looking, he was more interested in getting mud off his foot, but he managed to spread the dirt over his other leg.

'Ella, have you seen Nim?'

Ella shook her head and kicked the sand. From her hideaway by the reeds, Nim covered her mouth to keep the laughter quiet.

'Don't tell me you've lost Nim! Can't I trust you children with anything? We'll have to go and search for her.' Dee stood between the little ones and held their hands, leading the way. 'Where d'you think she is? Behind the rocks, over the other side, or near the reeds?'

Nim took the hint and holding her nose she dived under the water. All was quiet beneath the surface. Nim shut her eyelids tight as if Velcro fastened them. When her ribs began to twang, she let out a few bubbles of air. Her ears made a cracking noise but she stayed in place. Finally, when her throat felt like it was being twisted, she sprang to the surface, splashing out of the water like a dolphin.

'There she is.' Josh waved his finger, pointing at Nim.

'I tricked you!' Water streamed down her face and Nim coughed.

'No you didn't,' said Josh.

'You had me fooled.' Dee gave a wink.

They plodded across the sand. Nim's swimming costume dripped water and her wet hair hung like string so that when she turned her head, it was like being whipped. She didn't deserve to be beaten, but that's how it felt. Mum was laid out like a plank, her spine ready to be walked upon by pirates, but even Josh wouldn't dare to step on her. She stayed flat as anything, not bothering to turn over when she spoke. 'Did you have a nice time?'

The answers came: yeah, yes, yeah.

Mum didn't say any more but Dee got busy with the towels. As she wrapped one around Nim's shoulders like a cloak, a thought took shape. If children were able to choose a mum, she might go for one a bit like Dee.

FOUR

It was Dee who was the first mum to get up in the morning. Her pyjamas were creased but she went onto the deck and didn't care if anyone saw her. She left the breakfast bowls in the sink without washing them up and challenged the little children to a race to see who could get dressed fastest.

'Now they're sorted, how about you take Ella and Josh to the park?' said Dee.

'That's a good idea.' Nim puffed her chest like a peacock, proud of being asked to help.

'You enjoy the morning,' said Dee. 'C'est magnifique!'

The little children began by holding hands, but it wasn't long before Ella started dillying and dallying. Josh got bored with waiting for Ella to pick daisies so he wandered towards the shop where there was an orange Reliant Robin that looked like a wedge of cheese.

'Have a look around the back of the car, see if there's a GB sticker,' called Nim.

'What's that?' he asked, trying to stop himself from touching the car now.

'It shows the car's from Britain.' Nim enjoyed the fact that Josh was a bit of an idiot sometimes.

'I can't see.' He was too busy turning his head sideways and pulling faces in the wing mirror.

From the corner of her eye, Nim spotted a man with a newspaper tucked under his arm. He was walking towards the car. She didn't want Josh to get a telling off for hanging around. 'Come back now, Josh. The driver's on his way.'

Josh took long strides like his legs were poles. 'D'you think his name's Robin?'

'How should I know! Just come back here.'

Josh ran the last few steps and the man tipped the brim of his hat with a pointed finger.

'Let's get to the park,' said Nim. 'Before you get us into trouble.'

To keep the two of them in order, Nim gave chase, swishing her hands through the air as she rushed them around the shower block and into the playground. The place was deserted: the swing seats were empty and the top of the slide poked up like the point of a pyramid. Boggled by the space, Josh crept around as if searching for trouble. It was Nim who spotted the boy first, sprawled on the bench like he'd spent the night there. A baseball cap covered his face but the ends of his hair curled around his chin.

'It's rude to take up all the seat like that.' Ella jabbed a finger at him.

'He's dead.' Josh used a gurgling voice. 'No water.'

'Don't be silly,' said Nim.

'My mummy says you have to keep drinking water in the heat or you'll shrivel,' said Ella.

'You can drink squash if you want,' said Nim. 'Anyway, he's not shrivelled.'

'His face is.' Josh crouched, trying to sneak a look behind the cap.

'You don't know that, Josh. You're making it up,' said

Nim. 'If you look carefully, you can see he's breathing. Watch his T-shirt – his chest is going up and down. He must be asleep.'

'We should tell my mummy. She'd know what to do.'

'We don't have to do anything, Ella! You go and play with Josh. I'll stay and watch him. Make sure nothing happens.' Nim stood with her legs crossed, one over the other. This was a comfortable position whenever she was left to wait. She always stood like that when her class had to line up ready to go in for lessons. One of the boys called her a flamingo, like she was balanced on one leg, but that didn't bother Nim. She was good at ignoring boys when they were being stupid.

Ella darted towards the slide and gripped the rail so that it was impossible for Josh to get in front. He followed Ella up the ladder, closing the gap between them. When she reached the top Ella sat and hugged her knees waiting for him to sit behind. Josh shoved Ella and she squealed all the way down the slide, then she sat waiting for him at the bottom. Following her in a headfirst position, Josh stretched his arms and gave her a bump that sent her flying. She landed in a heap and, for a minute, Nim thought she might cry. Instead she dusted her hands and made a dash for the ladder. The chase around the slide began again.

Fishing in her pocket, Nim fingered her coil of rainbow string. It was always good to have something to play with, especially when the girls at school wanted to do handstands and they left Nim out. She never cared, so long as she had her string. She could make the figure of a witch's hat without any bother, gripping the point of the triangle between her teeth and stretching out the base. A cup of tea shape usually went right, too. As she hooked the string between her fingers, something sharp in her pocket scratched her skin. She realised it was the edge of a five pound note where she'd folded the corners sharply. Having the fiver gave Nim a sense of being superior. Josh could never be trusted with money: he'd either lose it or waste it. No wonder Dad put her in charge of the holiday spending.

Ella squealed for attention but Nim wasn't interested in watching the little children. Instead, she took a step sideways and slid onto the bench. The boy pointed his knees like an arrow to the sky so that Nim could sit more comfortably. She edged a little closer to him. Of course he was alive. She waited for another sign and this time he grabbed his cap, throwing it like a Frisbee onto the ground. Nim strolled over and picked it up. She flapped the cap against her hip and when she returned to the bench, he was sitting properly.

'Here's your cap.' Nim dropped it on his head and sat beside him.

'Merci.' He turned the visor to the back of his neck and cranked his eyes wide open. His expression made Nim laugh so loudly that Josh stopped in his tracks. After racing down the ladder, he ran over.

'He's alive,' Josh announced. 'What's his name?'

'I don't know – why don't you ask him?'

'WHAT'S YOUR NAME?' Josh shouted. The boy shrugged and Josh tried again. 'MY NAME IS JOSH.' He stabbed a finger at his chest with each word.

'Stop shouting, Josh!' said Nim. 'You know it's rude to shout.'

'He can't talk. He's losted his voice.'

'No, he hasn't. He's already said something to me.'

'What did he say?'

'Merci.'

'Me-see? What d'you see?'

'Stop being stupid, Josh. Just ask him nicely.'

The boy had a grin on his face, as if he was enjoying the argument between the two of them. 'Hallo, Josh.'

Josh took a step backwards, amazed.

'I Maxime,' the boy continued.

'Maxime?'

'Oui. Yes. I. Maxime.' The boy talked as if each word was bouncing on a trampoline.

'My neighbour's got a cat called Maxime. It's a black cat and it's got whiskers.'

'All cats have whiskers.' Nim walked over to Josh and tapped her brother's head. He didn't have a parting but his hair fell away from a tiny patch of skin, which Nim knew was called the crown.

'Maxime drinks water from puddles and lives at number eight. He's very good at catching birds. He wiggles his tail and jumps on them. A cat carries dead animals in its mouth.'

'Be quiet, Josh,' said Nim. 'You're talking too much.'

'My neighbour's cat catches birds and mice but he never eats them. My mum calls him killer cat but I don't. I call him Maxime.'

'Yes. A. Cat. Miaow.' The boy curled his fingers into claws and scratched the air.

'That's right,' said Josh.

The boy folded his arms and didn't say any more. Josh sat beside him, crossing his arms as well. When that wasn't enough, he crossed his legs too. This made Maxime smile.

'Let me sit down. I'm older and more sensible than you,' said Nim.

As if in slow motion, Josh collapsed onto the ground and lay there like an injured football player.

'Josh okay?' asked Maxime.

'He's messing about,' said Nim. 'He likes to be the centre of attention.'

'And me.' Ella collapsed on the ground next to Josh.

It was typical for the little children to show her up. She pressed her hand into her pocket and touched the five pound note. There was an idea.

'How about we buy ice creams at the shop?'

Josh sprang to his feet. 'I'm starving.'

It was only a little while since he'd scoffed a bowl of cereal, but he was always hungry.

'Me, too,' Ella joined in.

'Want to come?' Nim asked Maxime. She guessed the money would pay for four ice creams and she didn't want to leave without him.

Maxime shrugged. 'I go friends.'

'We're your friends,' said Josh.

'I go.' Maxime pointed to where some older boys were hanging around the shower block.

'They're smoking,' said Ella.

'Are they bad boys?' Josh screwed up his face.

Maxime laughed. 'Bad boys. Yes. Very bad.'

'We'd better go.' Nim didn't need Josh embarrassing her any more. She grabbed his hand and tugged him away.

'Bye-bye, Maxime,' said Josh.

Nim eyed Maxime through the strands of her fringe. 'See you again.' She wasn't going to let Josh have the last word.

'Goodbye.' Maxime fixed his cap on the right way and ran at full speed towards his mates.

32

'Trust you, Josh,' said Nim.

'What d'you mean?'

'Oh, never mind!' Nim stood stock-still as Maxime chased over the grass and bounded up to the boys. A cheer went up when he arrived and there was lots of backslapping.

'What are you looking at?' asked Josh.

Nim didn't reply. She concentrated her energy on watching Maxime.

'It's rude to stare,' said Josh. 'You're a rudey-pudey.'

'Shut up,' said Nim. But Josh didn't keep quiet. He went on muttering 'rudey-pudey' as if it were the funniest joke in the world. Although she was annoyed, Nim let Josh get away with it. At times like this, he was best ignored.

At the ice cream kiosk, a lady carrying a toddler was at the front of the queue.

'Bonjour, Madame.' She sang out a greeting to an assistant wearing a hairnet who replied in the same way. 'Bonjour, Madame.'

Josh sniggered with his hand over his mouth like something was very funny. He was behaving like a bit of an idiot, again. When it was their turn to be served, Josh bashed his finger at the glass cabinet, pointing to the vanilla. It might be easy to read words in French but it wasn't so easy to talk. Nim nodded at the lady and stuck three fingers in the air. It was easiest to order the same flavour but that didn't stop Ella from moaning. She was lucky to have an ice cream at all, seeing as Dad's money was meant for Nim and Josh. When the first cone was topped with a white wig, Nim passed it to Josh and the next went to Ella. When the last one arrived, Nim gave the lady the money.

'Non, non, non!' The assistant shook her head and wagged a finger.

Nim stood there. The little children licked their cones while ice cream ran onto Nim's hand. What was the matter?

'Zis English.' The assistant spat the words.

'Yes.'

'Non, non, non!'

'Is something wrong?' It was a relief to hear an English voice. The man had a tanned forehead and lines showed on his cheeks when he smiled.

'I don't know,' said Nim. 'My dad gave me the money as a going away present.'

'He should've given you francs. Never mind. Let me get these.' He passed the assistant a brown note and returned the five pounds to Nim. 'Save that for a treat when your holiday's over – you can spend it back in the UK.'

'I'm not sure.'

'It's not a problem. Let me do you a favour. Your dad would do the same in this situation, I'm sure.'

'Hmm.' Nim didn't know what to say. She'd been told not to talk to strangers, but it was too late. Josh crunched the last of his cone.

'What's your name?' asked Josh.

'Shush,' said Nim. Josh had been warned as well, but the man didn't look like a stranger. He wore a shiny top, and Nim hoped Josh wasn't going to say anything about football shirts.

'I'm Geoff,' he said.

'What's your job?' said Josh. 'And where did you get that shirt?'

'Too many questions,' said Nim.

'Don't worry. I know what boys are like. I've got nephews.

34

They're toddlers at the moment but I bet they'll be the same as Josh one day.'

'When I was little, I wanted to be a tractor,' said Josh. 'But now I want to be a policeman.'

'Interesting career choice,' said Geoff.

'We live at Sank-on-Seas,' said Josh.

'Sank-on-Seas?' Geoff repeated.

'He means fifty-six in English,' Nim corrected, but realising she'd probably said too much, she elbowed Josh. 'We need to go.'

'Goodbye.' Josh scampered to the steps, where he turned.

'You can come to my place any time you want ice cream. My freezer is full of it,' said Geoff. 'Just look for the caravan with the yellow door along the road from here.'

'Okay.' Josh skipped down the steps.

FIVE

On an errand taking rubbish to the bins, Nim discovered a piece of smooth tarmac tucked behind the trees. Making a return trip to check out the space, she found it was a shady spot, the perfect place to practise her scooter skills. Nim put her good knee on the ground to unzip the special carrying case. A scab had formed on her other leg from her fall, and although she was tempted to loosen the edges, she knew better than to pick. Besides, a chance to play on the scooter was much more interesting. There weren't many scooters as good as Nim's, with metal wheels that looked like hubcaps on a car. Nim organised the handlebar as Dad had shown her, allowing the metal to slide into place and turning the clip to hold it securely.

It was good to be alone without Josh bothering her for a change. Nim remembered how Dad had chased her down the road when the scooter was brand new, but the game had to stop when his coughing got too much. Instead, he took a photograph. Dad said it was important to mark the occasion of Nim's tenth birthday. Wearing her new denims, she stood straight and tall, but Josh's head stuck out from behind her at an angle. Trust Joshi, said Dad, to get his sticky-beak into the frame.

The ground slipped under her canvas pumps as Nim set

off. A few more pushes and she'd built up enough speed to put both feet on the platform. The wind made her hair fly, and sunlight flashed through the leaves. After a couple of laps, Nim became more adventurous and turned the handles so that she could travel in a figure of eight. It was like gliding through a kaleidoscope, with the pattern of shadows changing and dots of bright tarmac winking. Nim was the star of a new show, *Scooting in France*. She sang the title out loud, thinking it might be a huge TV success. Ella wasn't the only one who knew about being graceful. When Nim concentrated, she could point her toes and push the ground at the same time.

Stopping to catch her breath, Nim rested her elbows on the handlebar. Her throat was dry and her legs worn out. She noticed a mark on one of the rubber handgrips. With the hem of her T-shirt, she tried to wipe the dirt away, but the brown smudge stuck. She'd need hot water, washing-up liquid and a sponge to shift it. That was a good reason to head back. Twigs from a low tree branch caught in her hair and the wheels juddered as she dragged the scooter. Out in the sunshine, Nim shaded her eyes. She was startled to see Maxime sitting on the fence, watching her. An embarrassed giggle slipped from her lips and she hoped he hadn't heard her practising the song.

'Hallo,' Maxime shouted. He held a skateboard across his knees.

'Hello.' Nim put her foot on the scooter and gave it a push. She wanted him to say something more but he stayed quiet. He was too far away to talk to in a normal voice so Nim decided to get closer. This time she took a couple of paces and rolled the scooter beside her. Maxime pushed the visor on his cap upwards.

'What name you?' he called.

'I'm Nim.' She stood up straight, like she was really grown up, but her legs were mushy. She wiped sweat from her palms onto her shorts. 'You're Maxime, aren't you?'

'Okay.'

'Okay.' It was stupid to repeat every word he said and Nim noticed her cheeks pricking. She was famous for going red in the face even when she hadn't done anything wrong.

'You down?' Maxime spun the wheels on his skateboard and pointed to the bottom of the hill. Oh no! She had to think fast. There was no way she would race down the hill and risk another injured knee.

'How about you follow me?' she said.

'What?' Maxime stood up and held the skateboard under his arm.

'Come on!' Nim reached for Maxime's hand. This wasn't the kind of thing she'd normally do but there wasn't another way of making him understand. At least her hands were dry so that his fingers didn't slip through hers. 'I'll show you.'

Nim led Maxime back to the spot where she had been practising. Maxime stood on the tarmac and tapped his trainer. That showed he liked the place. Putting her foot on the platform, Nim rolled the scooter backwards and forwards, waiting for the right moment to start her routine. After one figure of eight, Maxime gave a round of applause and Nim noticed her face turning hot again.

'Good.' Maxime stood in front of Nim and tilted his head to one side. He smiled, reached for the handlebar and turned his fingers around the metal. Their faces were so close; Nim could feel his breath on her skin.

'One more circuit.' Nim finished a second routine

but this time he didn't clap. Instead, Maxime dropped his skateboard onto the ground. He stamped on the end and it flipped in the air, landing in a clatter beside Nim. She let out a squeal and stepped aside. Embarrassed, she studied the ground and she bit her lips together, determined to stop any more stupid noises from escaping. When she heard the wheels of the skateboard grinding, she looked up. There he was, sliding along, leaning in different directions, as if it wasn't any trouble at all. Skateboarding was cool but, well, having a scooter was cool, too.

'You like?' Maxime picked up the skateboard and tried to pass it to Nim but she wasn't keen on having a go. One minute on that thing and there'd be a disaster. She wanted to impress Maxime, not fall on her face. Instead she offered the scooter, and he took it. Worries crowded her brain as Maxime made the scooter jump. She hoped he wouldn't damage it but she daren't say anything. He might not want to see her again if she complained. He wheeled the scooter towards her. 'I like.'

There were bubbles in Nim's tummy, fizzing and popping. She wasn't sure whether he liked her or the scooter. She took the handgrip and he moved a step closer. She became all hot again and words tumbled from her lips. 'You've got brown eyes.'

'Oui.' He was so close that Nim's vision became blurry. She didn't like to say his eyes were like a cow's. She smelled his peppermint breath as he pressed his lips hard against hers. They stuck together for a second, like spit sealing an envelope, then they separated. Nim touched her lips, checking whether they were different now that Maxime had kissed her.

'You like?' said Maxime.

40

'I don't know,' said Nim. 'I think so.'

'You like more?'

'Yes.' This time she slanted her chin towards the sky and her eyelids closed like they were drawn together by magnets. This kiss was gentle. His lips were dry and smooth. They lingered a moment, then Maxime pulled away. The kiss was over. Maxime turned and barged through the trees, back onto the path. Nim stood alone, disappointed at Maxime leaving. He began talking in French and confusion rippled. She heard a bicycle skidding on the path and the voice of another boy. Nim didn't know what to do. Should she wait for Maxime to return or follow him? The talk sounded odd. She couldn't work out whether the words were teasing or funny or bullying. Then laughter boomed and one thing was sure: they both found something very funny. A minute later, Maxime returned to collect his skateboard.

'Will you come here tomorrow?' asked Nim.

'What?' Maxime's eyebrows were hunched together.

'You.' Nim pressed her finger against Maxime's chest. 'Here.' She pointed at the ground. 'Tomorrow.' She tapped Maxime's watch.

'No.' Maxime shook his head. 'I go park.'

'Okay,' she said. 'I'll see you there.'

'Okay,' Maxime repeated.

Nim spread her fingers like the ribs of a fan and patted them against her thumping heart.

SIX

By the afternoon, Nim had already made three trips to the playground and this time she'd dragged Josh and Ella along. On none of the other visits had Maxime been there. It was stupid to hang around all day in the hope of seeing him, but there wasn't anything going on at the caravan. At least the little children were company.

'Give me a push, Nim.' Ella grabbed the chains of a swing.

'When did your last slave die?' said Nim.

'Oh, please, please, please.' She clanked the chains, making such a noise that the French children scuttled away.

'One push to get you going.' Nim didn't really mind. She could do the work, no problem. Grabbing the seat and yanking it backwards, she sent Ella on her way.

'Now me.' Josh plonked his bottom on the swing that hung beside Ella.

'Just a minute.' She decided to make Josh wait. Nim wanted him to realise that she was in charge.

'Come on, Nim.'

'Just got to sort my hair out.' Nim curled the ends around her finger. 'Okay, here you go.'

Once they were both moving, Nim was very busy. Neither of them liked slowing down, so she had to dash about and give each of them a push. When Nim heard shouting, she turned to watch. The bad boys were taking it in turns to hurdle over the fence rather than use the gate.

'I go and watch,' said Josh.

'You can't.' Nim might've guessed he'd want to join them. 'They're not behaving properly.'

'Is that Maxime?' said Josh. 'He's wearing a football shirt. I want a football shirt like that.'

'I thought you wanted a red one,' said Nim.

'I don't really mind. I want to be with the winners.'

'That's not how it works, Josh. You're supposed to pick a team and stick with them whether they win or lose.'

Maxime didn't look the same without his baseball cap but his hair was nice and bouncy. Nim's heart beat like mad.

'We're here!' Josh stood up on the swing seat and shouted. 'This way.'

Maxime trudged towards them, giving a wave that sent his whole arm in an arc. Nim held her breath, wondering what he would do next. Her stomach was knotted.

'Hallo, Josh.'

'He knows my name.' Josh jumped to the ground and ran towards him. 'You've got a football shirt. Which team do you support? I found a red shirt but my mum wouldn't let me keep it.'

Maxime shaped his lips into an 'O' but didn't reply.

'Stop talking rubbish, Josh.'

He reached for Maxime's hand and dragged him over to the swings. Nim had something to thank Josh for if it meant she'd be able to talk to Maxime again.

'Maxime is going to push me,' said Josh.

'Yes.' Maxime turned to Nim and shrugged as if he didn't

have a clue. The bad boys stood beside the fence and jeered at Maxime but all he did was shake his hand like a flying saucer lifting-off.

Maxime was a good bit taller than Nim, and with the extra height, he was able to push Josh faster and higher than she could manage with Ella. When Ella complained, Maxime pointed, offering to change places. Josh was busy kicking the air, like he was riding a bike. He didn't notice that Maxime wasn't his pusher any longer until he caught sight of Nim. Josh ground his feet against the hard earth and dragged to a stop. Ella copied until she came to a halt as well.

With the four of them fed up with pushing and swinging, they made their way to the water fountain and took turns to have a drink. Maxime held his fingers over the spout and turned the fountain into a water sprinkler, showering droplets over them.

'Don't drown us,' laughed Nim.

'You can soak me!' Josh waited for another spurt to land on his head.

'Don't.' Nim pulled Josh out of the stream of water to stop the feathers of his hair from turning lank.

'I don't care.' Josh stuck out his tongue to lick away the drips running down his face.

'You'll get a telling off from Jenny,' said Ella.

'No, I won't.'

'It's only water, Ella. He'll be dry by the time we get back.'

'Water, it good,' said Maxime.

'Let's sit on the bench.' Nim pointed to the seat under the tree, deserted now that families were heading home. She walked ahead of Maxime and sat in the middle, so that he could be on one side of her or the other. It was good to shuffle up beside him, brushing hands and knees.

'I'm four and tall for my age.' Josh climbed onto Maxime's lap and Ella tried to copy until Nim grabbed her wrist.

'You sit with me, Ella.'

'I don't have to.' Getting to her feet, Ella scampered towards the slide. 'You can't catch me.'

That had Josh off on the chase, tearing after Ella, up and over and around the slide. Maxime watched them, fixing his hands behind his head so that his arms made the shape of elephant ears. Nim didn't want him to sit like that. She wanted it to be like the other day when they were alone and he was close beside her.

'You like park?' asked Maxime.

'Yes.'

'You like water?'

'I'm not thirsty.'

'No. You like water?' Maxime pushed his arms through the air, making out that he was diving underwater.

'I like swimming.'

'Yes. Swimming. La plage. You go?'

Nim guessed he was talking about the river. 'Yes, we like it. We like la plage.' The French words la plage were like marbles in her mouth and it was strange and nice to use them.

'You like swing,' he said. 'And water.'

'Hmm.' Nim didn't think there was a playground at la plage.

'Like this.' Maxime beat his chest as if he were Tarzan and gave the call.

Nim giggled. What was he on about? Then she

remembered. The rope. It was wrapped around the branch, but it could be a rope swing. 'I get you. There's a rope swing at la plage.'

'Yes, rope swing.' Maxime gave a thumbs-up sign. 'It good.'

'That sounds like fun.'

'I see you.' Maxime smiled and a star-shaped dimple dented his cheek. The shadow wasn't so different from Nim's mole. She tapped her skin where the mole stuck out. Perhaps, she was the same as Maxime, both with a mark on their faces.

'I'll see you at la plage,' she said.

Maxime stood up.

'You've only just got here.' Nim patted the bench. 'Stay a bit longer.'

Maxime shook his head and looked over to where the bad boys gathered. They were smoking and taking swigs from a bottle that they passed around. 'I go friends.'

One of the bad boys whistled. He was wearing black jeans that made his legs look as thin as chopsticks. Nim hadn't seen him before but he waved his arms and shouted like he knew her. This made Maxime laugh. Before Nim realised what was happening, the bad boy rushed over and tackled Maxime, grabbing his head in an arm lock. Maxime was helpless and couldn't get free but didn't stop laughing either. It was the way with boys; they liked playing rough. Nim giggled, there was nothing else to do. The bad boy turned to Nim. He blew kisses at her and sneered. What was he on about? Kiss-kiss-kiss. He did it again, pushing his lips together and turning his nose up.

For once she was glad Josh ran over but it wasn't Nim he wanted to help. He went up to the bad boy and stamped on his foot. 'Let go of Maxime!'

'Owh! Owh! Owh!' The boy screamed as if he were in real pain and let go of Maxime. The bad boy was laughing and shouting so much that he fell onto the ground. It was Maxime who offered a hand to help the boy up. They stood together, arms roped around each other's shoulders.

'He bad.' Maxime pointed to the boy. 'He Anton.'

'You kiss-kiss.' Anton stared at Nim, his eyes were huge and black, like liquorice ends. He puckered his lips again, as if he was going to blow more kisses, but instead he coughed and thumped his chest.

'You smoke too much.' Nim suspected that Anton was the boy on the bicycle. 'That'll teach you for spying.'

'Spying?' said Josh.

Maxime said a string of words to Anton in French. The bad boy rolled his eyes and used his finger to draw a circle on his own face in the exact same place the mole appeared on Nim's. She wasn't going to hang around to hear the insults.

'Come on, Josh. We need to get home.' She took Josh's hand and walked to where Ella watched.

'They're bad boys,' said Josh.

'What about Maxime?' asked Ella.

'He's okay,' said Josh. 'He's my friend.'

'He's my friend, too.' Nim tried to believe the words, but worry made her head hurt. 'Let's go to the caravan.'

SEVEN

Everyone needed a shower but the little children went first. Josh's chatter was so loud it could be heard above the pelting water. Nim went into the bedroom and slid the door shut. She needed some peace to think about what had happened. Tucking the pillow around her shoulders, Nim smiled as she remembered being alone with Maxime. The way her vision went blurry as he moved close, his breath hot on her face, the press of his lips against hers. Her stomach was a ball of string unravelling as she remembered the moment. She wished the kiss had lasted longer, but short or long, Anton had got to know about it, and the kiss wasn't their secret anymore. He'd made fun by blowing kisses. It was so unfair, but at least Josh hadn't twigged. She would never hear the end of it if he caught on.

Nim plugged her fingers against her ears to block out every sound. Why had Anton got it in for her? It wasn't just the kiss either – he'd joked about her mole. It wasn't right to let Anton get the better of her, especially as he might do his best to stop Maxime from liking her as well. That was too much. Nim pressed her lips together, determination made her jaw tight. She would take whatever chance was needed to see Maxime again. She would make it happen. And although Nim had set her mind on this, the exhaustion of wanting and needing made her limp.

Turning the pillow over to the cool side, Nim wished Mum had let her bring the Snoopy pillowcase she liked best. It wasn't a lot to ask and it wouldn't have taken up much space, but Mum had packed the linen for France and that was an end to it. The print of bright blue sky with a rainbow that Snoopy skipped through always made her feel better. Even back during the days when Mum and Dad argued the whole time and their voices travelled to where Josh and Nim lay awake, listening. It wasn't the sort of thing that was good to hear, so she used to slip into Josh's bed and place her hands over his ears to stop any upset from the shouting. Josh would press against her and they'd stay together until morning came. At breakfast, Josh would chatter away without noticing no one else was talking. At least those days were in the past, but she still missed Dad. The missing him made Nim think of all the things she should have done to stop him from going. But you can't turn the clock back, or so her teacher said in class.

Nim spun her feet onto the floor and cranked her body into a sitting position. Mum and Dee's voices filtered through to the bedroom and it sounded like a story was being shared. Joining them in the lounge, Nim saw the mums each with a child on their lap. Josh had his hair spiked as if it had been styled with gel, and Ella wore a towel twisted into a turban.

'Budge up,' said Dee. 'Make space for Nim.'

'I know how to speak in French,' said Josh. 'Bun-jaw mad-man.'

'*Bonjour* to you,' said Mum. 'Where did you hear that?'

'When Nim buyed ice creams.'

'Oh, she did, did she?' Mum gave a look and Nim realised there was explaining to do.

'It was spending from Dad.' She wasn't going to tell about the whole muck-up with the money and Geoff stepping in to help.

'I see.'

Now was probably a good time for Nim to make herself scarce. 'I'll go and have my shower.'

'Good idea,' said Mum. 'These two will be in bed and asleep when you've finished.'

'Not me.' Dribble ran from Josh's chin as he talked with his mouth full of thumb.

'We'll see about that.' Mum hid her face in Josh's hair.

'Stop it,' Josh giggled. 'That tickles.'

'There's some apricot shower gel on the shelf,' said Dee. 'Help yourself to that and you'll be good enough to eat.'

'And shampoo your hair.' Mum talked as if Nim hadn't bothered to do it in days.

By the time Nim returned to the lounge fresh and clean, or good enough to eat, as Dee said, the mums were washing up. Mum wore Marigold gloves and Dee held the tea towel, although she was more interested in whipping Mum's bottom with it than drying dishes. Mum couldn't help but screech, although she quietened down when Dee put her finger on her lips and told her to shush. If they wanted Ella and Josh to sleep, they should've known better than to make a rumpus.

'Can I help?' Nim didn't want to miss out on the fun.

'It's alright, love. Let's leave Dee to finish the job.' Mum put her arm around Nim's shoulder and guided her to the sofa. The bottle of wine was almost finished and the glasses were covered with fingerprints. 'You can have the last drop if you like.' Mum tipped what was left of the pink wine into a beaker. Nim wondered what she'd done to deserve special treatment. It would have been nicer to drink from a proper wine glass, but Nim had never been offered a sip before so was going to enjoy it.

'It tastes weird, but nice.' Nim tried to smile as the sour flavour hit.

'Neck it back,' said Dee.

'Take no notice,' said Mum. 'You drink slowly.'

'Is there any more?' asked Nim.

'Not for you,' said Mum.

'The end of another day.' Dee dropped the empty bottle into the rubbish. 'I say it's time for bed.'

Nim slipped through the partly open door of the children's room. It had been left like that because Ella was afraid of the dark. Nim patted her hand along the bed to find her pyjamas. The covers were lumpy and she guessed Josh was in her bed. They hadn't snuggled together since they'd arrived in France, and although she was tempted to take his place on the bunk, she squeezed in next to him. When she pressed her nose against his, Josh opened his eyes and blinked.

'Told you I'd stay awake,' he said.

'Move over.' It wasn't worth arguing with Josh, not when they were supposed to be quiet.

'Are you sleepy?' asked Josh.

'Not much.'

'I got a joke. D'you want to hear it?'

'Not if it's silly,' whispered Nim. 'I don't like silly jokes.'

'This one will make you laugh,' said Josh.

'It won't. Your jokes aren't funny.'

'This one is. This one's special.'

Nim didn't reply. She made a thinking face that bought her time. She knew she'd have to agree in the end. Being awake at night and mucking around in the half-light was only fun when she got along with Josh.

'Okay. What's the joke?'

'Knock, knock,' he began.

'Who's there?' said Nim.

'Nim,' said Josh.

'You can't have me in the joke!'

'Yes I can. Come on, say your line.'

'Alright. Nim who?'

'Nim, beep-beep.' Josh poked his finger at Nim's cheek, hitting her mole like a horn.

'That's not kind.' Nim gave him a shove. He didn't exactly fall out of bed but he got the message. 'Go away, Josh. Get in your own bed.'

He knew he wasn't wanted and he banged his way up the ladder to the bunk. Nim turned and faced the wall. Tears dripped from her eyes and her shoulders quivered. As if it wasn't bad enough having that bad boy make fun of her.

EIGHT

'Do as you're told, Nim. Go and play with Josh. We're only here because of you.' Mum spoke in a way that let everyone know she was angry. 'No one likes la plage when it's this busy. We only came here to keep you happy.'

'But Josh is being mean to me. He keeps saying "beep-beep".'

'Take no notice.'

Nim hung her head. Now was not the time to say any more about Josh's stupid joke.

'You're the oldest,' Mum continued. 'You should know what he's like.'

Mum turned to Josh. 'Play with your toys.' She opened the cotton bag and clanked a couple of engines onto the sand. 'Make a track around the edge of the picnic blanket. See if you can build a tunnel.'

'I want sticks,' he said.

'Nim, it's your job to help him.' Mum slumped her head onto the towel that had been folded into a pillow.

'Oh, alright,' said Nim.

It was just like Mum, ordering Nim to play with Josh, even though she had nothing better to do than lie in the sun. Searching for sticks wasn't going to be any fun. When they last visited la plage, it was easy to find them fallen onto the sand where the trees had shaken their heads and bits of wood had clattered down. But now la plage was jam-packed with people. You couldn't see the sand for towels and bodies. Men drank from beer bottles and left their cigarette stubs on the ground like sandworms burrowing. Babies in buggies cried and children paddling in the water shrieked. Next to base camp was a lady wearing turquoise eyeshadow that looked like tropical fish were swimming across her face. She sat under a tent without sides, her chair like a throne above the crowds.

Of course, the person Nim wanted to see was Maxime. She had a clear idea of what he might look like in swimming gear: quite thin, probably showing his ribs and his skin the colour of runny honey. No matter how many times she looked around la plage there was no one the right shape. She checked every boy who wore a baseball cap but none of them were Maxime. Disappointment made her curl over and hug her knees.

'Stop your daydreaming.' Mum prodded Nim's arm. 'Josh is waiting.'

He stood wearing his *Thomas the Tank Engine* trunks and his face was scrunched. There was no point in trying to hold Josh's hand because he'd snatch it away. Instead she caught his wrist and led him through the people. Once he broke free and stood with his hands on his hips, making it look like he could flap his wings and fly away. Nim wasn't having that. She doubled back and got him moving again with a tickle. He laughed for a second, then began to walk as if he were wearing flippers, staggering along. Nim went ahead and made for a tree with giant roots she could sit on. She leaned against the trunk and stretched out her legs like she was on a lounger. Mum wasn't the only one who could switch off from the world when she sunbathed.

'I don't like being pulled.' Josh crossed his arms, which showed brown against his chest. 'You're bossy.'

'Start looking for sticks.' Nim talked with her eyes shut. 'Or we'll have to spend the whole day here.'

'I can see the Reliant Robin again.'

'No you can't.' Nim wasn't going to be cheated into opening her eyes.

'It's over where the cars are parked by the café. It really is there and it's got a sticker on the back.'

'Perhaps the car does belong to a family from England.' It turned out there weren't many people at the campsite who understood English, and speaking in French wasn't so easy. Even Mum was stumped for something to say when the French people talked, but Dee liked to *tra-la-la* a few words. Nim wandered over and stood behind Josh, peering over his head.

'I see it,' said Nim. 'Shall we go a bit closer?'

They walked between the trees and up to the fence that blocked their path. There, Nim squinted to check she was right, that the car had a GB sticker. Josh began fidgeting at her side, waving his arm through the air like he was directing traffic. He was behaving like a bit of an idiot. 'What are you doing?'

'I'm waving to Robin.'

'Don't be stupid. The car can't wave back.'

'No, I mean the man. He's the driver.'

'What man?'

'Well, he waved to me first.'

'Stop your nonsense, Josh.'

'People like waving to me. They like me more than they like you.'

'You're talking rubbish. Go and find some sticks.'

'I expose.' Josh crouched. 'Can you help me?'

'Why should I?' Nim went back to her seat again and rested her head against the bark.

'Maxime would help.' Josh reached for a stick and tested its strength, poking it into the earth.

'Maxime isn't here.'

'Yes, he is.' Josh gave a crafty smile. 'He's on the big rock.'

'You're a liar,' said Nim. 'I've checked. I looked everywhere.'

'You missed him because you walk too fast.'

Nim's spine became stiff like a pencil. It couldn't be true. She stared at Josh and he gave a smile that was super annoying.

'Shut up about Maxime. He's got nothing to do with you.'

Josh didn't answer but moved across the ground like a duck, picking up twigs and chucking the duff ones over his shoulder.

'You can't be sure it was him.' Nim pressed her face into her hands, closing her eyes and blotting out the world. It wasn't beyond Josh to play a nasty trick, but the thought of seeing Maxime made hope catch in her throat.

'I'm sure,' said Josh.

'Definitely sure?' She spoke into her hands, collecting her breath. It reminded Nim of when Maxime's face was close to hers and his breath was warm on her cheek. She spread her fingers to peer through the gaps. Josh was scraping moss off a tree root, not searching for sticks.

'Stop mucking about, Josh. If we walk back through the

58

trees beside the road, there are bound to be some sticks.'

Nim picked up bits of branches as she went and Josh trampled alongside. As they came level with the swimming area, shouts and yelling from high up on the rock made it obvious that the bad boys were around. Like a horse wearing blinkers, Nim fixed her eyes ahead. Her target was base camp, where Mum lay on the blanket. It was too bad if Maxime was hanging around with that boy, Anton. Nim's mind buzzed. She couldn't blank out the picture of Anton's sneering. Even if he had been watching, there was no need to be horrible. It was natural to kiss someone nice, wasn't it?

Straightening the corner of the blanket, Nim sat down. Mum showed her spine. She was laid out like a fish finger under the grill and she talked into the pillow, muffling the greeting of hello. She pinged the elastic on her bikini bottom – it was clear she didn't want to talk. Josh set about sorting his find, chucking the rotten twigs aside, saving those that were dry and stiff. Nim shuffled towards Mum so that she could have a clear view of the rocks. She daren't get too close and spread shade over her. That would make Mum cross again. She should have 'do not disturb' written into the sunscreen on her back – that would be a warning. Nim thought about sitting on Dee's towel as she wasn't around. Dee wouldn't mind, but Mum might. Instead, Nim kneeled and poured sand through her fingers as if making mounds of flour and sugar and salt, ready to mix a cake.

Dee must've taken Ella to the toilet. Little girls needed the loo whenever it wasn't convenient, and when Ella returned she always shouted 'pooey looey' at the top of her voice, and that made Nim want to become invisible. The little children were always doing something embarrassing. Nim slapped her thigh where a fly had landed and her skin went pink. Not as pink as her cheeks, she guessed, sensing the heat flare. She tried not to think about what was happening on the rocks, where Maxime was messing about with the bad boys, but she couldn't stop her head from swerving in that direction. It was no good. Her cheeks pulsed, making her face feel hot and red like a tomato ripened in a greenhouse.

The boys wore shorts that dripped water and their wet hair was plastered to their heads. While they waited for a go on the rope swing, they pretended to shove each other off the rocks, pushing in front and mixing up their places in the line. The next boy on the rope swing gripped the knot with his feet. He swung above the river and back again, the boys giving him a push to keep him from crashing into the rocks. One boy was up there shouting, his hands around his mouth. Nim stared at him and, recognising the way he tilted his chin, she knew it was Maxime. He looked different with the dark strands of his hair pointed about his neck.

She wished she were up on the rocks – not exactly with those boys, but definitely with Maxime. She gave a little sigh, thinking it would never happen. Then, the boy on the rope swing let go and plunged into the river straight as a needle. When he came up, he spat like an angry camel. That had to be Anton. He flicked his head to make his hair swing out of his eyes and yelled at his mates. It was absolutely Anton. No one else would be so noisy or so rude. However much she wanted to climb to the top of the rocks and talk to Maxime, she'd never be able to go there if Anton was around.

Josh concentrated on the track, his fingers busy making a railway line appear in the sand. There was a junction and a signal, and with the twigs he'd built a tunnel, but whenever an engine tried to make it through, repair work was needed to stop a total collapse. Josh gave a commentary on the action but his voice became mingled with the others in a hum of talk. Usually Josh was easy to ignore, but when his voice became louder, Nim tuned into what he was saying.

'Nim loves Ma-ax, Nim loves Ma-ax!'

She could hardly believe it at first. Stupid idiot. Anger hissed in her throat, making all the things she should have said dash away. Three paces and she was next to him. Her foot sank into the earthworks and she pinched his jaw. His cheeks puffed into golf balls.

'You're such a pain,' she said in a low, slow voice. 'Just shut up and piss off.'

Josh made his arms fly about and he battled to be free. Nim had said enough and, satisfied, she stomped to her place beside Mum.

'Nim's broken my track,' wailed Josh.

'Never mind,' Dee chirped. 'Me and Ella will help to sort it out.'

'I'm good at helping,' said Ella.

Nim pressed her chin against her knees while her heart beat like a bongo. Dee was bound to have seen what happened. Frozen in place, Nim pretended she didn't exist.

'Not to worry, Josh,' said Dee. 'We can get a bucket of water to pour over the track. It's easier working with wet sand.'

Dee put out her hand and Josh took her fingers. A white stripe on Dee's shoulder showed where her strap had been, and against the pink skin it made her look like a piece of coconut ice. The idea made Nim cheer up.

'Who else wants a paddle?' said Dee. 'What about you, Jenny?'

Mum put her hands behind her back to do up her bikini top but the elastic escaped from her fingers. When it was fastened, she sat up and adjusted the front so that the straps were even. 'I'll sit here for a while longer. Keep an eye on Nim.'

'No need for that,' said Dee. 'Nim wants a go on the rope swing.'

Nim jolted with surprise. It was exactly what she wanted to do, but a quick glance over to the rocks told her it was still too busy to join the line. 'Perhaps I'll go when it gets quieter.'

'It's up to you,' said Dee.

'Is Nim brave enough to go on the rope swing? I'll have to stay and watch that,' said Mum.

'Suit yourself, Jenny.' Dee passed a plastic bucket to Josh, and Ella carried the other one with her Barbies inside.

Mum returned to her lying position while Nim watched the boys. They swung from the rope and dropped into the water one after the other. When they'd landed, each of them waded over to the other side of the river where Anton sat on the bank. One boy made a huge splash and nearly drowned. That sent Anton into fits of laughter and he shook his head so much that his hair sprang out, showering the others. He was like a dog trying to dry his coat. After a while, there was only Maxime left on the rocks. She had to take her chance now, or she'd miss seeing him.

It was the rule that Mum had to know exactly where Josh and Nim were, otherwise she might worry. But if Nim had to disturb Mum from her sunbathing and explain everything, Maxime would be gone. She scanned the paddling area where Josh and Ella were jumping in the water with Dee. She'd be back in no time, and besides, Dee knew that Nim wanted a go on the rope swing. Chasing around the edge of the water, Nim jumped over the pools and came to the tumble of rocks that made a staircase to the top. When she got to the ledge, Maxime was there, coiling rope.

'Hello, Maxime.' Nim puffed out the words, her chest heaving from the rush of getting there. She gave a smile that stretched her cheeks.

'Hallo.' Maxime slung the rope over his shoulder and put his foot on a stone, taking a pose.

'You like playing with the bad boys.' Nim didn't know what else to say.

'What?'

'You like playing with the big boys.' She thought better of calling his friends bad. She nodded her head to show she was talking about the boys now standing on the bank. Holding her arm up high, she tried to make Maxime understand. 'Big boys.'

'Yes. Big boys. Like me.'

'No. They're much bigger than you.' Springing onto her toes, she held her hand even higher.

'Okay,' he said but he shook his head. 'You want?' Maxime dropped the rope, which slithered onto the rock. He grabbed the knot that looked like the hooded head of a cobra. Nim's heart clanged as she curled her foot around the end. The rope was a bulky web of twisted twine that rubbed against her instep.

'Go.' He swung his arms like he was ready to push her.

Nim knew what to do – she hadn't been watching the boys on the rope swing for nothing. With one foot on the rope, she held fast with her hands and ignored the loose threads that itched her wrists. Ready with the other foot to push away, she decided on a stand-me-up ride and held tight. Above her the branch creaked as she set off, making her heart thump like mad. But as she swung, graceful as anything, she enjoyed the sheets of air that wafted by. When she was directly over the water, the rope circled, turning her like candyfloss around a stick. Ready to drop, Nim let go of the rope, and falling, falling, the colours smearing, she pointed her toes as she entered the water.

Gasping for breath as she came to the surface and winded with fright, Nim paddled her arms. Weeds strangled her legs, dragging her backwards. It was a fight to reach the bank and, exhausted, she sat in the shallows. Water lapped her thighs while she rearranged her hair, peeling away the layers that stuck to her face. When she could see clearly, she checked where Maxime had gone. He wasn't on the ledge any longer. The rope was secured around the branch and Maxime was sliding down the rocks ready to catch up with the bad boys heading for the fields. They called to Maxime 'kook-kook' and beckoned him over. Anton led the way, trampling a path through the crop and taking swigs from a bottle as he went. The others trailed behind, waist deep in wheat. She watched until the blobs of dark hair disappeared. It was a shame Maxime preferred to hang out with the bad boys, but at least Nim had seen him for a minute or two.

There was no choice but to head back to base camp. Nim searched for the tent with white sails. Next to that, she'd find Mum. After stumbling across the sand, her limbs weak, Nim fell onto the picnic blanket. Only Mum wasn't there. No one was there.

Nim dragged a towel and draped it over her head and shoulders. She was angry at first, thinking they'd gone to buy ice creams and she'd have to go without. Poking her head from under the trim, she scouted the space, checking for faces in the crowd, seeing if there was anyone she knew. Finally she saw Mum, who was standing with her hands flapping. Nim guessed Josh was in the water, that Mum was watching him play, encouraging him to make a splash. Then Dee appeared, hurrying next to Mum. Ella was having a carry, her legs wrapped around Dee's middle. It was strange to see Dee holding Ella; she usually said Ella was too old for that.

Nim got to her feet, thinking it was time to find out what was going on. It wasn't cold but something made her teeth begin to chatter. Mum linked her hands around her neck, as if she were going to throttle herself, and turned her head, almost like an owl, to take in the full view of the river.

Something was very wrong.

NINE

'Thank God you're here.' Mum's brows were pulled together and frown lines slit her forehead. 'Where's Josh?'

'I don't know. I just got back from the rope swing.' Nim's heart beat like crazy knowing she was in for a roasting.

'How many times must I tell you to let me know where you're going?' Mum let her breath come out in a huff. 'Anyway, where's Josh?'

'He didn't come with me. I thought he was paddling.'

'So did I,' said Mum.

Dee struggled up the beach and let Ella down to scamper the last few paces. 'Glad you're back, Nim.'

'But there's no sign of Josh,' said Mum. 'Where the hell is he?'

'He's bound to be somewhere close,' said Dee.

'Why did you send him back?'

'I told you, he got bored with paddling.'

'I must've been dozing. I never heard him.' Mum put her hand on her forehead and turned on Nim. 'Why did you go off like that? You should've been here to look after your brother.'

'That's not fair,' said Dee. 'And anyway, shouting at Nim's not going to help.'

'Well, I've had a good look around and I can't see him anywhere.'

'Stay calm,' said Dee.

'If only we were in England,' said Mum. 'I would've shown him where lost children should go. He can't even speak a few words of French to ask for help.'

'Let's not dwell on that now. We need a plan,' said Dee.

'I don't know what happened,' said Mum. 'He was supposed to be paddling.' Mum crumpled, as if her bones weren't strong enough to hold her up, and Dee gave her a hug. Nim folded over. If she hadn't gone on the rope swing, maybe Josh wouldn't have wandered off. But this wasn't the first time it had happened. When he got lost in Tesco, Josh had security men dashing around the aisles looking for him.

'I'm sorry,' Nim whispered, but Mum and Dee didn't break their huddle. She was left waiting for a reply that never came. Feeling awfully alone, Nim crossed her arms and gripped her shoulder blades, giving herself a hug. It was the only way of finding comfort as the worries niggled. Josh was asking for trouble, making up that stupid rhyme. But maybe if she hadn't hurt him, if she hadn't spoilt his track … Glancing around, she saw his engines and a patch of smooth, wet sand next to the empty bucket.

Nim dropped her arms and began running on the spot to stop the worries from spreading. If she kept busy, she wouldn't have to think about what she'd done. The teachers at school said jogging was good exercise and you wouldn't damage your feet if you landed on the balls. Pounding against the sand, Nim didn't care that she wasn't going anywhere. So long as she kept up the speed, Josh was sure to come back and everything would be back to normal.

'Stop that!' shouted Ella. 'You're flicking sand in my face.'

'I'm not.' Nim didn't want to take orders from Ella,

although she stopped running because she was out of breath.

'Shut up, you two.' Mum broke away from Dee.

'It'll be alright, Jenny. Josh isn't going to be lost for long when the place is this busy. There's a tannoy on the café roof. I'll see if they can make an announcement. All I need do is figure out the words in French. You do a search on this side of the river, Jenny. And girls, you keep guard of base camp. Watch out for Josh – he's probably trying to find his way back right now.'

After Mum had set off and Dee was away at the café, Nim put her arm around Ella's shoulders. It was her way of making up. She wasn't going to say sorry because she hadn't meant to get Ella sandy. This gave Ella the wrong idea, and she tickled Nim under the arm. Although this sent Nim into a bad mood, it wasn't Ella's fault. She didn't realise that concentration was needed to find Josh.

Nim took up position, sitting cross-legged in the centre of the blanket, her back straight and her eyes darting. Ella sat next to her, copying her actions. When Nim held her hand over her eyes, Ella did the same. She looked like she was wearing a baseball cap with fingers for a visor but Nim didn't say anything. Not when Ella was trying to help. Turning her head from left to right, Nim caught sight of Ella in the corner of her eye. Copying Nim had become Ella's hobby and it would've turned into another game if things had been different.

It didn't take long for Ella to become fed up. She started burying her feet in the sand and made out she was trapped. Nim gave a snigger but tried to ignore her. She had to concentrate on looking for Josh. Because Ella wasn't getting any attention, she pulled at her eyes to make them go slanted.

Then Ella started to sing, blasting a verse and moving her fists like she was building a wall. Nim took no notice; she continued to look for her brother.

Some of the children paddling at la plage were taller than Nim, but quite a few were younger. Most of them were French, and if they weren't French they were from some other country. You could tell from the way they talked. Not understanding a word was the first sign. The way they spoke was different, too. Their voices were like birds twittering, a kind of tune you didn't hear in English. They didn't look like English children either. For a start, their skin was tanned and they didn't have any patches of pink. With all these differences, Josh should be easy to spot. Only the old men in France had hair as white as Josh's and there was no mistaking Josh for one of them.

Nim fixed her mind to look for his blond hair like a torch in the shade. She could spot him if she stood tall. Jumping to her feet, she began again the routine of tossing her head from side to side, making her eyes skim over the bodies in the water, watching for movement on the banks, letting her hair slap around her shoulders. Knowing Josh, he could be anywhere. Perhaps he'd sneaked off and followed the bad boys into the field. Or maybe he got sick of paddling and decided to try a proper swim without his armbands. That would be dangerous, so Nim didn't want to think about it anymore. Instead, she got the idea that he'd accepted an invitation to join a family feast and was sitting at a picnic table stuffing cold meats. Josh liked his grub.

Startled by Mum lurching into the picture, Nim crossed her arms. She wanted to help, especially when Mum was worried, but she didn't know what to say. Mum was in a dither, her fingers tapping her chin as if she were trying to get her face to wake up. Her lips were apart but not in a smile, and she showed her tongue. Each time Mum took a breath, her tummy gave a quiver and a sigh whooshed out. Sitting down, Mum was like a heap of jelly.

When the ping-pong of the tannoy sounded, the whole area became quiet. Mum tilted her head, showing she was listening. The loud speaker crackled until the words came. It was a man's voice, and he sounded croaky. The French came in bursts, with little puffing noises between the gaps, like he was smoking to keep calm. The only word Nim understood was 'Joshua' and she clung onto his name, hoping there would be a sign of him, that something magical would happen if she held tight.

'Pourquoi les Anglais perdent-ils toujours leurs enfants?' the lady sitting under the sail next to base camp said into the air.

Mum glared. She would've bitten off the lady's head, easy as chomping on a jelly baby, given the chance. The husband looked up from his newspaper, twirled his finger in a circle by his temple and went back to his reading. Mum showed them her back and wrinkled her nose. It was as if a spotlight was on, making them the centre of attention. Faces turned towards them and each person stared. Nim straightened the edges of the blanket and smoothed the sand so that their patch of ground became neat. Everyone knew where the missing boy should have been, playing with his trains on the sand, but no one shouted 'the boy's here' or 'I've found the boy' or words with that meaning in French. Silence stabbed the air, making everyone squirm. It was only by talking again that the holiday spirit returned. Children in the river restarted their games, splashing and paddling and filling buckets, their voices rolling. Someone turned up the volume on a radio. No one bothered looking for the four-year-old English boy called Joshua, last seen paddling, wearing blue trunks.

'Any sign of him?' Dee approached.

'Nothing.' Mum held her hand over her forehead. 'What should I do now?'

'Try walking beside the river,' said Dee. 'If he followed the path of the water, he'll be on the far side of the café.'

'I'm not sure that's good logic.'

'He's got to be near. It's only been ten minutes. You look along the river. You're sure to find him, Jenny.'

'He'd never have gone missing if …'

'Sniping isn't going to help.'

'I didn't mean …'

'I'll watch Nim and Ella, you get off and find Josh.'

Mum pulled on her trousers and, walking alongside the water, she kept turning her head. Every now and then she called Josh's name but the noise was more like a howl. She was a wolf-mother searching for her cub.

Glued to the spot, Nim watched for the way Josh stuck out his knees and elbows. She listened for the splatter of his laughter. Left, right, left, right, her eyes moved across the space; in and out, her breath pumped. Watching and breathing, watching and breathing. Putting her hands over her ears, Nim blocked out the noise. She needed quiet to concentrate. If she concentrated hard enough, she'd find Josh. But as time went by, she realised silence didn't make any difference and she started to lose hope.

'Have you got any idea where he might've gone, Nim?' asked Dee.

'I'm not sure.' Nim racked her brains. It was easy to think of where Josh might be hiding at home, but not at la plage. Then, as if a shooting star had lit up an idea, Nim thought perhaps Josh had gone to check out the Reliant Robin. 'Can I take a look around the car park? Josh kept going on about a car he liked when we went that way to collect sticks. I'll go over and see if he's there.'

'There's an idea,' said Dee. 'Perhaps we should go together.'

'But someone needs to stay at base camp and I'm the only one who knows where to look.'

'Okay, but don't be long and don't talk to anyone you shouldn't. I'll keep an eye out for you.'

Nim darted through the people and along the road to where some cars were lined up in the shade. Most of the spaces in the car park were taken and the paint gleamed hot in the sun. Walking along the rows, Nim tried to remember where the Reliant Robin was parked. But after one or two laps of the car park, Nim came to an empty bay where she guessed the car must have been. She couldn't believe it wasn't there. She turned round and round in a circle until she was giddy. But it was not good acting crazy and getting all hot and floppy in the sun. Josh had to be found. And if he wasn't looking at the Reliant Robin, where was he?

Back at base camp, Nim shared the bad news. 'I really thought I was going to find him. Josh reckoned the owner was called Robin, you know, because the car was a Reliant Robin.'

'But if it's not there, Josh has no reason to hang around the car park. It was good thinking, Nim.'

Mum wove a path through the crowds, her shoulders

hunched. She was staring at her toes, not looking around. She'd never find him if she carried on like that. Nim knew how to look for Josh. She'd done it often. Sometimes when he was playing, he'd go off and hide. There was the time he got into the toy cupboard. Nim never guessed it could hold him. She got the shock of her life when the doors shot open and out sprang Josh, his face beaming. He was a life-size jack-in-the-box. Perhaps it was a good time to remind Mum about the trick. Make her remember that Josh was crafty. He wasn't afraid to wait it out. But when Nim saw Mum's face, she knew she had to be careful. Anything could set Mum off when her nerves were on edge. Keeping out of the way, Nim made room for Mum to sit next to Dee. That was a good idea. Dee tucked her hand around Mum's waist, giving her a tug that made Mum fall against her, as if she were the last of the ten pins to wobble then drop. At least Dee knew how to make Mum feel better.

'We'll find him, Jenny. Don't worry. He's okay paddling in the water.'

'It's not the water I'm worried about. There are plenty of people around to stop him from drowning. But too many here to mask an abductor.'

'Ductor,' Ella repeated.

'Shush.' Dee put her finger to her lips, like the teachers did at school, and she gave Ella a stare that kept her quiet.

'Why did you give his name as Joshua?' asked Mum.

'What?' Dee pushed her eyebrows together so they almost met in the middle.

'When you asked them to make the announcement. Why did they call him Joshua? You know he never answers to that name.'

'I didn't think, Jenny. I was under pressure. You know what it's like trying to speak in French.'

'But if you'd said Josh, we might have him back by now!'

'I did my best.' Dee dropped her arm to the ground and Mum moved away.

'You could've called him Joshi,' said Nim. 'That's what me and Dad call him when we're together. He likes that name best.'

'Shush.' Dee held her finger to her lips one more time.

Nim was on lookout duty while the mums became friends again. No one said thank you for the work she did searching. She stood on her tiptoes and watched, rolling her fingers into binoculars to get a better view. The mums pressed their heads together, foreheads touching, and they talked in voices so quiet it was impossible to hear what they were saying. You could've called it whispering, and everyone knew how rude it was to whisper. Ella sat on the edge of the blanket and sucked her fingers, the two middle ones. At bedtime she was allowed to do this but Nim was surprised when Dee didn't give her hand a tap, reminding Ella that sucking wasn't okay during the day. After ages of muttering, Mum came up with an idea.

'Nim, I'm going to walk you and Ella over to the café. You'll be safe indoors. That'll leave me and Dee free to spread the search.'

'I'll start by looking further along the road,' said Dee. 'Nim's already checked out the car park.'

'Has she, indeed?' Mum didn't look too pleased.

'We need to draw on all our resources.' Dee folded the towels as she talked. 'We'll leave our stuff here so that if Josh finds his way back, he'll know we haven't gone without him. I'll have a word with Mr and Mrs Tight Lip.' Dee nodded in the direction of the couple under the tent. 'I'm sure they'll keep an eye out for him. Our mobiles are switched on so anyone can ring with news.'

'You girls will be okay in the café. You won't have to put up with everyone staring.'

'Keep it down, Jenny. We need all the friends we can get right now.'

It was cool in the café. Mum gripped the counter as if she needed something to keep her upright. She talked to the staff who stood on the other side. Mixing English with French, her words were a jumble, and during gaps in the talk, tiny gasps came from Mum's lips. The lady in charge wore an apron with a special badge that read 'AMIE'. She nodded as she listened. When Mum had finished speaking, the lady covered Mum's hand with her own. They stood like that for a minute, Mum blinking back tears. Then Mum got into a fluster again and, searching through her bag, she found her purse and handed over a note. The lady took the money, gave Mum's arm a stroke and waved her away. Everybody tried to smile as Mum tugged on the door and made her way outside. Nim understood that Mum had Josh on her mind, but she should've remembered to say goodbye.

Ella walked over to an empty booth and bounced along the seat until she was beside the window. Nim climbed onto the bench opposite. Through the glass, Nim watched Mum run towards the river. The wind caught Mum's hair, making it stand on end. Halfway along the path, she turned around and gave Nim a kind of smile, but her mouth soon hung down at the edges again. Nim waved back, trying to be brave.

The table was long and marked with lines to make it

seem like wood but the surface was smooth and shiny. Ella held the squeezy bottle shaped like a tomato, then she shot it along the top with a swipe. Nim blocked the journey, her arm a hockey stick protecting the goal.

'You need to behave nicely in a café.' Nim returned the ketchup to the wire basket that held the salt and pepper pots. 'We're to wait patiently, and they'll bring us some chips.'

'How do you know?'

'I overheard Mum. She paid for a great big plate.'

'I like chips more than I like Josh,' said Ella.

'You mustn't say that.' There was a pang deep inside Nim and a tear drained from her eye. She pulled a napkin from the metal box and wiped her face. 'You wouldn't like it if your brother was lost.'

'I don't have a brother. I was born in an incubator.'

'You can't have been. Everyone knows babies come from their mummy's tummy.'

'I mean, I was made in an incubator.'

'Okay.' Nim wasn't about to argue. 'Why don't you play with your Barbies?'

Ella undid the buckles on her satchel. The bag wasn't as bright as it had been at the start of the holiday. It kept the purple colour but there were scratches on the side and dull patches where the shine had rubbed off. As Ella turned the bag upside down onto the table, three Barbies clunked out and sand scattered. Using her hand as a brush, Nim organised the sand into a tidy pile, but Ella made the Barbies walk scissor-like through the heap and the tabletop was in a mess again.

'Look what you've done – now I'll have to clean up for the second time.' Nim began the work, getting rid of the sand, shoving it onto the windowsill.

'My Barbies are tired. I'll put my Barbies to bed.' Ella snatched a napkin and used it to wrap the Barbies into a paper sleeping bag. When they were all covered up, she put them to bed inside the satchel, giving each one a goodnight kiss on the forehead.

'They'll sleep well tonight,' said Nim.

The café was thick with the smell of chips frying. Ella stretched her legs under the table, placing her feet beside Nim. She was trying to be friendly but because she was so little, she almost disappeared from sight.

'Don't put your feet on the chair.' Nim gave her leg a playful slap. 'Sit up straight, the chips are coming.'

'Alright.' Ella did as she was told.

'Voila!' The waitress made the chips crash-land on the table. 'Okay?' The lady smiled, moving the plate so it was placed exactly between the two of them. From the pocket of her apron she offered two forks, but Ella was busy using her fingers and a chip was already between her teeth.

'Merci.' The word felt strange in her mouth but Nim was pleased to use it.

'D'accord.' The lady tapped the table with her knuckles and she walked away.

Ella dropped her half-eaten chip on the table and Nim wondered what Dee would have said about her table manners. Perhaps she'd say something like 'you're being a Little Miss Greedy'. The chips were too hot to eat without dunking the end in ketchup. Nim set a dob of red on the rim of the plate but she squeezed too hard and a whole line squirted out.

'Watch me.' Ella stuck out her lips and put the chip on top to make a corn-coloured moustache. 'Ouch.' They were even too hot to play with.

Most of the chips remained uneaten and the table was messy, spotted with ketchup and the salt Ella had been playing with. Nim couldn't tell her off if chucking salt over her shoulder brought the luck needed to get Josh back.

'Do you want any more chips?' asked Nim.

Ella shook her head and began stamping her feet on the floor. Nim tried to think of something that would keep Ella entertained. It was her job to keep Ella busy while the mums searched. Outside, wind made the honeysuckle bush scrape against the glass, and Nim stared out of the window. A panel in one of the fences had blown down and it reminded Nim of the gap-tooth Halloween pumpkin Josh brought home from nursery. Her heart clanged, and worries filled her mind like foam. It was hard to think straight, but when she grabbed a napkin from the shiny box to wipe her nose, an idea formed. She could fold the napkins into a star. That would be something to guide Josh back.

'Watch me – I can turn this paper into a star.'

'It won't be a proper star.'

'Look.' Nim folded a triangle and placed another one, upside down, on top of the first.

'That's cheating. You can only use one bit of paper.'

'Okay.' Nim made a diamond shape this time and held it up. 'Look!'

'That's not a star, the points need to stick out.'

'You have a try. See if you can do one.'

When the waitress came to collect the plate, paper napkins covered the table. Rolling them into a bundle, Nim gave a yawn.

'Are you tired?' asked Ella.

'A bit.' Nim slid her feet from her sandals and turned on her side, tucking her toes under her so that she sat like a mermaid. 'What about you?'

'If my Barbies are asleep then I should be as well.' Ella flapped open the satchel and checked inside. 'They're asleep.' She planted the bag at the end of the bench and, lying down, used it as a pillow. Nim made a bed on her bench, tucking an arm around her knees. The girls stared at each other. The table was like a roof above them and gave somewhere to rest. Ella sucked her middle fingers and her eyelids closed. Listening to Ella's breathing, Nim fell into a doze and when she turned over, she drifted to sleep.

'Nim and Ella.' The tone of Mum's voice skidding through layers of sleep confirmed things weren't right. Nim split her eyelids open but when she didn't see Josh's chubby knees beside the stalks of her mother's legs, she clamped them shut again. It was Dee who carried Nim to the car. She stayed limp in her arms, her head bouncing against Dee's bosom, and she was put onto the back seat. She fell sideways, trying to make her pretend-sleep convincing. When Ella was lined up beside her, they set off. The ride was over in minutes. Again, Dee did the carrying. She put Nim into her bed and tucked the cover over. There was no need to bother with undressing or washing. None of these things mattered with Josh missing.

Under the covers, Nim lay on her back and stared up at the mattress on Josh's bunk. Usually the wires sank under his weight, but not that evening. Not that evening, because he wasn't there. Sticking her finger through one of the gaps, Nim prodded the foam. This usually made Josh grumble and woke him up when she wanted to play. That night there was no sound from Josh, but the mums' voices in the lounge sparked. It wasn't exactly an argument. Not like the ones Mum and Dad used to have before he moved into the flat. They would shout all night and Nim could hear the words from under the duvet in her bedroom. The mums didn't often argue, or if they did it was over silly things. Like the time Dee wanted to sing karaoke and Mum couldn't stand listening to 'Dancing Queen' one more time.

Nim lifted her head from the pillow so she could hear exactly what the mums were saying. The words were clear because she listened with all her strength. Dee was walking about the lounge, her footsteps heavy. When she stopped moving, Mum's words streamed like lava down a volcano.

'Stop telling me what to do. It's not your child that's gone missing. Put yourself in my position.'

The silence was interrupted with sighing. Nim couldn't tell whether it was Dee or Mum.

'You have to ring Gary,' said Dee. 'He needs to know what's happening.'

'I can't.' Mum's voice was sharp. 'He'll kill me if he knows I've lost his boy.'

'That's not the point.'

'Besides, the police will find Josh. They have to. There's no point in worrying Gary.'

'I'll do another walk around the grounds when you've made the call. I want Josh found as much as you do.'

'We'll take it in turns,' said Mum. 'I'll go when you come back.'

'Yes, but in the meantime, you have to tell Gary. Imagine if the boot was on the other foot.' Dee's voice was serious.

'You'd want to know.'

'Of course.' Mum sucked a breath. 'Pass me the phone.'

'And tell him to bring a photograph. The police will need that to move the search on.'

'Christ! Why didn't I pack my camera?' asked Mum.

'There's no point in fretting about that now. Besides, they won't be interested in a few blurry snaps. Haven't you got a proper portrait? Something recent?'

'His nursery photograph was taken at the end of term.'

'That'll do the job.'

'D'you think?' asked Mum. 'Those boys at la plage. This isn't going to be another Jamie Bulger story ...' Her sobs muffled the end of the sentence.

'It can't be, Jenny. Nothing so terrible could happen twice.'

TEN

In the morning, cool air whipped around the bedroom and Nim was sure this would wake Ella, but there was no sign of movement. The curls on Ella's head looked like a daisy chain and she slept with her lips apart. Ella gurgled and Nim thought about replying in a dream language she might understand. Nim made a warbling sound but Ella didn't twitch. She didn't even move when Nim got out of bed. Standing at full height, Nim's head was level with the top bunk. She pressed her chin onto the mattress, but there was no bundle of boy under the sheet. It was true. Josh wasn't in bed like he should've been. There was a rip inside her body and worry filled the gash. He'd never been lost this long before. Nim needed to be a detective and work out the clues.

Sliding the folding door against the frame, Nim entered the lounge. It was strange going into the room with the curtains closed. Dee lay on the sofa and her eyelids sprung open as Nim approached.

'Why are you sleeping here?'

'I've just got back from pacing the campsite.' Dee yawned and her tongue looked like there was cress sprouting. 'I'm sorry, Nim, there isn't any news.'

'What happens now?'

Gail Aldwin

'We keep looking for him. He's got to be out there, somewhere.'

'I hope he's okay. It's too bad he's always doing stuff he shouldn't.'

'We can't change what's happened.' Dee made space on the sofa so Nim could sit down, and the cushion was warm where Dee's legs had been. 'Let's put our thinking caps on and work out where he might've gone.'

'He likes it at the playground but he can't hide there for long. Not with all the kids and families.'

'D'you think he's hiding somewhere?'

'He might be.' Nim hung her head and counted the cornflakes under the table. There were six whole ones and another that'd been stepped on and broken into crumbs. Josh must've scattered them when he last upturned the cereal box. Everyone else preferred a French breakfast: croissant or pain aux raisins.

'He's not at the playground. I've been there several times.'

'Did you search the bushes?'

'Everywhere,' said Dee. 'Got any other ideas?'

'He made me cross.' Nim found the words, and when more ideas came, she let the sentences pour. 'He was being annoying. He said stupid things about me and Maxime. I wanted him to shut up.' Tears ran over her cheeks. 'Poor Josh, he's only wearing his trunks and he won't sleep without Blankey.'

'I hope he's not been too cold,' said Dee.

'He kept saying "beep-beep", making fun of my mole.'

'Come here.' Dee threw out her arms, giving Nim a hug. 'These things happen. Brothers and sisters fall out all the time.'

84

'Do they?' Nim's tears made a wet patch on Dee's top.

'Never mind, Nim. We've got to keep our minds on the job. Wipe your face.' Dee reached for the kitchen roll on the counter and tore off a piece. 'Blow your nose. Everything is a whole lot better in daylight.'

Nim opened the curtains but the day was cloudy. 'You know Josh is brave. He's ever so brave for a little boy.'

'That's the trouble, Nim. He's a very little boy.'

'Don't let Josh catch you saying that. He thinks he's as big as Dad.'

'And that's the other bit of news,' said Dee. 'Your dad's on his way.'

'That's good, isn't it?'

Dee didn't answer, just rubbed her eyes.

A switch clicked on in the mums' bedroom and a spike of light showed under the door. Nim wanted the loo but wasn't sure whether she should go through the mums' room to use it just yet. It was awkward going in there, so she waited. The room was always stuffy with a clinging smell of something Nim could never quite name, but the tang reminded her of hotdogs. Tucking her hand between her legs, Nim held her fingers where the wee came out and used them like a plug to stop the leak. Then she jiggled, moving her legs like she was walking.

'You don't need to stand there, Nim. Your mum won't mind you using the toilet.'

Nim slid through and saw Mum curled in the centre of the bed, holding her ankles. The covers had fallen onto the floor, so Nim's path to the bathroom was spongy under her feet. She didn't check to see whether Mum's eyes were closed but went straight to the bathroom. Nim's face was a shadow

85

in the mirror but her mole showed like a blob from a felt-tip. If Josh came back soon, she'd forgive him. She'd let him say that stupid joke again and again. She rehearsed the lines in her head, remembering Josh's opening knock-knock, and her reply, who's there? She'd let him jab her mole again and it wouldn't matter.

Nim swallowed spit that filled her mouth and tried to stop her eyes from making tears. His joke was horrible but things were even worse with him being lost. Nim patted her eyes dry with a piece of toilet paper and practised smiling. It was hard work making her lips point upwards – it was like her cheeks had rusted and her muscles could do with oiling to get them working better – but she managed it in the end.

Going back through the bedroom, Nim noticed Mum had shifted position and her fish-eyes stared. Her breathing was like a string of hiccups, stopping the words from coming. Mum stretched an arm across the mattress, beckoning. Nim took a seat on the edge of the bed and toppled sideways. She lay looking at Mum, her face was an upside-down reflection of her own. Nim breathed more quickly than Mum and she slowed the pace so that the gushes of breath came at the same time as Mum's. When Mum put her hand on Nim's face it was like an iron on her skin, but Nim didn't move. Staying close to Mum was important.

ELEVEN

Watching from the caravan window, Nim kneeled on the sofa. With the extra bit of height, she saw right over the campsite. As a car wormed along the road, Nim followed its progress and realised it was an estate with a huge boot, same as Dad's. He needed a lot of space so that he could fill it with rubbish whenever he went to the dump. That was one of Josh's favourite Saturday morning outings. He loved hearing the glass shatter in the bottle bank when Dad pushed the jam jars through the porthole openings. There were recycling bins at Le Camping but Mum didn't like hanging around them because of the stink from the rubbish.

The car groaned as it took a turning, and gravel pelted as the wheels moved. No one else would bother driving to the top of the hill so Nim decided it must be Dad. She rushed onto the deck, ignored Dee and Ella sitting at the picnic bench, and darted for the road. Focusing on the driver, she recognised Dad's hair kinking over his ears and his face all red from being hot. The engine stalled as Nim hurtled towards the car and the driver's door swung open. Out lumbered Dad, using one hand to rub the small of his back. With the other arm he made a coil around Nim's waist, lifting her into an off-the-ground hug.

'There's my girl.' He pressed his nose into her collarbone

and she closed her arms around him. His shirt was damp and drips of sweat ran along his cheeks. 'I'd better put you down, love, before I do my back in. Has Joshi been found?'

Nim shook her head and slid from his grip.

'Where's your mum?'

'She's gone to the police station but Dee's over there.' Nim nodded in Dee and Ella's direction.

'Who's she?' Dad's eyebrows pointed down in a confused face.

'Mum's old school friend. That's her little girl, Ella. We've spent the holiday with them.'

'Quite a party,' said Dad. 'As soon as I got the news, I set off. I've been driving through the night and day. There must be some word. What the hell is going on?'

'I don't know. Mum doesn't say much. The only thing is, Josh hasn't been found. He's still lost.'

'Don't you worry about Joshi. He'll be alright. He's got a compass between his ears.'

'I hope so.'

'Are you going to introduce me?'

Before Nim had a chance to do the work, Dee was striding towards them, her hand stretched out ready to shake Dad's. Her huge hips wobbled with each step. Nim remembered when she first met Dee and how she felt embarrassed about the size of her. Her clothes drew attention, too. The flappy red dress was as big as a sail on a boat. It was okay now because Nim had got used to Dee and she was wearing flared trousers that actually looked quite nice. Besides, Dad had no reason to criticise when some evenings he ate a whole tub of ice cream straight from the freezer. Nim knew this because the stack of empty containers grew like a beanstalk and was taller each weekend when she and Josh stayed there.

'I'm Gary.' Dad gripped Dee's fingers then released them quickly. 'You've been helping Jenny?'

'Yeah. I'm Dee. The thing is … Perhaps it's better if we go inside. I'll make us a cup of tea.'

'Right you are.'

'Can I have juice?' shouted Ella.

'I'll bring some out,' said Dee. 'Be a love, Nim. Give Ella a hand with the puzzle or we'll be there until midnight.'

Nim hated jigsaws, especially when all the corners and straight edges were found. It had to be a fairy picture, making the wishy-washy pink pieces hard to place. She had a go with one or two of the pieces, trying to see where they might fit, then she shook the box to find another colour that would be easier to match. Without success, Nim became bored. She waggled her foot and retied the laces on her trainers. When she looked up, there was Geoff standing at the end of the hedge which divided their plot from the neighbouring one.

'So this is Sank-on-Seas.' Geoff had his arms behind his back, making it look like there were only stubs coming from the sleeves of his T-shirt.

'Who's that?' Dad called from inside the caravan.

Geoff took a few steps closer and Dad appeared on the decking.

'This is Geoff, who saved the day,' said Nim. 'He paid for our ice creams when the lady wanted French money and I only had the five pounds you gave me.'

'I should have realised.' Dad smacked his forehead. 'Let me pay you back.'

'No need, no need at all,' said Geoff. 'I only came to offer my help. I heard Josh is lost. Is there anything I can do?'

'My ex is due back from the police station any minute. Do you want to hang on?'

'Best if I come back later. I'm staying down the hill.' Geoff turned to point to the caravans lined up beside the shower block. 'Sometimes the police ask for volunteers and I'm happy to help.'

'I'll tell them to let you know. What's your last name?'

'Reardon. Geoff Reardon. He's a lovely boy, is your Josh. I'm sure he'll be found safe and sound.'

'Yeah.' Dad took a sip of tea from the mug he was carrying. 'Thanks, mate.'

Geoff nodded, and where the ends of his lips hung down you could see creases like tiny speech marks. He turned, taking strides so long it took only three paces for him to get back on the path. Dee followed Dad and carried a tray of drinks to the table.

'Who was that?' she asked.

'Some bloke offering to help.'

'Word's got out.' Dee found a deckchair stored beside the caravan and slipped the frame together so that Dad could sit down.

'Don't mind me,' said Dad. 'You get on with the game.'

'I've got a better idea, Dad. I'll show you round the caravan. I've been tidying everything.'

'Let your dad have a rest, Nim. He's been driving for hours,' said Dee.

'It's no bother. If Nim wants to show me around, that's what we'll do.'

Opening the windows in the caravan didn't make much difference to the heat, and sweat streamed down Dad's face. He kept turning his head, as if he was checking to see whether there were cobwebs in the corners. With the work she'd done that morning, Nim could guarantee the place was perfectly clean.

'Let's start the tour here. We have our breakfast at the table. And over there is the kitchen area.' She pointed to the cupboards and the sink but Dad didn't bother looking that way.

'I'll show you our bedroom. You'll be more interested in where we sleep.' Nim launched into the room like a sprinter from starting blocks. She twirled around, admiring her efforts. The covers on the twin beds were straight and she'd folded Blankey on Josh's bunk. Finding a partner for each of the shoes, she'd lined them up in a row. Standing between the beds, she ran her fingers over the curtains so that they stayed neat. 'What d'you think?'

Dad poked his head around the doorway like a tortoise stretching from its shell. 'Very nice, love.'

'Come and have a proper look.' Nim gripped Dad's hand and pulled him inside the room. He stood beside the wardrobe while Nim danced between the beds. 'I like to keep the bedroom clean and tidy.'

'I can see,' said Dad. 'The bunk's for Joshi, I take it. He always wanted to sleep in a tree house.'

'That's right. D'you want to look in the drawers?' She pulled the handle without waiting for an answer. 'The clothes are in here.'

'Good job.' Dad backed out of the room, rubbing his eyes.

'What's the matter?' She didn't really need to ask. All the tidying in the world wasn't important when Josh was missing. She might've known Dad had other things on his mind.

'I'm okay.' Dad tapped his trouser pockets and found a handkerchief. He covered his face and gave a good blow.

'You're thinking about Josh, aren't you?'

'Ahem.' Dad's lips trembled. 'It doesn't mean you haven't done your best. The whole place is spick and span.'

'You haven't seen everything,' said Nim. 'Are you ready to continue the tour?'

'Not really, love. Think I'll stop here for a bit.' He sat on the end of the sofa.

'Well, you might like to know that Mum and Dee sleep in there.' Nim pointed at the door. 'And the bathroom's through their room.'

'Now you're talking. I need to splash my face with water.'

'There's a clean towel hanging on the rail,' said Nim. 'I put it there myself.'

Nim waited in the lounge, wondering what Dad was doing on the other side of the folding door. He was taking ages to wash his face – Nim hadn't even heard the tap running. Mum always said that their bedroom was a private space and it was rude to go poking around. She wouldn't even let the little children play monkeys jumping on the bed, and whenever they tried to get in there, Mum always shooed them out. What on earth was Dad doing?

The sound of water running through the pipes brought a sense of relief. Dad had found his way into the bathroom and he wouldn't hang around in there for long because he got claustrophobia. Mum said it was only because he couldn't fit into small spaces that he didn't like them. When she was in a bad mood she said hurtful things and sometimes said sorry afterwards. That was because it made Nim sad to hear her say unkind things.

Dad returned holding the towel. It was like a tiny rag in his giant hands. He used it to mop the water dripping from his wet hair. He'd done more than wash his face – his whole head was wet!

'You should have said if you wanted a shower. There's shampoo and everything in there.'

'No, no. Just needed a cooling off. It's all come as a bit of a shock. First Josh and now I've got to come to terms with your mother and that woman.'

'Dee takes a bit of getting used to,' Nim admitted. 'But she's okay once you get to know her.'

'I won't bother doing that,' said Dad.

Uncertainty whooshed out of Nim like air from Crocshanks. Why had Dad taken against Dee? His face was stern and Nim knew better than to ask questions. Perhaps Dad needed to be on his own.

'I'll go and help the others fix the jigsaw.'

Dad stepped sideways and blocked the double doors.

'Stay with me,' he said. 'The less you have to do with that woman the better.'

It was clear that for some reason, Dad didn't like Dee. Perhaps Dad needed a bit more time. To make the best of the situation, Nim tried to keep Dad company, although he wouldn't keep still. He walked around the caravan, tossing his head like a polar bear in a cage. When he did sit down, Nim drew a noughts-and-crosses grid on a scrap of paper and started the game with a nought. This usually began a kind of argument where Dad said he deserved to have the first go and Nim reminded him of the rule about the youngest player. Josh often pushed in because the rules said so, but he couldn't that day. She tapped her chest, thinking there'd be the sound of a hollow ding, like her innards had been turned out. It happened to people in the past when they were hung, drawn and quartered as punishment for a crime. Nim hadn't done much wrong, every brother and sister argued, Dee said so.

Nim picked up the pencil and went over the lines, making the grid dark, and she ground the nought onto the page. She hoped the activity would remind Dad to start the game but he didn't want to play because of Josh. Nim hung her head and concentrated hard, thinking she could guide Josh home. She used up her energy holding fast, but it didn't make any difference. Dad picked up the pencil and he marked the page without speaking. It wasn't much fun when Dad didn't play properly. He made a silly mistake and Nim became the champion without trying. There was no point in saying yippee.

A police car arrived a little later but its light wasn't flashing and the siren didn't make a noise. That must be a good sign – they didn't think Josh going missing was an emergency. Dad went outside, saying he'd have to move his car, but it was okay, the police were allowed to park in the middle of the road. A French man opened the door so that Mum could get out. You could tell he was French because he had a moustache, one that went right the way along his top lip and fell down at the sides of his mouth. Mum clasped his arm. Although she wasn't wearing high heels, her ankles turned outwards. It was as if she was too tired to stand. Everyone was quiet and Nim wondered if the saying she'd learned at school was true: no news is good news. Judging from the blank faces of the adults, that was not the case. When Mum and the policeman got close to Dad they stopped walking. Mum opened her mouth as if she was going to say something, but instead she clamped her teeth together.

'What have you done, Jenny?' asked Dad.

Mum and Dad eyeballed each other.

'I've been working with the police.' Mum found her voice. 'He hasn't come back.'

'No,' said Dad.

'This is Josh's father.' Mum turned to the policeman as if she preferred talking to him.

'Hello, my name's Pierre Abel.' The policeman and Dad shook hands.

'I'm Gary Mashard. Are you in charge? What's the latest news?'

'I'm sorry, there's been no development but we're doing everything we can. I was asked to liaise with you. My mother's English so the chief thought I'd be the best person for the job.'

'Are you half-French, half-English?' Nim tried to make sense of this.

'That's right.' He smiled at Nim. His eyes were gentle. 'I need to talk to your parents. Shall we go inside?'

Dee led the way, abandoning the jigsaw and Ella in one go. She stood alongside the sofa, plumping the cushions and placing them diamond-shaped against the backrest.

'Take a seat,' she said. 'I can make some drinks.'

'Don't put yourself out,' said Dad. 'You'd better go and mind your daughter.'

'Ella's here, Dad. She joined the end of the line with me.' Nim lifted Ella's hand in the air to show that they were together.

'This discussion is for family members only.' Dad tapped his fingers on the table.

'Please, Gary. Dee and Ella can stay,' said Mum.

'No, Jenny. You need to get your priorities right. This is family business.'

'Don't mind me.' Dee held her arms out to Ella and gave her a lift and carry.

'We'll go down to the shop and buy a bit of lunch. I've got my phone on if you need me, Jenny.'

Mum didn't reply. She was too busy fiddling with the trim on the nearest cushion.

'Come over here, love.' Nim scrambled onto Dad's lap but there wasn't much room. His belly rested on his legs so there were only his knees to balance on. The commotion brought Mum to attention.

'Pierre's been telling me how things are progressing. They're stopping cars on the road out of town, there's a search party organised,' said Mum.

'I wish there was a different sort of party. Josh loves sausage rolls and lemonade,' said Nim.

'What are you going on about?' Mum shook her head.

'Perhaps we can have a party when Josh gets back,' said Dad.

'Okay.' Nim wasn't sure but she thought it was more likely that Josh would get a slap and a telling off, like the other times he'd wandered off.

'He's been gone for hours.' Mum slid her watch around her wrist but she didn't need to read the time.

'The more we can do in the early stages of the investigation, the more likely it is that we'll find Josh. That's what's happened in other cases where children have gone missing.'

'I thought he was lost,' said Nim.

'He is lost but the police think of him as missing,' said Dad.

'Or taken,' Pierre butted in.

'Please, no,' Mum gasped. The silence that followed made Nim's mouth go dry. She remembered Dad saying how he'd pay someone to take Josh away whenever he was naughty. Like the time Josh hid his dinner in a cupboard saying he didn't want to eat the chops because they were brown. That got Dad really mad.

'I'm going to change my clothes. Pierre can fill you in on all the details, Gary. You don't need me around.' Mum headed for her bedroom.

'I want to know exactly what happened,' he shouted after her. 'Find out where the negligence lies.'

'You mean point the finger at me.' Mum turned and glared at Dad.

'This is not the time for allocating blame,' said Pierre. 'We need to focus our energies on finding Josh.'

'Too right,' said Dad. 'What can I do to help?'

Dad listened while Pierre described the measures that had been taken to try and find Josh. The nearby fields and outbuildings were being searched. A door-to-door of the caravans on-site hadn't revealed anything. The more Pierre talked, the more hunched over Dad became. He was concentrating on the details. But Nim wasn't. She didn't want Dad to know that she'd argued with Josh and then gone off and played on the rope swing at the very moment Josh had gone missing. Nim held her hands over her ears, blocking out the talk so that she'd never have to listen. If she had a magic wand, she could make sure the right words came from

Pierre. But she knew she couldn't fix what had happened, so she held her breath as well.

She slipped off Dad's knees and made her way into Mum's bedroom. Mum already knew the truth and she was still talking to Nim, so that meant she wasn't holding a grudge. Sitting in front of the mirror, Mum wiped her nose. The end had started to peel from too much sun, and with all the blowing, her whole face had become blotchy. Nim bent her arm around Mum's neck, and she noticed her collarbones sticking out under her skin. It was hard trying to be helpful when Mum didn't seem to notice she was there.

'I miss him.' Mum's voice was a whisper.

Nim took the hairbrush from on top of the chest of drawers and waved it. Mum gave a nod and lifted her chin so that Nim could run it through. Mum's hair was knotted and snagged on the brush, but Nim didn't want to be rough. She knew not to brush right to the ends so Nim fluffed the hair around Mum's parting.

'That's better,' said Nim.

'That's better,' said Mum.

TWELVE

Pierre and Dad were still sitting on the sofa when Nim closed the mums' bedroom door.

'Come here, love, just for a minute.' It was Dad calling so Nim rushed over. 'Can you tell Pierre whether Josh has made any special friends since he's been here?'

'There's Maxime, but he's more my friend than Josh's.'

'He was at the river yesterday, that's right, isn't it?' asked Pierre.

'Maxime was with some friends.' Nim wondered whether she should mention Anton. Her thoughts were tangled, the ideas coming slowly because she didn't want to get Maxime into trouble. As her doubts grew, she remembered Josh stamping on Anton's foot. Her face became hot with worry. She didn't want to tell Dad about kissing Maxime or the mocking from Anton. It was horrible to think that a friend of Maxime would do anything to Josh. He jeered and made nasty faces but wouldn't hurt a little boy, would he? Nim held her face in her hands.

'There's nothing to worry about,' said Dad. 'Just tell Pierre what you know.'

'And there was Geoff, who just called by.'

'That's right. Geoff Reardon. Says he'll volunteer to search if you need extra help,' said Dad.

'He knew you were here,' said Pierre.

Nim took a deep breath. 'I told him we lived at caravan fifty-six.' There was no need to tell on Josh by saying what actually happened.

'That's not very wise.' Dad frowned.

'Don't worry. I'll check everything out.' Pierre stroked his moustache like it was the tail on a cat. He looked strange doing that. If Josh had been watching, it would've made him laugh. 'Did you bring a photo of Joshua?'

Dad went to his car and groped around the back seat, bringing out his football bag with the broken zip. Dad didn't actually play football but the bag must have been the first thing that came to hand. Nim noticed her cheeks heating up, standing there, watching Dad. You could see his bum like a wonky heart under the tracksuit bottoms and a cord hanging between his legs because he hadn't tied it. Dad looked like he was coming undone. Finally, he pulled out an old plastic wallet, one that Josh used when his reading book came home from nursery. Josh quite liked books, but they weren't real ones because they didn't have any words. He used to point at the pictures and say the names for the things he saw.

'Got it.' Dad turned the flap and gave a photo of Josh in a frame to Pierre.

'I'll get this back to you as soon as possible.'

When Pierre had gone, Dad gave the folder of photos to Nim. 'Wait in the car, love, and we'll go into town for ice creams. I'll pay for them properly this time.'

While Dad hurried back to the caravan, Nim sat like an obedient child in the passenger seat and sorted through the photographs. The prints were higgledy-piggledy so she arranged the corners to line up in a neat pile. There were all sorts of snaps: Josh and Nim with messy faces eating spaghetti, one from her birthday when she wore her denims and Josh barged into the scene, and another with Josh dribbling a football at the park. He looked so small with the ball bigger than his head. Poor little Josh, all he wanted was a football shirt. Nim squashed the memory and slotted the photo back into the pack like a playing card. Switching her mind to something different, Nim imagined the bright colours of the different ice creams lined up in a freezer behind a special glass counter. Poking her tongue between her lips, she tasted the flavours: a sharp lemon with slivers of ice, a dollop of creamy strawberry. The chocolate in France was too dark and bitter – no one even liked pain au chocolat. Josh got away with calling it 'pan-o'-poo', which put everyone off trying one again. It seemed that all her ideas led back to Josh, and a growing sense of being without him made her forehead splinter with worries.

Dad had been ages in the caravan and it was never a good sign when he wanted 'a word with your mother'. Nim's shoulders pinched as she wondered what was happening inside. The clouds above were stitched together but sunlight flicked through the seams. It was warm enough to walk around in a T-shirt and shorts, but at Le Camping the weather couldn't make Nim happy.

Shifting her position, Nim crossed her legs and sat like she did at school, although she was more comfortable in the car than on the wooden floor of the hall. She tried to remember the words of the prayer they said during assembly. She'd said the words often, but it was hard to remember things when life was turned upside down. Squeezing her eyelids shut she tried mouthing the words, and some of them came quickly, but the old fashioned lines were harder. Nim pressed her hands together and that helped, but her tongue got mixed up and she had to break off. All she wanted to do was ask for Josh to come back, and for the shouting coming from the caravan to stop.

First it was Dad's voice bellowing. If the walls of the caravan could've moved, they'd have sprung outwards, like in the cartoons whenever fighting happened. Nim found that making pictures in her head was a good way of coping when things got stressful. She used to do it a lot when Mum and Dad argued before they split up. The pictures she drew made things less real, as if the shouting was between some other parents. Imagining it differently at Le Camping, she could see Dee and Dad and Mum sitting around the sofa, drinking tea and nibbling on the Hobnobs that Dad had brought with him as a gift. As it was, Dad's voice kept hammering, and when he stopped, Mum took her turn. Mum's words started off a bit louder than normal, but as the talk splattered, her voice cranked up so that she was screeching. This wasn't unusual. This was the way Nim remembered the arguments.

Dad was the one who had started this row, and Nim thought it must be about Josh getting lost. He was upset, but so was everyone. Then she heard a different word: dyke. The secondary school kids sometimes shouted it, but she'd never guessed the meaning. She repeated the word in her head, thinking that if she heard it loads of times she'd understand it. When the shouting stopped, Dad appeared in the doorway and trampled down the steps. Nim straightened her legs, getting ready for going into town, but Dad turned back. With his pointing finger ready, he gave one last blast.

'If that dyke isn't gone by the end of the day, I'll out you both. I mean it, Jenny.'

THIRTEEN

When Nim and Dad returned, they found Mum alone in the lounge. Although the strip light hummed, it wasn't much company.

'About time, Gary.' Mum tossed the newspaper aside. 'You could've sent a text if you knew you were going to be this long. You said you were only going for ice cream.'

'Sorry,' he said. 'I didn't realise the time.'

'What was so important that you had to keep Nim out till this hour?'

'I thought it was worth driving round for a bit. We were just checking – trying to spot Josh.'

'We didn't find him.' Nim stared at the sofa, not wanting to look at Mum. During the time that she'd been out with Dad, half her head was concentrating on looking for Josh while the other part of her was worried about Dee. Of course, she couldn't say anything to Dad, not after the way he barked at Dee and wanted to send her packing. That was one of the most confusing things. Dad was normally friendly to other parents; he chatted to the ones at the school gate when he came to collect Josh and Nim for a weekend at his place. He didn't even mind Josh's friends calling him Gappy on account of the space between his front teeth. Nim spun in a circle, taking in the lounge. There wasn't anything different about the place: cups on the counter, kettle plugged into the wall, but there was no sign of Dee either.

'Don't look so worried,' said Mum. 'Dee and Ella have moved into a caravan two doors down.'

'That's a relief.' Nim flopped onto the sofa and angled her head to give Mum a smile but her hair fell over her face like a curtain. Mum ran her fingers through Nim's fringe and scooped her in for a hug. Nim was secure with Mum's arms pressed around her. She rested her head against Mum's shoulder and felt safe. But it wasn't the same for Josh. Where had he gone? He was there one minute and not the next. She should have stayed and helped build his track. Everyone knew Josh needed watching. If only she'd kept an eye on him instead of grabbing the chance of a go on the rope swing. The thought made her hot and panicky. Mum's arms became heavy and she broke free.

'Can I go and see Dee?'

'In the morning. You know Dee would never go off and leave you without saying goodbye. You're one of her favourite people.'

Nim drew her lips into a smile that made her cheeks swell and she nodded as the words settled.

Mum kissed Nim's forehead. 'You'd best get ready for bed.'

'Not so fast, young lady.' Dad held out his arms. 'Give your dad a hug before you go.'

She fell against the bulk of Dad and his hands patted her back.

'That's more like it,' he said.

As she slipped into the bedroom, she kept her listening ears ready to hear the talk between her parents.

'I hope Dee's move satisfies you, Gary.'

'It's a compromise. That's all.'

Dad's footsteps clomped on the deck as he headed off.

The ceiling lamp tinted the walls of the bedroom. Ella's bed had been stripped of sheets and the duvet was folded, making the place bare, but Josh's bunk was ready for when he returned. She'd lined up his engines on the bunk beside the wall. That way he'd easily get to his favourite. She put his covers in a pile and grabbed the yellow blanket. Some of the threads that held the binding had torn and the silky edge was coming away from the mesh. Wrapping it around her fingers, she sniffed the strip and the smell of Josh filled her nostrils: sweet and dirty and sticky. He had to come back. Nim ripped the ribbon free and laid it under her pillow. Next, she turned the blanket into a triangle and let the point hang down from under Josh's mattress so Blankey was like a flag to welcome Josh back.

Nim admired her work then stared at her reflection in the mirror. Pressing her shoulders back, she stood up straight. In Science lessons at school she'd learned that the purpose of the skeleton was to give shape to the skin that covered her body. It was a frame, a bit like the poles that hold up a tent. Although she was glad to remember, she couldn't help feeling there was something wrong with her bones. They were heavy, for a start, and her legs ached even though she hadn't done any running. As for swimming, well, she'd better not think about swimming. Nim fell onto the bed. The thin mattress stopped her bottom from banging against the wooden base, but it wasn't exactly comfortable. The floor was empty where Ella used to drop her shorts, leaving them body-shaped alongside her T-shirt.

Although Nim was tired, her mind was too busy for sleep. At the end of Nim's bed was a wardrobe with a round knob. Moving from the bed, she stood in front of the door and twirled her fingers around the handle like she was holding hands with Maxime. Pressing her lips against the shiny flat surface, she remembered kissing him. Excitement fluttered in her tummy but it quickly turned to a dull ache. A reminder that it wasn't a good idea to think of happy times; her energy should be concentrated on Josh. She opened the wardrobe door and a blast of air made the wire hangers jangle. There weren't many clothes hanging there now that Ella had gone. She climbed into the wardrobe. Her head bashed the rail and a dress swamped her shoulders, so she bent her knees and sank down. Her legs were cramped and her back lined the wall. She was rammed in, only able to move her head. She gripped the underside of the door and pulled it shut. In the darkness, the tight little space brought relief, a kind of escape from the mess of life. Scrunched into place, Nim was able to think. Too much went on in the world of noise and light, too many people, too much talking. It was good to be in the quiet, where she could hear her breath; good to be in the dark, where she had her own skin to feel. Winding a strand of hair around her finger, Nim whispered, 'Come home, Josh.'

She imagined her words drifting out of the caravan, floating over the campsite, carried with the air or with angels until they reached Josh. She thought of the words comforting him, giving him courage to find his way. Her voice was a marker. If he followed the trail, she'd see Josh in the morning. The thoughts steadied her heart. The blank screen of darkness allowed her to imagine that everything was going to be fine and Josh would come back.

The bedroom door shunting open startled Nim. It was sure to be Mum coming for a last check, or perhaps she wanted a tuck-you-in or a cuddle-up. She often did that to Josh even when he was asleep. It was stupid to be hiding in the wardrobe when she was supposed to be grown up. The floor creaked as if Mum was pacing but Nim stayed put. If she tumbled out of the wardrobe, she might give Mum a fright and that would be no good.

'Nim.' It was Mum speaking. 'Are you okay?'

Inside the wardrobe, Nim didn't make a sound. It was too embarrassing.

'Where are you, Nim?'

Still she waited, wondering what to do. There were scrabbling and ripping noises. It sounded like Mum was tearing down the walls. Nim pushed the wardrobe door open a crack and the light streaking inside made her blink.

'It's alright. I'm here.'

Mum turned around, her eyes shiny. She jerked the door wide open. 'What the hell are you doing in there?'

'Looking for a button.' It was a poor excuse.

'Christ.' Mum held her face between her palms. 'For a moment I thought I'd lost you as well.'

'It's okay, Mum.' Nim toppled onto the floor, banging her hands and knees as she found a way to stand up.

'You stupid girl!' Mum wrapped her arms around Nim and squeezed her, but it wasn't long before she went weak and droopy, her arms falling away. On the floor were the covers, all mucked up. After a while, Mum grabbed them and shoved them onto the bed.

Nim picked up her pyjamas. 'I'd better put these on ready for bed.'

'You're right.' Mum took the bottoms and gave them a shake so that Nim could step straight into them.

'Hang on a minute – I need to undress.'

'No hurry.' Mum stretched the elastic making the waist extra large while Nim dumped her clothes. 'You've grown so tall, Nim.'

'My pyjamas are miles too short. They end way above my ankles.' Nim flashed her leg, showing where the material stopped.

'You're not wrong,' said Mum. 'Now for the top.'

Nim sprung her hands up, shooting her arms through the sleeves. It was the routine Mum usually did with Josh but there was no harm in playing along.

'I'll have to get you some new pyjamas,' said Mum.

'And when I go back to school, I'll need some new trousers, too.'

'I've already got Josh's uniform.' Mum let her head sink, showing where her hair parted like a lightning strike. Nim thought she might be crying but no sound came. She roped an arm around Mum and they stayed like that, stuck together with Mum's bony shoulder pressing into Nim's tummy. It was uncomfortable but she didn't want to complain. The thought of going to school was like having pins and needles. It made Nim want to get moving yet at the same time she was numb. Ideas of what to say spurted but the nuisance of finding the right words made Nim hesitate. Eventually she decided on a line. 'When will we get back home?'

'God knows,' said Mum.

Nim wished she'd never asked.

'Get into bed and I'll kiss you goodnight.' Mum's lips were cold on Nim's forehead.

FOURTEEN

'I'm waiting to find out what the police have learned from their interview with Geoff Reardon. He's got to know something. Why the hell did he leave the campsite after all that fuss about wanting to help? You don't think …? Thank Christ they tracked him down.' Mum spoke into her mobile and she nodded as she listened to the reply. It must have been Dee on the phone. Nim knew by the way Mum talked. Nim was glad they'd found Geoff; he was sure to tell the truth. He had to. She held her breath, willing him to say something that would help find Josh. And from what she understood, a Reliant Robin had been stopped as well. With all this going on, there were bound to be clues, some way to get to Josh. 'Pierre wants me and Gary to make a public appeal. D'you think that's a good idea?' More nodding. 'Buy something for Nim's breakfast, would you? Okay. See you in a bit.'

A little while later Dee burst through the double doors of the caravan. She tossed the morning's shopping onto the counter. The lady assistant at the shop was an expert at swinging paper bags by the corners and twisting the edges into ears, but that morning the horn of a croissant poked out. Nim broke off the end and starting chewing. There was no point in waiting to be offered breakfast – there was too much commotion. Ella hung onto Dee's shorts, pulling the waistband and whimpering. It was just Ella doing her pretend crying routine and making a show. Dee was having none of it; she ignored Ella and continued to stride about the place.

'Gary's going to have a job getting through the mob at the gate today,' said Dee.

'He's already grumbling about photographers outside his hotel,' said Mum. 'He's complained to the Embassy about it.'

'You need the press onside, Jenny.'

'I hate the idea.' Mum sagged onto the sofa.

'It's getting hot.' Dee unwound the cotton scarf that she was using as a disguise. 'I feel like a bloody Egyptian mummy bound up in this thing.'

'That's funny, Mummy.' Ella stopped snivelling and let go of Dee. She held her arms out and started swaying like she was a mummy from Ancient Egypt. It wasn't a realistic performance. From a project at school, Nim knew all about the Egyptians. Instead of pointing out Ella's mistakes, Nim decided to join in the game. She dashed into the bedroom and yanked a sheet off the bed. Hiding underneath it, she made ghostly noises and sprang into the lounge.

'Good grief.' Dee stumbled like she was shocked to the core. 'I give up. First a mummy and now a ghost!'

'That had you scared, Mummy!' shrieked Ella.

'You're not really scared,' said Nim.

'Startled, not scared,' said Dee. 'Now I know it's you, Nim.'

Dee was, for the most part, normal. It was Mum who was different. Nim never could guess what sort of mood she'd be in, and now it was even harder. That morning Mum wandered about wearing screwed-up trousers that had been in the washing bag, and she hadn't brushed her hair. She

110

didn't seem to care what she looked like anymore.

'Come on, Nim,' said Dee. 'Finish your croissant then we can head off.'

'Where are we going?'

'You want to see our new place, don't you?'

'I'll eat this on the way.' Nim packed the rest of the croissant in a paper towel.

'You're keen,' said Dee. 'We'll have to go around the back, through the trees, or the photographers will cop us with their zoom lenses.'

'You be careful,' Mum said to Dee. 'You don't want to end up on the front page.'

'It'll be fine.' Dee smacked her lips against Mum's cheek. 'I'll take good care of Nim.'

'I know,' said Mum.

Dee's new caravan had exactly the same material on the sofa but it was smaller with only one bedroom. The tour didn't take more than a minute. Ella settled at the table and started a new page in her colouring book. She passed over some felt pens but Nim didn't want to help. Instead, she walked over to the kitchen counter where Dee was making a drink.

'You know about Maxime, don't you?'

'He was one of the boys at la plage.' Dee scratched her arm where she'd been bitten and a circle of red showed. 'I can't believe he's done anything.'

'He hasn't. He was kind to Josh.'

'The police have questioned the ringleader.'

'His name's Anton.' Nim wished she hadn't met him, never seen that horrid boy. 'But I don't care about him. It's just … if I hadn't been playing with Maxime, if I'd been looking after Josh, maybe he wouldn't have gone.'

'You don't know that.' Dee held Nim's shoulders and gave her a shake so that her head rocked from side to side. 'It's not your fault.'

'That's not what Mum thinks.'

'Come here.' Dee tugged Nim into her arms. The folds of her skin were soft. 'Jenny doesn't mean anything.'

'She does.' Nim repeated the words Jenny had used. 'If only Nim had stayed put, if only Dee hadn't gone for a paddle, if only la plage hadn't been busy.'

'Let's not think about it.' Dee held the back of Nim's head and looked into her eyes. 'There are too many "if onlys" in life. It's no one's fault. Things happen.'

'Like when Mum nearly ran over someone on the drive here.'

'Did she?'

'You should have seen it. The man was pulling a box on wheels and Mum had to swerve to miss him. The cardboard split and sent football shirts spilling over the road.'

'Was he hurt?'

'I don't think so. Josh helped collect the man's things and he wanted to keep one of the shirts but Mum said he had to give it back. It was too big for Josh anyway.'

'I wonder if Jenny's mentioned this to Pierre.'

'Josh kept going on about wanting a football shirt.'

'Perhaps I'll send Jenny a text. You never know, it might be important.'

Nim watched while Dee's fingers got busy. Then she snapped the phone shut.

'If we were living in a fairy tale, there would be a happy ending.' Nim's eyes pricked, as if she was going to cry. She knew the sign and opened her mouth to gulp a breath. This was a good way to stop the tears and to make her voice strong. She started again. 'If we imagine the trees out the back are a wood, and Josh is lost in there, he is sure to make his way home. He knows the story of Hansel and Gretel. Even if the crumbs got eaten by birds, Josh will find a path.'

'Course he will,' said Dee.

'My teacher says every fairy tale ends well. The last line always says they lived—'

'Happily-ever-after.' Ella made the words join up in her race to speak. Trust her to butt in.

Nim pulled the loop of rainbow string from her pocket. She'd planned to ask Dee for a game and now was exactly the right time. Ella could buzz off. 'Want to play cat's cradle with me, Dee?'

Dee gave a smile. 'I haven't played with string in years. You'll have to remind me.'

'Let me have a go, Mummy.' Ella scrambled over.

'Not right now.' She moved Ella's pens and books away. 'You get on with your colouring. Nim's got to teach me how it goes.'

Dee shuffled up close to Nim, and for once she triumphed. Ella was left to sulk.

'It goes like this.' Nim arranged the string around her hands and used her middle fingers to make a shape. There was something pleasing about stretching her hands and watching the different colours create a cradle. Although it was made for a cat, Nim would be more than happy to curl up with Dee. 'You have to pinch the crosses between your thumb and first finger.'

'Like this?'

Dee's grip was the wrong way round.

'No, your hands have to be straight. Like horizontal.'

'I get you.' Dee picked the strings and dived her fingers under the lines, taking the string figure from Nim. 'You don't forget stuff like this in a hurry.'

Nim considered the new shape. 'I think this one is called candles.'

'Watch out for a flame,' said Dee.

Nim smiled as she hooked her little fingers and stretched the cord to dart between the lines. Her head bobbed close to Dee as she admired the new figure. She loved the warmth of their closeness. 'We're making pretty patterns.'

'Absolutely,' said Dee. 'C'est magnifique.'

Sirens split the silence as police cars tore up the road. Sitting on the couch, Mum stared out of the caravan window. She raised her knees and hugged them. Beside her, Nim became dizzy as her brain sprung into gear and she tried to think of all the things this might mean. Hope gushed in her tummy while fear made her muscles ache. She grabbed her foot and spent time crossing her toes, pushing one little piggy over the next until they were plaited like the crust on a pasty. The noise of footsteps distracted her and the room filled up with people she'd never seen before, but Pierre was in the group. For extra luck, she crossed her fingers as well. When she couldn't hold the position any longer, she rushed into the crowd. There were too many adults taking up space, but she searched between the gaps for any sign of Josh. She could tell from the way the adults were all hunched together that Josh wasn't there, but it was worth taking a look. She didn't want hope to vanish altogether.

Mum jolted into action. She took her notepad from the counter and held the biro ready to write. She told Dee she would do this so she could share all that was said. It was too difficult for Mum to remember things when she got in a flap. Pierre shook his head. Mum stared at him, turning the pen between her fingers. She didn't need to write that down, although Pierre did look strange when he shook his head again. She guessed it was possible for someone with a French dad and an English mum to be confused.

'No, don't tell me …' Mum collapsed against the table, gargling sounds coming from her throat.

'Let's leave Pierre to explain things to Mum.' Dad was there. He hooked Nim under her arms, picking her up like she was a baby. 'We'll go outside for a minute.'

Dad staggered as he carried Nim, tears streaking his face and dropping from his chin. Howling came from the caravan and Nim wished Dee was there to give Mum a hug. Finding the deckchair collapsed behind the caravan, Dad slipped the frame into place and sat down. Nim scrambled onto his lap but a chill ran through her as she waited for Dad to speak.

'Let's look at the sky, Nim.' Dad's voice was croaky. 'Let's have a good old think about Josh.'

There was a patch of blue between the leaves. It reminded Nim of the colour of Josh's *Thomas the Tank Engine* trunks. 'It's bad news, isn't it?' said Nim.

'Hhhm.' Dad didn't open his lips but the tears kept dripping.

A policewoman approached, holding her head at an angle. She was quiet, too, and just stood beside the chair.

'You wait here, Nim, while I go back to check,' said Dad.

Staring at Dad's back, Nim watched his legs fumble. Something awful had happened, Nim was sure. The realisation made her limbs stiff and her blood pump through her veins. She heard an echo of her heartbeat deep inside her ear. It was like she was closing down. The dread of finding out what had happened to Josh gnawed away at her skin, her bones, her brain.

When Dad came back into the picture again, he stumbled down the steps of the caravan. A policeman caught his elbow and helped him straighten. As he got closer, Nim wished she could freeze the moment. Stop him from talking, moving, stop the news from coming.

'I'm sorry, Nim.' Dad sounded strange, as though his voice was stretched.

'What's Geoff said? Did they find the Reliant Robin? What's happened?'

Dad's face was smeared with pain. Nim curled into a ball, not wanting to know the answers.

'I'm sorry, love.' No more words came.

PART TWO

The Worm
Five years later

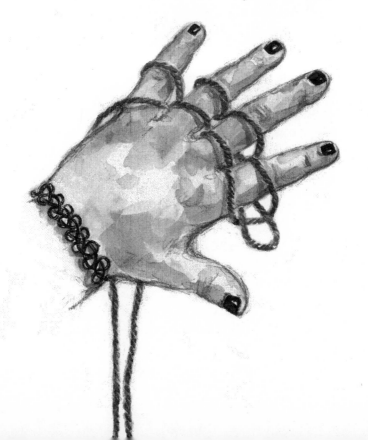

SIXTEEN

It was the first time Nim had worn her new high-leg Speedo swimsuit and she ran her fingers under the shoulder straps. Shame her tits were no more than a couple of mosquito bites under the sleek covering. Alice took every opportunity to remind Nim, with a self-satisfied gloat in her voice, that there was still time for her boobs to grow. Alice, with her size 34D bra, was maddening to listen to when they sat together on the school bus. She pushed the thought from her mind. After scooping the ends of her dyed brown hair into the swimming cap, Nim snapped her goggles in place. The sounds of swimmers pounding the lanes and the voices of spectators in the gallery echoed around her. She gripped the edge of the pool with her toes and dived into the medium-speed lane.

Nim liked the drill of stretch and pull, the flick of her head as she took a breath, the burble of underwater sounds. It wasn't as if she was ever going to make the fast team but her stroke length was reasonable and her turns were tidy. Bashing through the lanes, Nim came up for air after the final stroke. Her goggles were steamed and leaked water. She plucked them off and lingered in the shallow end until her breathing settled. When she was ready to exit the pool, Ben finished his session in the adjacent lane. They climbed from the pool simultaneously, water sluicing from their bodies.

'Shall I wait for you?' asked Ben.

'Okay.' Nim smiled.

It took ten minutes for Nim to get changed. Her face was tight and hot from a blasting with the dryer to sort her hair. She skimmed gloss over her lips and traced her eyebrows into arches. Without her full make-up kit, it would have to do. Entering the foyer, she saw Ben slouched against the reception desk. His damp hair was lank and there was a smudge growing on his top lip. A whiff of shower gel drifted. Ben's grammar school blazer was rucked up where he had his hands in his trouser pockets.

'You don't usually come to this session,' said Ben.

'Glad you're pleased to see me.'

'It's not that.' He cuffed Nim's shoulder.

'Mum's doing hot wheels on the sewing machine again and it's driving me nuts.'

'The lanes are good for clearing your head.'

'Tell me about it.' As the doors to the exit slid open, Nim sucked the icy air. The night was thick with mist and the moon a blur. 'Let's walk along the trail.'

The route took them on a meander through town. The pedestrian paths were lined with trees, globe lights strung in rows illuminating the bare branches. Dropped leaves had gathered into piles and a single brown one danced ahead of them.

'How's your dad?' asked Ben.

'What have you heard?'

'My dad said Gary's been laid up. He missed quiz night at the pub – not that they ever win.'

'He's in hospital having a few tests. If he'd lost a few pounds when the doctor told him, he might never have got in such a state. People must reckon he deserves it, being so fat and all.'

'No way. Everyone likes your dad. In fact, they're a bit jealous. There aren't many blokes his age with a full head of hair. He looks the part when it's slicked back.'

'You are joking. He single-handedly keeps Brylcreem in business.'

'What of it? My dad drinks Bovril.'

'That's better than Horlicks.'

'What the hell? A whore that licks. Now you've got me thinking.' Ben sniggered.

Nim crinkled her nose. 'I thought you knew about food products, Ben. Isn't food tech your thing?'

'Yeah, but I've never heard of it.'

'Horlicks is a milky drink for old people. A geriatric version of hot chocolate but not nearly so nice.'

They walked on, Nim listening to the pattern of their footsteps. It didn't matter if she was quiet with Ben. There was no need to keep up the banter. He was a friend from primary and she thought of him more like a cousin, or perhaps a replacement brother, a sort of family friend who had always been around. She guessed he might be thinking about rowing or his ambition to get to Oxbridge. They weren't in the same league. Nim took pleasure in being nothing more than ordinary but it didn't stop them from being mates. Ben turned to Nim while they waited at the pedestrian crossing for the lights to change.

'What are you thinking?' he asked.

'Nothing much.' Nim let out a sigh that made a plume in the air.

They walked on, cold seeping through the soles of Nim's

pumps. 'You don't want to hear about my group at school. They're obsessed with hair care and make-up. That's all they talk about. I could give you a few tips, if you want.'

Ben tested the girl's voice he sometimes used. 'Like, how do you protect your hair from chlorine?'

Nim laughed and gave his shoulder a slap. 'None of my friends actually sound like that.'

They reached the corner of Nim's road and she looked over to the town houses braced in a row. A lamp illuminated the blind across their lounge window. Nim gave a sigh. Mum thought she had good taste in fabric, but to Nim the pattern appeared more like an ultrasound scan. It was evidence of her mother's latest obsession. As if her fascination with collecting china hadn't been enough. Some of the items were weird, and the hobby became another excuse for Alice to pick on Nim. She turned to Ben and smiled. At least he knew better than to take the piss.

'Catch you later, Ben.' Nim crossed the road, knowing that Ben would wait until she'd made it through the door. Before stepping inside, she turned and rippled her fingers as a way of saying goodbye. With his hands in his pockets, Ben nodded and slunk into the shadows.

Everything was quiet in the hallway, and Nim hoped Mum had cleared away the mayhem of her latest home furnishing efforts, but the 'chukka-chukka' of the sewing machine announced otherwise. In the living room, Mum sat hunched over, feeding a strip of material with purple flashes under the needle.

'What are you making this time?' asked Nim.

Mum didn't answer but turned to show the pins gripped between her teeth. Nim picked up the end of cloth that swept the floor. 'You haven't started on curtains for my bedroom. You know I don't want any new things. I like my stuff the way it is.'

Mum pulled the pins from her mouth like she was extracting teeth. 'Thought I'd make a start on a pelmet. It doesn't have to go in your room. It's just I don't like to see the fabric in the cupboard reproaching me. I spent quite a bit of money on it.'

Nim rolled the tail of cloth into a bundle and passed it to Mum. 'I've been at the pool.'

'I guessed as much from your school bag dumped on the stairs. Let me tidy this up and give you some space.'

'Don't bother. I can eat my dinner on a tray.'

'It's no trouble.' Mum unplugged the machine and turned the cable, ready to fit everything back into its box.

'I'll make some beans on toast.' Nim barged into the kitchen and started searching cupboards.

'Help yourself to the casserole from the fridge instead. Three minutes in the microwave and it'll be piping hot. I know you're always starving after a swim.'

Nim stood beside the counter, listening to the hum from the machine. The bleep interrupted her concentration, mesmerised as she was by the stew twirling in the microwave. She used a tea towel to carry the plate to the table while Mum slithered into her armchair. With her kitten heel slippers abandoned on the rug, Mum stretched. Her legs weren't in bad shape, even with the standing she did at the library. This was one of the few ways in which Nim didn't mind being like her mum. If only she hadn't inherited her dad's knobbly knees. It was a reason not to shorten her school skirt too much. She could roll the waistband once, but more than that and she'd risk getting a torrent of snide remarks from Alice or one of the others.

'Mind you don't burn your mouth,' said Mum.

'I'm not a child.'

'I know.' Mum sighed.

Nim demolished the meal and glugged a glass of water. She was tempted to burp (for the sake of annoying her mother) but thought better of it. Stacking her plate in the dishwasher, Nim avoided criticism.

'Have you got much homework to do?' asked Mum.

'The usual.'

'And how was your swim?'

'Sixty lengths.'

'Would you like a cup of tea?'

'No, thanks.' Nim collected her bag and made for her bedroom, a good way to end the interrogation.

'You don't have to spend the whole evening in your room. We could watch something on TV together. I know you like *Grey's Anatomy.*'

'Not tonight.' She'd never enjoy an episode if she had to sit through it with Mum.

'What's the point in being hostile, Nim? I'm only trying to be a good parent.'

'That's what you call it.'

'I don't always get things right, but I do care.'

'Is that so?' Nim had her now. 'You've forgotten to ask something.'

'What?'

'About Dad's health,' said Nim.

'Indeed.' Mum pulled her lips into a tight little smile. 'How's Gary?'

'They're keeping him in hospital,' said Nim. 'Not that you give a shit.'

'He's your father. Of course I want to know how he is.'

'He texted to say I can visit him tomorrow after school.' Nim trudged up the stairs.

'I'll hang your costume and towel to dry.' Mum's voice spiralled but Nim didn't reply. Not when she was trying to do her caring mother routine.

On the top floor landing, Nim's school bag butted the door to the study and it swung open. She reached to catch the handle and pull it shut but something had become wedged underneath the door, and Nim was forced to enter to investigate. Going into the space that had once been Josh's room was something she tried to avoid. Never once had she used the exercise bike that stood in front of the window. She set aside the image of Josh's bed that it replaced, tried to blank out the picture of his engines parked next to the pillow. The artificial Christmas tree that stood in the corner had toppled over and was jammed under the door. She dragged it away and laid it against a wall. While she was in there, she opened the door to the wardrobe where Josh's clothes once hung. Mum had converted the space to shelves, where she stored fabric for making stuff: cushions, table mats, you name it. Spreading her fingers under a layer of loose weave on the nearest bolt, Nim studied the intersecting strands of silver and beige, the pattern like mesh on a security fence. It might make a nice scarf for Mum, Nim thought, smirking. Something to match her Crème de Nude lipstick. There was no way she wanted to become part of Mum's new fixation for home décor – the latest in a string of hobbies that prevented Mum from living in the real world.

In her tiny bedroom, Nim slammed her school bag onto the shelf. Torn pages from magazines wafted on the corkboard where she hadn't enough drawing pins to secure them properly. A picture of Keira Knightley in a crop top and low-slung jeans floated featherlike to the floor. Picking it up, she scrunched the paper into a ball and hurled it at the bin. Hole in one. Switching on her laptop, Nim checked for emails. Her friends were sharing photos online, showing off their latest fashion purchases, and Nim was being left behind. If she did something new with her hair, maybe dying it a different colour from the faded brown it had become … She had to do something to show she was her own person.

Nim dug to the bottom of her bag and found the concertinaed worksheets. She was well behind in Maths. It wasn't like Nim to neglect her GCSEs. She usually took satisfaction from doing well and liked it when her teachers gave her positive feedback, so long as their comments were out of earshot from the class. She didn't want to be labelled a swot, but getting her head down somehow controlled the thoughts of all the rubbish going on in her life: Dad's health and Mum being a pain. Stress made her belly tight and the pain sizzled.

Calculator questions were usually the easiest. Nim set about pressing the first worksheet flat and began to formulate the answers. It wasn't so bad. If she got one or two completed, her teacher would shut up. He was easy to get onside, but if the Head of Maths got to hear about her unreturned assignments then there'd be trouble. Mrs Winchester might send her down to the mixed ability lot. If that happened she'd never hear the end of it from her mother. Dad wouldn't be so bad. He stayed calm when things went wrong.

She heard Mum tapping her fingernails on the bedroom door. What did she want?

'I've brought you some tea.'

Nim went to answer the door but before she reached it, Mum was there beside her desk looking at her emails. Nim minimised the page.

'I'm entitled to a private life,' said Nim. 'It's written into the UN convention of rights.'

'I'm interested in your homework, actually.'

'Look, one set of questions completed.' Nim flashed the page.

'What a mess! Why don't you take some pride in your work?'

'So long as the answers are right, the teachers don't care.'

'I don't believe that for a minute.'

'Whatever.' Nim reached for the mug of tea and slumped over the page, feigning concentration.

SEVENTEEN

The rubber soles on the nurse's shoes squeaked as she edged around Dad's bed. Her blue uniform was sharply pressed and gave her more authority than the staff wearing pale green.

'Don't look so glum,' said the nurse. 'He's on the mend, really.'

The words were meant to reassure, but the yellow tinge to Dad's face made Nim believe otherwise. His cheeks were hollow and the skin around his neck looked baggy.

'Come and help me straighten these sheets,' the nurse said. 'Let's turn the covers.'

Nim folded the blanket and placed Dad's arm on top. He always joked that his large bones accounted for his excessive weight when really his eating habits were the problem. His elbow sagged and Nim studied the covering of hairs on his skin. Dad gave a snuffle but his eyelids stayed closed.

'You can give him a kiss.' The nurse's words were an order more than an invitation.

'I don't want to wake him.' Nim hesitated.

'He won't mind.' The nurse stood there watching like one of the lunchtime supervisors at school, ready to insist that her instructions were carried out. Nim pressed her face against Dad's and his bristles scratched as she pulled away. The reek of pine acted like a decongestant, making Nim want to cough. Poor old Dad. He was in a state with his health taking a downward turn, and there she was stiff, not knowing what to do. It was scary. But not the sort of scared she felt when he lost his temper and shouted. Not even when he was quiet and wanted to talk, which was always a signal she was in deep shit. In that hospital ward, next to his bed, Nim began to feel the terror of Dad's illness.

'That's better.' The nurse adjusted the plaster that kept the cannula in place and checked the fluid in the IV bag. Her fingers were long and thin, the colour of cinnamon sticks. 'He'll be fine.'

'You're sure?'

'Hmm.' The nurse scanned the ward, checking on the other patients. There was an old boy asleep in the bed under the window. The curtains were drawn around someone in the corner and the last showed the unmade bed of a patient who'd escaped.

'You're sure he'll be alright?' Her voice was a whine that made Nim's throat sore and she sank onto the chair.

'That's right. You sit down.' The nurse bustled towards her. 'All this fretting isn't good. I'll get you a cup of tea and a biscuit.'

'And one for me,' Dad croaked.

'Your daughter's here and you must promise to get well for her sake,' the nurse bellowed as if Dad were hard of hearing.

'Right you are.' Dad gave a limp salute with his good hand. 'I'll do my best.'

The nurse cleared off and Nim drew the curtain around Dad's bed. She pulled the chair close, flicked off her pumps and tucked her feet beneath her. A ladder ripped along her tights as she bent her knees. She sighed. She'd have to buy a new pair on the way home or risk wearing the black woollen knits Mum thought were an appropriate alternative. Mum would never understand how important it was to avoid the jibes, even when they were done in a friendly way from people she thought of as mates. What was it her form tutor said? The social hurdles of school were as challenging as the academic. Right. That's why she hadn't told anyone about Dad being in hospital. She imagined Alice offering a sympathy hug that lasted a few seconds, something just for show. Nim had learned the trick of survival at school: trust no one.

'So how's my best girl?' Dad's head flopped to the side and he gave a weak smile.

'Don't call me that, Dad. It makes me sound like a child.' Nim watched her father swallow, like even that was a huge effort. It wasn't right to give Dad a hard time. 'I'm totally fine.'

'You've not been worrying about your old dad, have you?'

'You're in the right place. Lots of people here to get you well again.'

'I'll be better in no time.' Dad tugged on the IV tube. 'With this stuff pouring into my veins. It'll knock the angina right on the head.'

'Absolutely.' It was okay Dad getting better in hospital but he had to stay healthy when he got out. She might as well tell him. 'When you get home, Dad, you're going to have to make some lifestyle changes. No more buckets of ice cream eaten in front of the telly. Definitely more exercise than a stroll to buy a newspaper in the morning.'

'Guess you're right, love.'

Nim let a sigh whistle through her lips. 'You promise to do things differently?'

'Cross my heart,' he said.

'I'll be checking on you. Don't think you can hide food from me. I'll be sniffing out anything containing fat. It's no good eating green beans on the weekends I'm over and then stuffing junk the rest of the time. I mean it, Dad. You really do have to try all the time.' Nim's eyes stung and she blinked back tears. She hung her head, wondering what else to say.

'I know you're right,' said Dad. 'I will try.'

'Thank you.' Nim wrapped her fingers around Dad's hand and gave him a little shake.

'Watch yourself,' he said. 'I'm a man on the mend. It won't do to mess with me.'

'Yeah,' said Nim. 'I'll take you on any day.'

The nurse appeared through the curtain and presented a tea tray. Nim accepted a mug and took the single digestive from the plate. Slurping his tea, Dad watched as Nim dunked the biscuit. When she'd finished eating it, she chased the crumbs around the plate with her finger. Dad said nothing, just watched.

'It's time I was going.' Nim collected her things and buttoned her school jacket.

'You should be wearing a coat in this weather,' said Dad.

'It's only October.'

'What about a kiss?' Dad puckered up.

'Goodbye, Dad.' Nim brushed her lips against his cheek. 'I'll check on you again tomorrow.'

'There's no need, love. I'll be home for the weekend. Come and see me then.'

EIGHTEEN

On Saturday morning, Nim walked to Dad's. The key to his flat chinked on the beaded chain attached to her bag. When she opened the door, a blast of Dad's favourite song greeted her. She never understood why he loved 'Mr Blue Sky' so much and she wasn't ready for another conversation about the merits of ELO but it was definitely better than her mother's habit of listening to *The Archers*. Dad was stretched on the sofa. His stomach seemed shrunken, perhaps from the regime of hospital food and missed opportunities for stuffing snacks.

'It's good to be home,' he said. 'Come over here and give your old dad a hug.'

'I was worried about you.' Nim fell into his arms and pressed her head under his chin. She listened for his heart and, counting the beats, tried to reassure herself that he'd be around for years to come.

'Fit as a fiddle now,' said Dad.

'Did you see a dietician?'

'Not sure one of those is going to help much. It's simple: eat less, do more exercise. It's hardly rocket science.'

'Are you going to stick to it?'

'Day two and nothing but low-fat food has passed my lips.'

Nim scanned the coffee table piled with strips of medicines and packages sprung open at the top. 'You're a right pill-popper.'

'Modern medicine is a wonder. Fancy a grape?' Dad whipped a bunch from the fruit bowl and dangled it above Nim. 'I've gone off them.'

Nim picked a couple and Dad dropped the rest back. Biting into the rubbery skin, Nim checked for seeds then munched her way through. One or two grapes wouldn't kill him. It wasn't about saying things were going to change, but doing it. 'You could at least try one.'

Dad reached over and seized a grape. He rolled it between his fingers and, opening his mouth, he aimed the grape and scored a goal. Two chews and he swallowed. 'Happy now?'

'No.' Pushing away from Dad, she sat up. 'No, not really.'

'You can't stay angry with me forever. I can't help getting ill.'

'It's not that.' Nim made her lips go flat and creased her forehead into a frown. She wanted to tell him, make him realise, that he needed to stay healthy. He was her Dad after all and he should be around for a good, long time. It was enough that her family had been reduced to three. One loss was one too many. She tried to find the words to explain, to tell him what she was feeling, but it became too difficult. Besides, there was no point in going on and on. 'I'm ready to go shopping in town.'

'You'll want your pocket money.'

'It's called an allowance, Dad.'

'Right you are. Go find my wallet. It's in the red jacket I wore home from hospital. It'll be in my room somewhere. Have a scout around.'

The bedrooms in Dad's flat were on either side of the hall. Before she went in search of the wallet, Nim poked her head around the room where she slept. She'd long grown out of wanting to lie under a Pocahontas duvet, but there was something comforting about holding on to it. Dad had painted the walls purple when it had been her favourite colour and nothing much had changed since. She opened a drawer, letting the shiny jewels from a broken necklace slide around the empty space. The strip of yellow ribbon from Josh's blanket tempted her to rub the silky surface against her chin. She resisted and instead prised the lid off an old custard tin where she found a few coins. Dad would have to be more than a bit generous if she was going to buy the special hair products she wanted.

Dad's room was full of shadows because he hung his suits from the curtain pole rather than in the wardrobe. Knobs on the cupboard were used to drape damp towels, and giant-sized pants were chucked about the place. Dad was a man of habit. His room was always a mess, but maybe that was because he lived on his own. Nim gripped the cagoule and tapped the pockets to find which one contained Dad's wallet. The leather was bulky with credit cards and, flapping it open, she noticed he still kept her last school photo behind the plastic sheet. She hated the way she looked with her skin all shiny and her mole jutting out like a swotted fly. Roll on next year for a new and improved portrait showing only her best side. Maybe she could even get away with a bit of eyeliner. As she closed the wallet, a business card fell onto the carpet. She picked it up and read the details. Strange that Dad was carrying around the card of a solicitor. The law firm had an office on the high street, but she couldn't imagine why Dad was involved with them. She memorised the name of Sally Jenkins at Ellis Solicitors. She could save the questions for later.

Returning to the lounge, she found Dad reading a car magazine.

'Here.' Nim dropped the wallet onto Dad's lap.

'Your usual for the fortnight.' He whipped out a ten-pound note. 'And there's another tenner for being my best girl.'

'Sweet.'

'I used to spend every Saturday afternoon at the cinema when I was your age. You could get in dead cheap and watch all sorts of films. If no one turfed you off the seat, you could watch the show over again for free. Value for money or what?'

'They'd arrest you for trying that at the Odeon.'

'True,' he said.

'I'm going on the spend.' Nim fanned the notes. 'Thanks, Dad.'

Taking the path into town, Nim reflected on the secrets she kept. Perhaps she should've said something about her school grades dropping. Dad was more reasonable about stuff like that than Mum could ever be. When the flack hit, Dad would stick by Nim rather than drill into her. With a bit of warning, he'd stand up to Mum. Recalling past incidents where Dad had sounded off, Nim gave a little smirk as she pictured Mum speechless and Dad with the upper hand. She kind of enjoyed having the two of them in battle. Dad never said anything really nasty about Mum but referred to her as 'a woman without reason'. That put Mum in her place.

NINETEEN

The carrier bag was bulky with bottles and boxes. Nim wanted straight raven hair and the purchases promised to make it a reality. The afternoon light was beginning to darken as she took a route through the recreation ground and went up the steps on the railway bridge two at a time. Making her way over, she stopped to stare at the parallel tracks. A voice on the speaker announced leaves on the line and apologised for delays. Nim pressed her chin against the railings; the metal was as cold as a knife against her neck. She fixed her gaze to the point where the railway lines merged. The lure of London made her heart fizz. One day she'd make it to the city and enjoy the bars and clubs of the capital, none of which existed in Fording. The town was a pit, but she wouldn't have to live there forever.

Nim had the house to herself whenever Mum was on the rota for a weekend library shift. It was total luxury to roam around the place, especially with the heating turned up high. Without Mum in the way, Nim advanced the hot water as well. Celebrity gossip from the radio accompanied Nim as she headed for a shower. Mum had mounted a blue plaque to indicate BATHROOM. It was meant to be funny, like a sign to show where a famous person had lived. Things got beyond a joke when the nameplate IMOGEN appeared on her bedroom door. Two dents remained in the wooden grain after she'd insisted it was removed. No one ever used the name on Nim's birth certificate, and besides, the illustration was of a bow and a sheaf of wheat. What was her mother thinking?

After a good long shower, Nim wrapped her hair in a towel and put on her shaggy dressing gown ready to watch Ant and Dec. The show was compulsory viewing on Saturday evenings and when Mum got home, it would be too late to argue over dinner and Mum would be happy to shove a pizza in the oven.

'How's your day been?' Mum sorted through the post Nim left on the mat. She appeared to need no reply. 'Pass the paperknife.'

'Pass the paperknife, *please*.' Nim loved the opportunity to correct her mother but she was too busy reading to notice.

'What's this about uncompleted Maths work?' Mum flapped the page and stared at Nim. The frown that scored Mum's forehead was permanently on show during conversations with Nim. The words 'shit' and 'fan' came to mind.

'I've fallen a bit behind, what with Dad being ill.'

'You have explained to the school, haven't you?'

'Teachers don't need to know every detail of my life.'

'I could've given them a ring. They do make allowances for when things go wrong.'

'Course.' This was news to Nim.

'Never mind, they've got the situation covered. They've decided to move you up a set where there'll be more supervision of work in progress. That way, you'll be more

140

than ready for the final GCSE exams in the summer.'

'Christ.' Nim reached for the letter and read for herself about the imminent disaster. 'There's no way I'm spending the rest of the year in Mrs Winchester's class.'

'The staff have obviously spotted your potential, Nim. This sounds like a really positive move.'

'You think so?' Nim's mind was clogged with anxieties. She'd done nothing of merit. In fact, she'd done the opposite. Girls in the top set were stuck-up bitches and the boys were fools. Mrs Winchester was bound to have it in for her as well.

'We need to celebrate. How about a glass of wine, Nim? I'll go and look for the bottle of cava I put under the stairs.'

Now there was a surprise. Nim had never thought to search for stray alcohol in that particular cubbyhole. While she waited, Nim read the letter and worries about moving sets crowded her brain. At least some alcohol would blur the inevitable. She couldn't get her head around what was happening. Okay, she'd quit doing her Maths homework, but she never expected this. The news was a whole lot worse than going down a set.

Mum returned, studying the label. 'It's only nine per cent alcohol so it won't have us rolling.'

'We could knock back the whole bottle.' Nim had had no trouble downing her share when a bottle had been split at Alice's party, but when a second one was opened, something had gone horribly wrong. Nim ended up spewing out of the window and became the joke of the party. Fortunately Alice lived in a ground floor flat and there were rose bushes to disguise the globs of sick so none of the adults found out.

'Get the champagne flutes out of the dresser. There aren't many opportunities for using them.'

Nim unlocked the glazed doors where Mum stored her collection of items bought at local auctions. That phase had occupied her for at least a year with a rotating display of all the new things she'd purchased. When Mum moved onto a new hobby, it was the set of tiny Susie Cooper coffee cups with a buttery pattern that remained on show. They replaced the pinch pots Nim and Josh had made at a pottery class. She was never sure what had happened to all the reminders of Josh. 'Gone into storage' had been a phrase used while Mum got busy with the bubble wrap and boxes. Once Mum had installed decorative replacements, there was no point in asking about the things that had gone.

As Nim set the glasses down, the towel on her head began to unravel and the tresses of her dark hair fell about her shoulders. Mum's tut was almost inaudible but it registered. Turning to glance in the mirror, Nim ran her fingers through the strands and checked for an even colour. 'I've moved onto soft black.'

'You'll damage your hair doing that. Such a shame to cover your natural colour.'

'I never liked it.'

Mum fiddled with the bottle, tearing the foil and unhooking the wire. A pop announced her success in opening it. Nim examined the flute Mum offered, watching the bubbles race to the surface. It didn't exactly hold a lot.

'Cheers,' said Mum.

Nim clinked and gulped, unsure exactly what she was celebrating. It was more a case of drowning her fears.

Even while watching *Saturday Night Takeaway*, it was impossible to stop her mind from frothing. She nibbled the last crust of pizza as scenes from an imagined Maths session in Mrs Winchester's class layered over the TV screen. Mum was glued to the set, keen to watch anything of vague interest to young people. She said it was helpful in planning and preparing for her job. Little did she know of the crap Nim had to take about her mum getting down with the kids at the library's after school club.

When Mum went to the loo, Nim glugged a few mouthfuls of wine straight from the bottle. The bubbles went up her nose and she thought for a moment she'd either sneeze or puke but neither happened. Mum found a stopper for the bottle and put it straight in the fridge without even thinking to offer another glass, which made Nim pleased she'd taken the chance.

'You seem distracted this evening.' Mum turned off the set as the credits rolled.

'I was watching that,' said Nim.

'Come on, love. What's on your mind?'

'Isn't it obvious? I don't want to go into Mrs Winchester's class. Everyone knows she's a bitch.'

'That's not very respectful. She's only doing her job, and a good one, I think.'

'Why d'you ask me if you don't want to hear the answer?'

'You're a bit nervous, that's all. They wouldn't have decided on a change unless they had confidence in you. It's a great opportunity. You're bound to do even better in your GCSEs with Mrs Winchester.'

'All you think about is exam results!' Nim's anger erupted and her voice was high and loud. 'I'm going to be so unhappy. There's no one in her group I know. They're all up themselves and I don't want to be part of it.'

'Calm down, Nim.' Mum reached out her hand but Nim

pulled away before she had time to land it. 'Don't be like that. I'm only trying to help. It seems to me you'll feel better about the whole thing once you've had a good night's sleep.'

'That's your answer to everything.'

Mum shrugged. 'It works for me.'

'It's too early to go to bed.'

'Not with a good book,' said Mum. 'I'll see you in the morning. Don't stay up late.'

It was Monday morning and Nim wanted to make herself look reasonable for her first day in the new Maths set. The school rule about no make-up was rarely enforced and it was easy to get away with a sheen of foundation and a coat of mascara. Alice was an expert with dark liner, but when Nim had used an eye pencil a clot had crusted in the corner of her eye. When she'd dug it out with her finger, no one had told Nim about the trail this left across her face and she'd become a laughing stock. After that, she'd abandoned the pencil and stuck with navy mascara.

Nim was pretty sure Alice would notice the extra shine to her hair, and using straighteners helped. She had to do something to match the henna streaks Alice was so proud of. Nim wasn't sure Alice's favourite trick of using dry shampoo added to her look, but Alice couldn't be separated from the container always in her school bag. With her new hair products, Nim would never need to borrow a squirt, so long as the gloss impressed the stuck-ups.

Spotlights in the kitchen kept the gloom of the thick morning sky away. Once she'd finished a bowl of cereal, Nim shouted goodbye and slammed the front door shut. The early crowd at the bus stop hogged the bench. Alice stood next to the wall, her shirt buttons undone to expose her cleavage and her tie hanging from her pocket like a dog's tongue. Nim tapped her iPod, halting the closing beats of 'Mr Brightside' as she unhooked the headphones ready for a girl hug.

'What's that smell?' asked Alice. 'You haven't bought some cheap perfume from the market again?'

That purchase had been a mistake but Alice liked to rub it in. No, it was Nim's hair that gave off a fruity perfume and she shook her head trying to get Alice to notice the soft black tint to her hair.

'I get it.' Alice turned her head so that her fringe fell over her eyes. 'You're going Goth, are you?'

Trust Alice to make the suggestion. 'I wasn't thinking of that.'

'Buy a wardrobe of black clothes and you'll be one of them.'

It wasn't exactly true; the soft black simply deepened the shade of Nim's hair. 'The conditioner's made it extra shiny, don't you think?'

'Get a whiff of that.' Alice leaned forward and snuffled Nim. 'You smell of apples!'

The day wasn't starting as Nim had planned. The texts Alice sent over the weekend with ideas for how to get on in the new Maths set meant nothing now. With one comment, Alice undid the shreds of confidence Nim had gathered. Ideas for a come back to Alice's remark wove through Nim's mind, then she struck on a line. 'That must make me good enough to eat.'

Nim didn't wait for a reply but strode to where the bus pulled in, her head buzzing as she remembered Dee using the phrase. It wasn't long after they'd returned from France that Mum had broken up with Dee and Nim hadn't seen her again. It was like a double desertion, first Josh and then Dee off the scene. In Nim's house, stuff that actually meant something never got talked about. Mum wouldn't allow discussion of anything connected with Le Camping, and as Dee was hardly flavour of the month with Dad, her name and all the fragments of her were lost.

All through registration, Nim stared at the whiteboard, imagining she was somewhere else. She didn't want to sit with the girls gossiping or join with the banter of the boys. Being on her own wasn't so bad. It meant she could put together a plan for how she would operate in the top set. The first hurdle would be working out who to sit next to. Not that there'd be much choice. Mrs Winchester was known for having seating plans which she stuck to without considering friendship groups. Apparently she never moved away from the prepared lesson, never enjoyed a little distraction or conversation or questions that might be a bit off the mark. Straight down the line was Mrs Winchester.

When the bell sounded, Nim joined the scrum as everyone barged through the door and spilled along the corridor. Mrs Winchester's classroom was on the first floor and as Nim made for the stairs, she walked past a boy who pushed chewing gum into a hole in the brickwork as if it were putty. When he saw Nim watching, he crossed his arms and nodded his head mechanically. Nim thought better of commenting, wanting to avoid getting a mouthful back. Instead, she made her way to the Maths room and peered in from the doorway. A couple of girls were already seated and Mrs Winchester was battling with the vertical blinds. She was as broad as a tree trunk with her head balanced on the top like a pea. The thought made a giggle escape.

'What you laughing at?'

Nim turned around and came eyeball to eyeball with Michaela Judd from 11F. She stood there, the knot in her tie so big it was like a rosette. God knows how she managed to get hold of an academic tie when Nim and almost everyone else was stuck with a clip-on. Michaela was just the sort who might want to hang someone with it and that would completely stuff the school's health and safety policy.

'Nerves.' Nim mumbled and hoped Michaela hadn't heard. It wasn't a good idea to admit weakness to the most notorious girl in school.

'Hey, are you joining this class?' Michaela removed a hairgrip that dangled from the backcombed mound on her head. Biting it with her teeth, she made the prongs open and stuffed it into the pile on top of her head. Nim guessed she was trying for an Amy Winehouse look but couldn't quite pull it off without the tattoos.

'Yes,' said Nim. 'How about you?'

'Didn't have much fucking choice. Head of Year yapping in my ear first thing this morning. Said there'd been a letter sent home but I haven't seen it.'

'My letter came on Saturday.'

'I don't give a crap. All I want to do is finish with this shit house and get a life.' Michaela made her eyes roll to the back of her head.

Nim dropped her gaze and mumbled, 'Exactly.'

'Cool,' said Michaela. 'We're on the same page.'

Mrs Winchester approached with her hands on her hips. This made her too wide to get through the doorway. She showed them to an empty table right in front of her desk.

'You two can sit here.'

'Ta,' said Michaela.

'I know you have light-sensitive eyes, Michaela, so I've drawn the blinds. There will be no need for wearing sunglasses in my lessons.'

'Left my Ray-Bans at home, Miss.'

'Yes, and that's where they can stay.' Mrs Winchester turned to welcome other students with an overly cheery 'good morning'.

'We're screwed.' Michaela spoke in a loud voice but Mrs Winchester ignored her. 'What's your name, anyway?'

'I'm Nim Mashard.'

'Weird sort of name.'

'Nim or Mashard?'

'Both.' Michaela swung her bag onto the desk and started sorting through her stuff. Out came a paddle hairbrush, a zipped make-up bag that bulged, a rolled-up copy of *Cosmo* and finally her Maths book. 'You can't help what you're called – blame your parents.'

'Well …' Nim wondered whether to admit her given name was Imogen but thought better of it.

Mrs Winchester bustled towards their desk, a pile of workbooks in her hands. 'You won't be needing that old thing, Michaela.' She positioned two sets of pristine books on the table. 'Take these. We'll call it a fresh start.'

Michaela shoved her things back into her bag and pulled from her pocket a stub of pencil and a biro with a chewed end. She wrote her name on the cover of the first book and Nim did the same with hers. The two of them were drawn together in a task that didn't involve anyone else. Nim took darting glimpses around the classroom and noticed most of the students were facing front and listening as Mrs

Winchester started the lesson. Michaela leaned back with her hands behind her head and Nim rocked on her chair to keep Michaela company.

It was a whole different experience. Nim was seated in a classroom at the school she'd attended for years, yet nothing was familiar. Mrs Winchester's voice, normally projected with full force, seemed to be drifting through the murk, a cascade of maths Nim didn't care about. It was much more interesting sitting with Michaela, wondering what she might do next. A flash of heat to Nim's neck rose up until her whole face beamed. Blushing like that was about as obvious as admitting to something she hadn't done. Christ knows what Michaela would make of it.

'Why've you gone all red?' whispered Michaela.

'It's a bit hot in here.' Nim flapped her hand like a fan. 'I'm roasting.'

'Your hair looks blue under these lights. Bit like a plum.'

'Stop that whispering, you two.' Mrs Winchester was poised to write on the whiteboard but instead fixed the cap to the pen. 'It's time I introduced you to the rest of the class.' She folded her arms across her chest while she waited for the class to pay attention. 'I doubt it's escaped your notice that we've two new members of our group. Michaela and Nim have joined us now that the twins have moved overseas. This class has a full quota of students. There'll be no more changes before GCSEs, so it's best if we all rub along together until then. Is that okay with everyone?'

'Yes, Mrs Winchester,' the rumble of voices replied.

'Oh my God.' Michaela turned to Nim with her cheek pushed into a bulge by her tongue. 'Get a load of those fools.'

Sitting in her bedroom, Nim stared at the blank page that should be filled with answers to the maths questions Mrs Winchester had set. Clattering from the kitchen made her wonder what kind of muck her mother was making for dinner. There was a time when Nim texted photos of her meals to friends. She got a few replies, but then the nudges at school started and the behind-the-hand whispers. Everyone knew her mum worked at the library in town and ran the after school club that a whole bunch of losers attended. It didn't take much for gossip to spread, especially when one of the no-hopers came in wearing a neon badge that her mum had awarded for effort. *Please.*

Nim closed the cover of her workbook but the pages didn't lie flat. Taking the lump of stone that sat on her desk, she let its smooth coldness fill her palm. As if her hands were a pair of balancing scales, she passed the stone between them. It was one of the few mementoes she'd brought home from France. Staring at the dents and markings, she became used to the strange phenomenon of memory. Images jostled and scrambled for attention and she waited to see which one would dominate. It was Dee's laughter that hooked. There she was, Dee with her hair sprigged and her cheeks bulged like a gerbil. She leaned against Mum's shoulder, letting the laughter pour. Ella and Josh chased up the hill and took one last turn to race roly-poly down. No one could manage it as fast as Dee. She was the champion and there was no denying it. As the laughter slipped away, Dee wiped tears from her eyes. Turning on all fours, she got to her feet and pulled Mum's arm to make her stand up. They draped their arms around each other, their clothes patched with green and brown stains. Tilting her head, Nim tuned into the sound of Josh's chanting, and involuntarily she echoed his words: 'Stains on your arse, arse grass!' Nim's tongue moved around her mouth as the words escaped from her lips: 'More stains on your arse, arse grass!' One last juggle then she landed the stone to hold her book flat.

After heading down to the dinner table, Nim observed the massacre on her plate.

'The meal doesn't look quite the same as when Nigella makes it.' Mum used her knife to press a quantity onto the back of her fork. 'I couldn't remember all the ingredients from the TV show so I had to substitute.'

Nim lifted the chop and stared at the goo underneath. She dissected a bit of meat from the fat.

'Perhaps using beetroot wasn't such a good idea,' said Mum. 'But at least it looks colourful.'

'You could say that.' Nim pushed the stalk of broccoli to the edge of her plate.

'Eat up,' said Mum.

Nim took a couple of mouthfuls and drew her cutlery together. 'I'm not very hungry.'

'There's Bakewell tart for afters if you eat a bit more.'

'I'm not a child.' Nim pushed the plate away.

'All the more for me.' Mum lifted another forkful to her mouth.

'You treat yourself, Mum.' Nim pushed her chair back. 'I've got to finish my homework.'

'How is Maths in your new group?' Mum caught Nim's eye and held her gaze.

'Fine,' said Nim. 'I've made a new friend.'

'That's good,' said Mum. 'You're in the top set with ambitious students. They'll help you reach your goal.'

'And what exactly is my goal?'

'To do well in your GCSEs, especially in proper subjects like Maths. Do that and you'll go far.'

'If that's what you think.'

'Of course,' said Mum. 'You'll make a whole new group of friends in that set. More suitable than the girls you've known so far.'

'What's wrong with my friends?'

'Nothing really.' Mum pushed the rest of her dinner to the edge of her plate. 'But there are one or two who aren't, you know, suitable.'

'Who d'you mean?'

'Alice, for a start. Bit too pushy, a bit too forward.'

'Good God.' Nim smirked. Alice was nothing compared to Michaela. And what the fuck did Mum know about friends? It wasn't as if she had any. 'I never realised you had it in for her.'

'I heard it was Alice who spread that ghastly story about the girl in the Science lab who used a test tube inappropriately.'

There was no way Nim wanted to get into a conversation with Mum about that. Heat rose from her chest, sending her ears tingling. It can't have been true, anyway. Nim's group agreed that you couldn't masturbate in class without somebody noticing. Ben said the same rumour had circulated at his school and he was pretty sure a test tube would need more force to shatter. Yuck. The thought of going to hospital to have glass removed from … It made Nim wince to think about it.

'Well, maybe you could invite your new friend over one day? That would be nice. You so rarely bring your friends over anymore. Why not invite her for tea?' Mum gave the sort of smile that was intended as encouragement.

'Right.' As if that was ever going to happen.

TWENTY-TWO

Nim sat in the car waiting for Dad. It was okay getting a lift to the pool, but he was so slow at wiping down the windows. Anyone would think he was actually cleaning the car the way he set about the job with a sponge. She switched on the radio. A crackle came but no music. Gadgets in Dad's life were half-cocked and it was never a surprise when things stopped working.

'Right you are.' Dad lowered his bum onto the driver's seat. His side of the car sank as Dad swung his feet inside.

'Thanks for the lift,' said Nim. 'It's the midweek time trials tonight and everyone has to show up, but I don't expect there'll be much difference in my time.'

'Keep at it, my girl. You never know what'll turn up.'

The exhaust rattled while Dad stopped at the crossroads waiting for the lights to change. Further along the road, the golden 'M' for McDonald's invited. Nim stiffened but Dad did nothing more than tug his hair and drive straight past. It was progress that neither of them mentioned burgers.

'Think I'll take the road through town. There's never much traffic in the evenings.'

'You're telling me,' said Nim. 'Fording needs a kick up the arse.'

Dad turned into the one-way street and the plate glass

windows of the closed shops made Nim wish he hadn't bothered. The empty street was another reminder of the dead-end place that was Fording. Dad pulled into one of the parking bays. 'There's a letter I need to drop off. Won't be a minute.'

Dad took an envelope from his pocket. He tapped it against his arm as he crossed the road and bent down to reach the letterbox at the door. With Dad posed like that, virtually on one knee, Nim paid attention. She read the sign and realised it wasn't a shop but an office: Ellis Solicitors.

'Glad that's out of the way,' said Dad.

'What are you doing writing to a solicitor?' asked Nim.

'Bit of business,' said Dad. 'Nothing to concern you.'

At the pool, the time trials had already begun and Nim was directed to a lane. Above the chatter of swimmers who'd done their turn, the whistle sounded and Nim launched into the water. Slicing into another existence, Nim's diving technique made her like an arrow. Her underwater strokes were powerful, and when she reached the end of the length, the turn was neat. Having mastery over her limbs, long and thin as they were, gave Nim a sense of achievement, even though she wasn't nearly so fast as the rest of the swimmers. The trainer shook his head and marked Nim's time on a clipboard. She hadn't been there for the warm up session and there was no point in asking about her result.

Ben was waiting in the lobby, leaning against the hot drinks machine wearing a white T-shirt under a dark jacket. Nim twirled a strand of hair around a finger, wondering if Ben would notice the new shade.

'Cool jacket,' she said. 'Is it leather?'

'The real McCoy.'

156

'Nice one,' said Nim.

'What's been happening with you?'

'This and that.' She let the silence hang, testing whether it was safe to reveal more.

'Come on, Nim. I can tell from that look on your face there's something going down.'

'I've made a new friend.'

'Cool.' Ben coughed into his curled fingers. 'Boy or girl?'

'Girl, of course. You know what it's like at my school. The boys are all losers.'

'Right,' he said.

'So, I've made this new friend.' Nim cocked her head. 'She's called Michaela.'

'That name's familiar.' Ben made his eyebrows ripple. 'She's the one with the big hair.'

'That's right,' said Nim.

'And the rep-u-tation!'

'Shut up.' Nim stared at the ground while anger threaded her veins. 'Don't judge.'

'I'm only repeating what everyone knows.'

'You're happy with your stuck-up mates at your school. Let me find my own friends.'

'Michaela's bad news, Nim.'

'She's not.' Nim tapped her foot on the tiled floor. 'Everyone thinks that because she's different.'

'I heard she's been done for shoplifting.'

'That's gossip. You don't know anything.'

'And there's worse.'

'Oh yeah?'

'Apparently she's crawling with STDs.'

'That is so obviously a lie.' Nim turned her back to Ben

while annoyance seethed through her. 'Why don't you just call her a slut? That's what you mean, isn't it?'

'Let's not fall out. Especially not over Michaela.' Ben gave Nim's arm a nudge. 'How about we take the trail and I'll tell you all about my mate at school and his latest trick?'

Nim was tempted. Learning about Ben's dramas were usually a laugh, but she weighed the possibilities and a stab of indignation grounded her. 'You can't go around calling my friends tarts, slags, whatever. You don't live in the real world, you and all those little shits you hang out with.'

'Now who's calling names?' said Ben.

'Stuff it. I'm walking home on my own.'

TWENTY-THREE

On the whiteboard, Mrs Winchester's calculations spread like messages from outer space. Her explanations came in bursts with the squeak of her pen filling the gaps. It was more than Nim could cope with, especially as Michaela hadn't made it to school. Although Nim had space to spread her books and pencil case across the table, there was no fun in sitting on her own. Nim's ribs tightened. Everyone else had a partner and she'd wind up having to work with other students if Mrs Winchester gave out shared tasks. Swallowing, Nim took a sneaky glance at the pair sitting in the next row. Michaela would never give those boys a chance. Not with their pencil shavings in a pile and their four-colour retractable pens.

It was easy to lose concentration when Mrs Winchester explained stuff. When Michaela was around, it was important to keep up. Michaela might ask Nim a question and it was wonderful to have the answer like they were real friends helping each other out. Otherwise, the two of them would ignore what they should be doing to hold a conversation of scribbled lines on the last page of Michaela's book. It was part of the fun of having a Maths mate.

Nim watched through the window as latecomers straggled into the school grounds. Her heart beat a little faster when she saw Michaela at the end of the line. A few people hanging about the entrance separated, making room for Michaela to reach the door first. Nim checked the time on the clock. She reckoned it would take five minutes for Michaela to make it to class.

Time passed slowly. Mrs Winchester's rambling explanations continued. Just before the bell was due to sound, Nim spotted Michaela through the glass panel on the door. She'd obviously organised her arrival to coincide with the end of the lesson. Nim wondered whether she'd make a big entrance but instead she loitered outside. It was a relief when the bell sounded and Mrs Winchester told the class to pack up. Nim rushed around the desks and bumped through the line to reach the corridor.

'What kept you?' Michaela stood against the wall, chewing gum turning in her mouth.

'I could ask you the same question.' Nim smiled so broadly her face ached but Michaela ignored her reply. Instead, she sniggered at the Year Sevens who went past. A tall girl who wore a scrunchie had the nerve to stare.

'Want a photo?' Michaela yelled. The girl ducked her head and grabbed the arm of a friend. 'Fucking loser.'

'Forget about her,' said Nim. 'Get me up to speed. What's been happening?'

'Had to travel over from Cornhill this morning.'

'That's where the executive homes are.' Nim bit her lip, conscious of pitching a ridiculous comment.

'Yeah, and?'

'Nothing,' said Nim.

'Got a new boyfriend,' said Michaela. 'Sleeps in a four-poster.'

'Tell me more.'

'Not with old Winchester in earshot.'

Nim smirked and Michaela grabbed her arm just as the figure of Mrs Winchester appeared in the doorway. Together they chased along the corridor, catching their breath at the bottom of the stairs.

'What lesson d'you have now?' asked Nim.

'How the crap should I know?'

'I think it's English. We can walk together. I'm in the History room above you.'

'Give us a stamp on the floor when you get bored.'

They parted at the entrance to the new block. Michaela gave Nim a goodbye hug that brought them close enough to whisper and Nim wished she could think of something funny to say. She needn't have worried because when Michaela released her grip they shared a smile. It was amazing to be standing with the girl Nim had once done her best to avoid. Everyone knew getting on the wrong side of Michaela had consequences, so up until this point Nim had kept out of the way. Now, she was wrapped in the possibilities of this new friendship and life was exciting.

Nim's heart pumped as she entered the History class a few minutes late. It was unlike Nim to be anything but on time. She said sorry to the teacher and made her way to an empty desk behind Alice. It didn't matter that she had to sit alone in this lesson; there wasn't going to be much work done with the pricks on the back row about to kick off. Nim flicked through the textbook that had been slung onto her table. She liked History and had several good marks from her coursework, so she was predicted an A grade in the final exam. It took the pressure off. One lesson full of boys' banter was no loss.

etGail Aldwin

Stretching her legs, Nim kicked Alice's chair. For a minute, Alice ignored her, then she turned around and showed a lopsided smile. She didn't bother talking quietly. 'She's your new best friend, is she?'

'You mean Michaela?'

'She's known by plenty of other names,' said Alice.

'What are you getting at?'

'Nothing,' said Alice.

'Good.' Simply knowing Michaela gave Nim a kind of power and influence she'd never experienced before. 'Michaela will have you if she hears you're spreading rumours.'

A table slamming over brought the class to silence. The teacher and a pizza-faced boy glared at each other. On a clipboard, the teacher wrote across a page ending with the jab of a full stop. 'That's the incident recorded.'

The boy scrambled to set the table straight and gathered the pens. 'It was an accident.'

The teacher put the clipboard on his desk. 'Let's get on with the lesson.'

The commotion was loud and likely to be heard by the class in the room below. Michaela was sure to be impressed and Nim wasn't about to confess that the drumming on the floor had nothing to do with her.

TWENTY-FOUR

After school, Nim saw Michaela at the gate, but she wasn't with the group who lit up as they left the school grounds – she was actually standing there waiting for Nim. Michaela cocked her head to the side, and a rush of excitement gave Nim the confidence to approach.

'Let's walk into town,' said Michaela.

With arms linked, Michaela charged through the rabble, dragging Nim with her and knocking a few midgets off balance. It was hard to breathe with laughter ripping through Nim's stomach.

'That'll teach them for being in the way,' Nim puffed.

Michaela grabbed Nim and spun through another group where the girls stepped off the kerb to avoid a collision. 'That's how to do it.'

Another girl who walked alone was swinging a rainbow string like a lasso and the sight of her distracted Nim. She wasn't arranging the twine in a pattern of loops and tucks as Nim used to do. Side-lined by a memory, Nim imagined draping the string around one hand and threading it between her fingers, making the figure of a worm appear. Josh used to love it when she pulled the string to make the worm vanish like a fish had taken the bait. That girl was messing about, turning the string above her head like she was out in the

Wild West. A simple shove sent the girl with the rainbow string off balance. 'Odious kid.'

'Knock her out!' Michaela held up her palm and Nim slapped a high five. 'Odious kids, look out!'

In the centre of town there was a shopping mall. It was nothing to get excited about, but Nim's heart beat out a tune because she was with Michaela. It was something like being a celebrity, hanging out with the girl everyone knew. Kids had to have the right face if they watched Michaela, otherwise she'd have a go at them. Nim noticed the shy ones drop their heads, checking out the laces on their trainers so as not to look at her. It wasn't long ago that Nim would've done the same, yet there she was, mates with a girl who was famous in Fording.

Michaela took a seat on one of the empty benches like it had been reserved for her and Nim wasted no time in sitting down. When a silence descended, Nim sieved her brain for things to talk about. Ideas about swimming came to mind but were immediately dismissed. The one thing they had in common was the Maths group.

'Winch-y-poos got her knickers in a knot when she realised you weren't in class,' said Nim.

'Stuff her,' said Michaela.

Nim laughed.

'Take a look at the smokers.' Michaela nudged her head towards a group who slunk into a porch. 'Who'd have thought they'd get into town this quick with their diminished lung capacity. I gave up smoking when I was fourteen, but I don't mind a spliff.'

'Yeah,' said Nim.

'Very ageing, is smoking. I don't want to end up like my mum, coughing her way to forty.'

'My mum's forty next year.'

'Odious,' said Michaela.

'You're right,' said Nim. 'Odious.'

Nim stretched her arm along the back of the bench, an action to fill the swelling silence. A taxi whittled along the bus lane and stopped outside the solicitors' office. Out tumbled Dad, his jacket flapping with the wind. Hunching her shoulders, Nim wanted to disappear into the collar of her shirt.

'What's wrong with you?' asked Michaela.

'Nothing.'

'You're curled up like a hedgehog.'

Nim pinned back her shoulders. 'My dad's over there.' She didn't move her head but darted her eyes.

'The fat guy?'

'That's him. Christ knows what he's doing with that solicitor. He's got a business card in his wallet from a woman called Sally Jenkins. He keeps delivering letters to her.'

'Maybe he fancies her! One way to find out.' Michaela hitched her oversized bag onto her shoulder and walked towards the shop.

'Where are you going?' Panic raced as Nim tried to guess what Michaela was up to.

'You wait here.' Michaela prodded Nim and she took a step aside. 'Pretend you're reading the adverts in the newsagent's. I'll go check what's happening.'

'Be careful,' Nim pleaded. 'Don't let him see you.'

'No probs. He doesn't know who I am, anyway.' She crossed the road and stood slap in front of the shop. Nim hunched her shoulders, trying to pretend she wasn't there while she watched Michaela in the reflection from the window.

'Your old man's sitting at a desk,' Michaela's voice belted. She wasn't even using the pretence of a stage whisper.

Nim stared so hard her eyes ached as she tried to make out what was going on inside the solicitor's. Mostly there were shadows, but she could see the outline of her father sat at the desk and the stick insect of Sally Jenkins.

'They're shaking hands. He's moving in for a snog. It must be tongues.'

Nim checked the reflected silhouettes. Motionless figures were sitting on either side of the desk. 'You're kidding me.'

'No.' Michaela strutted to the newsagent's entrance, her eyes clouded with lies. 'Your dad's got a girlfriend and he's heading out of the shop right this minute.'

Michaela sped along the pavement and Nim dashed after her. Taking refuge in KFC, their shrieking made diners turn. Nim found her purse and bought fries. Balancing on high stools, they shared the stack, poking ends into ketchup.

'Gotcha now,' Nim wielded a chip like a blood-soaked spear. 'Confess!'

'What you on about?' said Michaela.

'You didn't really see my dad snogging in the solicitor's office.' Hearing her voice say the words made the whole suggestion completely ridiculous.

'Course not,' Michaela scoffed. 'You're so easy to wind up.'

'I guessed as much. Come on, fight.' Nim dabbed Michaela's hand with ketchup and she lunged back. The sparring began and the laughter. Nim gripped her side because it ached so much and Michaela's chest heaved, showing the extent of her cleavage.

'Seriously, though.' Michaela cleared her throat. 'Have you ever thought of plastic surgery?'

Nim gripped her shoulders so that her arms crossed. 'I'm just a late developer.'

'I didn't mean your tits.' Michaela rolled her eyes. 'It's that mark on your face.'

'I don't know.' Nim closed her eyes and wished to be covered with Harry Potter's invisibility cloak.

'If it was above your lip, a bit smaller and sparkled like a stud, you'd be the same as Amy Winehouse.'

Nim spread her fingers and touched the mole. It was like a clod of soil on her face.

'You can't hide it,' said Michaela.

A rush of insecurity surged, bringing Josh to mind. The joke she wished he'd never made, the chaos that followed, the bastard that got him. Blinking away the memories, Nim returned to the moment.

'Ignore me like that again,' said Michaela, 'and you'll be asking for it. Not that I'd really do anything to you.'

'We're mates, aren't we?' asked Nim.

'Course we are.' Michaela let her skirt ride up as she stretched a leg to reach the floor. Turning her head, she scanned the diners, like she was checking who was watching. 'No point in sticking round here. Why don't you come to my place?'

'I should go home.'

'Come and help me with Maths.' Michaela made her lips pout. 'Please, Nim. Pretty please.'

Michaela's house was on the big estate at the edge of town. They walked, their breath showing as puffs in the cold air. A large area of grass held the houses apart as if separating

Gail Aldwin

rival tribes: those with the white uPVC doors and the others painted in racing green or indigo blue. They stopped in front of a semi-detached overlooking a block of garages. One had the cross of St George painted over the steel struts.

'Who parks there?' asked Nim.

'Member of the EDL,' said Michaela.

Nim frowned. A boy at school had been excluded for distributing fascist propaganda and she didn't want to get mixed up with anything like that.

'He's no friend of mine,' said Michaela.

Nim blew a long stream of air. 'Cool.'

Inside the lounge, a flat screen TV took up most of the wall. The very size of it impressed Nim so much that Michaela clicked her fingers to free Nim from a trance. Nim giggled to hide her embarrassment. The pile on the carpet was pressed into arcs, like a vacuum cleaner had recently done its work. This house wasn't so different from her own, even if it was on the other side of town.

They sat at the kitchen table and when the first page of calculations had been completed, Michaela biffed Nim on the arm. Taken by surprise, Nim grabbed the edge of the table for balance. She wasn't used to getting a bashing. Perhaps it could be called exuberance: a celebration of success. Nim stuck the lid on her biro and stuffed it into her pencil case. It was time to go home.

'You don't have to leave yet,' said Michaela. 'How am I going to finish the rest of the work without you?'

'Copy from me in the morning.'

'Sweet,' said Michaela.

'No worries.' Nim repeated the phrase from *Home and Away*.

'Tell you what,' said Michaela. 'I'll get you back somehow.'

'Oh, yeah?' Nim gave a smug little smile, aware that Michaela was no bright spark when it came to equations.

'No, I mean. I'll fix you up with Jez.'

'Jez?'

'I've been seeing him.'

'Is he your boyfriend?'

'Sort of ... he's really cool. Nineteen and he's got a proper job in town,' said Michaela. 'Have you lost your V-plates yet?'

'What?'

'You are.' Michaela grinned. 'You're still a virgin.'

'So what if I am.'

'I did all my sleeping around when I was fourteen,' said Michaela.

'You didn't!'

'Just kidding. You're so easy to wind up.' Michaela flicked Nim's arm. 'I'll talk to Jez. He's got a motorbike, you know. I'm sure he'll like you.'

'Great.' Nim wanted to meet Jez for sure. Michaela was a proper friend if she was willing to do that for her.

TWENTY-FIVE

By Friday, Dad was still on sick leave and he promised to be home when Nim visited after school. As far as Nim could make out, he had barely left the flat apart from the one trip into town she knew about. Suspicions roused by Michaela niggled but she had been kidding. There weren't any lingering looks between Dad and the solicitor, absolutely no sign of a kiss. Trust Michaela to have a laugh.

It was quiet at the flat and Nim wondered what Dad was doing. There was no music blasting, no chatter from the TV. She poked her head around the kitchen door and saw the washing-up stacked on the draining board. In the lounge, Dad was flat-out on the sofa. Nim collapsed into the chair opposite and, stretching her legs, she waggled a foot. A curl of hair fell onto Dad's forehead and sprang up each time he breathed. Nim smiled as she watched it bounce. After a snuffle, his eyes opened.

'Must've dropped off for a minute,' he said.

'Really?'

Dad checked his watch. 'No more than forty winks.'

'Really?'

'Okay.' Dad showed his palms. 'You've got me. But there's no harm in a nap, is there?'

'You should be feeling completely better by now. When

are you going back to work?'

'After the weekend the routine will kick in. I'll make salad sandwiches every morning and I've stocked up on low-fat spread.'

'Really?' asked Nim. 'What about exercise?'

'I have a plan.' Dad waved a pointed finger in the air like he'd come up with a genius idea. 'I'm going to leave the car a few streets away from the office. That way I won't have to pay for the car park and I get to do a walk each morning.'

'Make sure it's a long one.'

'Right you are.' Dad gave a salute and swung his feet onto the carpet. It didn't look like he'd changed his socks all week. 'We can take a stroll to the shop right now. I haven't collected my newspaper yet.'

They went along the railway path, which wasn't the quickest route. Perhaps Dad really was making an effort. Terraced houses overlooked the track and dog walkers paced along. Nim had to slow her walking speed so that Dad didn't get out of breath. It was more like a wander than a healthy burst of exercise but at least it was something. Whenever a dog approached, Dad stopped to give a stroke and exchanged a few words with the owner: 'lovely breed', 'healthy coat', 'good companion'. In truth, Dad didn't know the first thing about dogs; it was simply an excuse to take a break from walking.

'You don't have to talk to everyone,' said Nim.

'Can't help being friendly,' said Dad. 'Let's do a circuit around to the shops, go through the railway arch. You know how Joshi used to love playing echoes in there.'

'Daaad.' Nim wasn't in the mood for thinking about Josh. No one ever wanted to talk about her brother when she needed to. It was always Nim who had to swallow back the words whenever Josh came to mind, never allowed to say anything out loud. Mum would silence the conversation before she'd even got his name out. It was different when Dad wanted to do the talking.

'He was a lovely lad.'

'Walking that way will give us an extra few metres ...' Nim conceded.

'Remember how he used to yell and giggle at the same time?'

'Let's walk a bit faster, otherwise it'll be Christmas before we get there.'

'He loved Christmas.'

'Pity he loved talking to strangers,' Nim mumbled.

'What's that?' asked Dad.

'Nothing. By the way, what's with you and that solicitor?' Nim would have said anything to stop him going on about Josh. 'I saw you in the shop.'

'Just a little business.'

'Like what?' She tugged Dad's sleeve.

'Who's the sticky-beak now?'

Dad sat on a chair set out for family members while Nim completed her Saturday morning training. It was usually the parents of the younger kids who stuck around, but Dad said he liked watching Nim and it wasn't too embarrassing. As soon as Ben and his mates had finished their lengths, they headed for the poolside showers. Practising breaststroke allowed Nim to see what they were up to as she swam towards the shallow end. Bubbles dripped down Ben's face and he lobbed the shower gel. It crashed and skidded on the tiled floor, a football for them to dribble. It wasn't long before one of the trainers yelled, and the boys scattered. When it was time for Nim to get out, she noticed Ben eyeing her through the café window. It didn't seem right to have fallen out with him. All she needed was a mediator to help patch things up.

'Dad, why don't you go and have a coffee with Ben while I get changed,' said Nim. 'Make sure you ask for skimmed milk.'

'Right you are.' Dad tucked the newspaper under his arm.

With Ben to keep Dad company, Nim didn't have to rush. She dried her hair and applied some gloss to her lips. The wet and the heat made petal-pink circles appear on her cheeks. She didn't look too bad.

'Here she is.' Dad's voice boomed across the café and

made Nim want to turn around and pretend she had nothing to do with him. She twisted her lips.

'Why d'you always have to show me up by shouting like that?'

'I'm in trouble.' Dad nudged Ben.

'Buy me a cappuccino and we'll call it even,' said Nim.

Dad went to the counter, leaving Ben and Nim at the table.

'Your dad's okay,' said Ben. 'You can have a laugh with him.'

'So long as it's not about me.'

'Course it's not.' Ben rested his elbows on the table and Nim tidied the sachets of sugar in the container, separating the white from the brown.

'Bet you're both shattered after all those lengths.' Dad slid the mug onto the table, trying not to make the drink slop. 'And Ben's in the Enfield gala tonight. I don't know how you do it, mate.'

'Ben likes to notch up awards in the speed trials,' said Nim.

'Have you checked the results?' asked Ben.

'Yes,' said Nim. 'I'm always looking out for you.'

Ben ducked his head. 'I do the same for you. You're a brilliant distance swimmer, Nim.'

'What's that you're saying?' Dad barged into the conversation.

'It's nothing.' Ben shook his head.

'I've been telling Ben you can help with his Maths project,' said Dad. 'You being in the top set.'

'Keep your voice down. I don't want the whole world knowing.'

'Don't see why,' said Dad.

'Stop going on about it.' Nim necked her coffee and dashed the empty mug onto the tray. 'We better go.'

'Keep your hair on,' said Dad. 'I've promised to run Ben home.'

Ben was too tall to sit comfortably in the back and his knees dug into the passenger seat. Nim wriggled to get comfortable. Perhaps she should have offered to swap places with him. But, the atmosphere in the car was tight because Nim had zapped into a bad mood at the mention of her Maths set. Although it was childish to sulk, she couldn't do anything to haul herself out of it. Dad began whistling a ridiculous tune that had a chorus of 'do-dah-do-dah'. She hoped that if she huffed, he'd get the message and shut up.

'Can you drop me at the corner?' asked Ben.

'No problem.' Dad pulled over.

'Cheers.' Ben almost fell onto the pavement in his bid to scramble out of the car. He slammed the door and waved. Drumming her fingers against the glass was Nim's way of saying goodbye but the gesture was too small for Ben to notice.

Dad kept his eyes fixed on the traffic while silence elbowed between them. Fiddling with the dials on the dashboard, Nim got the heater working and warm air trickled onto her ankles.

'You don't have to be short with everyone,' said Dad. 'Nice boy, is Ben.'

Turning her head, Nim stared out of the side window.

'Ever thought, you know, that he might make a good boyfriend?'

Nim latched her fingers around the seat belt.

'That's if, you know, you're interested in boys.'

Nim sensed her blood surging. 'What's that supposed to mean?'

'Nothing. Although, maybe you've got feelings for girls instead.'

'Christ.' Nim's forehead pulsed. Trust Dad to go and dream up the idea she was gay. Images darted across her retina. There was Dee leaning against Mum, with her arm around Mum's waist. There was a searing sensation in her chest. 'Just cos Mum was with Dee doesn't mean it runs in the family.'

'I know.' Dad's voice sounded a measure of panic. 'I didn't mean anything. It's just that if you were *that way inclined*, I'd understand. Really I would.'

'You didn't show much understanding towards Mum.' It was strange to be on Mum's side for once.

'Not where that bloody woman was concerned.'

'You mean Dee? You always had it in for her.'

Dad shook his head as the line of cars slowed. They drew up to the traffic lights. The rattling heater filled the silent void. It was easy to gang up on Dee, as if losing Josh was all her fault. Yet Nim remembered Dee differently. There she was with a tea towel tucked into her shorts as she turned the meat on the barbecue. Heat from the charcoal made it look like the end of the caravan had turned into a wavy line. Sausages sizzled. In a salad bowl, tomatoes appeared like tiny rubber balls on a nest of leaves. When everything was cooked, Dee brought over a plate piled high, and using tongs, she shared the meat out. Josh took a bite from his burger, turning the disc into a crescent moon.

'Is it too early for a Big Mac?' asked Nim.

Dad shrugged.

'You can have a salad,' she said.

TWENTY-SEVEN

Nim's phone kept bleeping while she watched TV with Dad after dinner. Any text from Michaela required an immediate response. It was fun thinking of a snappy reply and Michaela took banter to a new art. She began teasing Nim about Swimming Saturday and called her choice of TV programmes odious. About as odious as, well, Michaela's choice in boys. But then Nim remembered Jez and ideas about him powering along on his motorbike came to mind. That was something else.

Give u a go on Jez. Came Michaela's text. *Meet 10 clocktower.*

Cant. Staying at Dads.

Sneak out!

!?!!

Nim put her phone in her pocket, determined to ignore Michaela's taunts and invitations. But as the programmes changed on television and her dad suggested going to bed, Nim was invigorated with the thought of escaping. Her dad slept soundly. There'd be no need for him to find out about a night-time adventure. Her fingers itched to type a reply. *B there 30 mins.*

Fear and excitement brought a bitter taste to Nim's mouth.

She waited while the wind whipped her skirt. Wishing she'd worn jeans, she stood in the doorway of Zara. It was better to wait in the shadows until Michaela appeared. She didn't want to stand out, or worse, have some creep approach her. The town centre was deserted but a disco beat drummed from the Fire Station nightclub on a parallel street. She'd been in the place once, when there'd been a half term under-eighteen night. Alice had worn a skin-tight dress with tinsel sewn along the seams. She'd called it her Tinker Bell impression, but Alice was no fairy. The whole evening was an embarrassment: plastic cups of cola and a sticky dance floor.

Nim adjusted the collar on her military jacket. The button over her pocket was loose so Nim picked the strand of cotton and wound the end around the shank, hoping to hold the button in place. Suppose Michaela's text had been a wind-up and she was left standing in the cold for nothing? That would give Michaela a laugh, leaving Nim hanging by a thread like her button. She didn't want to feel like she was dangling, but knowing Michaela had its compensations. For one, Alice was jealous of the way Nim had jetted up the social strata at school. Of course, Ben's view was different but that didn't matter as he belonged with the stuck-ups at the grammar school.

A cackle announced Michaela's arrival. She hung onto the arm of a figure in a leather jacket. They walked in a zigzag until they reached the clock tower. Stepping from the shadows, Nim made her way over.

'Hey.' Michaela's eyes were as large and black as olives.

'Are you okay?' asked Nim.

'Sure she is.' A cigarette hung from his lips and turned bright as he took a drag. 'One too many vodkas.'

'I prefer white wine,' said Nim.

'Course you do.' Michaela slumped against him.

'We'd better keep her walking.' He took Michaela's arm across his shoulder and heaved. 'You get the other side.'

Michaela wobbled between them.

'Jez and Nim, sitting in a tree.' Michaela stumbled and her ankles turned out. 'Fuck it.'

'Where are we going?' asked Nim.

'Let's get to the taxi rank.' They swayed sideways as Michaela lurched. 'I'm Jez, by the way.'

'Hi, I'm Nim.'

'Yeah.' He took a last drag from his cigarette and threw it on the ground. 'She can't stop talking about you. Says we're made for each other.'

'Hmm.' Nim ducked her head as her cheeks stung.

When they reached the bus shelter, Michaela refused to walk further and became grounded on a seat.

'You wait here with Kala,' said Jez. 'I'll go and sort a ride.'

Michaela's eyelids closed and her breath whistled through her lips. A snort brought her back to consciousness and she blinked. 'God, I feel awful.'

'Don't worry.' Nim patted her shoulder. 'Jez's gone to find a taxi. You'll be home soon.'

Michaela gave a crooked smile. 'You like him, d'you?'

'Well …'

'He's a good kisser, he is. Why don't you give him a snog?'

'Not if you're still going out with him.'

'No way. Jez is all yours.'

The silhouette of Jez legging it through the glow of tangerine street lamps made Nim wonder. Her last kiss had been with a boy at Alice's sleepover, and the slime from his soggy tongue was best forgotten. Kissing Jez needn't be as bad. A moment of distrust drizzled. Michaela was a game player, and using Nim as a pawn wasn't beyond her.

Along the road, a coach manoeuvred into the one-way system, halting Jez's progress. She hoped there weren't going to be people getting off at the bus stop. Michaela gagged as if she was going to throw up. Nim checked her pockets in case she had something to mop up a spew. The coach bashed against the kerb and faces peered onto the street. Nim wanted to hide. She didn't want anyone to see the debacle that was Michaela. Pressing her chin to her collarbone, Nim pretended she was elsewhere and waited for the chortle of the engine to pass. Glancing sideways, she noticed a line of dribble hanging from Michaela's lips. The coach reversed and caught the other kerb making the brakes sigh. The passengers continued to stare. Christ, the evening was turning into a complete fiasco. When the coach finally straightened, Nim shot a look at the departing vehicle and clocked the boy on the back seat. He turned his face so that he didn't meet Nim's gaze. Trust Ben to see Michaela at her worst.

'The black cab's not up for the ride.' Jez's sideburns were shaved into points. Under his leather jacket, she guessed his arms were covered in tattoos. Tasteful ones, she hoped: compass points and billowing clouds.

'Give us a hand with Kala,' he said. 'A minicab's going to swing by.'

Nim twisted her arm through Michaela's, and together they pulled Michaela onto her feet. She staggered, tossed her head and blinked. 'What's the problem?' she asked.

'Cab's coming,' said Jez. 'Stand up straight or he'll drive past us.'

She grabbed Jez's shoulder. 'Just need something to hold me up.'

'Feel free.' Jez tossed his head and smiled as if he was used to the routine.

'I'd better get home,' said Nim.

'Might as well,' said Jez. 'There's no clubbing for her tonight.'

'Another time.' Nim tilted her head to stare up at Jez.

'Sure.' His breath spooled in the air.

TWENTY-EIGHT

Mrs Winchester perched on the edge of her desk. This made her proximity to where Nim and Michaela sat unusually close. The other students had swarmed out when Mrs Winchester swung her arm in the direction of the door – she didn't need to use words to dismiss the class – but Nim and Michaela had to stay put. An enamel brooch like a jade eye was attached to Mrs Winchester's shirt. It was easier staring at the piece of jewellery than trying to work out what Mrs Winchester was going to say. Folding her hands in her lap, Mrs Winchester waited. Under the table, Michaela flicked Nim's leg. The ping startled her, but Nim disguised the surprise by tugging the hem of her skirt.

'It's not like you to be quiet, Michaela. You must have something to say.'

'You wanted us to stay behind.' Michaela used a pen to chip varnish from her fingernails. 'What d'you want to talk about?'

'I would've thought it was obvious.'

'Not to me, Miss.'

'Let's talk about your coursework.' Mrs Winchester searched through a pile of books on the shelf and pulled free a folder. 'There's been concern expressed by a number of teachers.'

'I'm behind with my Geography,' Nim volunteered without thinking what effect the admission would have on Michaela. She scowled but continued to strip nail varnish. Nim stared at the pattern of flakes on the table.

'Thank you for your honesty,' said Mrs Winchester. 'So long as you get everything completed before the end of term, that will be acceptable. Michaela, you've work to do in Textiles. Such a shame to be lagging behind when you were predicted a B grade.'

'What's the point in Textiles?' said Michaela. 'Stuff in Primark's much cheaper than anything you can make.'

'That's not the point.' Mrs Winchester's eyes focused on the page. 'Looks like you need to get on with your English work, too.' Mrs Winchester snapped the folder shut before Michaela had a chance to reply. Kids in the playground started a game of tag and squeals from the girls made Mrs Winchester turn to the window. Michaela nudged Nim with such force she nearly shot off the table. This made Nim want to laugh but instead she pressed her lips together in a flat smile. Michaela rolled her eyes.

'I don't want to labour the point. You two are intelligent students. Don't let the chance of success slip through your fingers.' Mrs Winchester spun the folder onto the desk and it landed with a clunk. 'You've got your name down for sixth form, Nim. There's no guarantee of a place for existing students. You have to get the grades.'

Michaela stopped scraping her nails and Nim could sense her eyes boring. It was enough to make Nim's skin become hot. As if in slow motion, Michaela licked her finger and pressed it hard against Nim's cheek.

'Sizzle,' she said.

Nim jerked away and, using the sleeve of her jumper, wiped off the spit. 'I don't have to tell you everything.'

'Course you don't.' Michaela let her chair grind against the floor as she stood. 'Keep your little secrets.'

'There's no need to go falling out,' said Mrs Winchester. 'Seems to me you two could be good for each other.'

'As if you'd know, Miss.' Michaela grabbed her bag and bundled out of the room.

Nim brushed Michaela's pile of varnish flakes onto the floor. 'I'm not completely sure what I want to do after GCSEs.'

'You've got time to make up your mind. If you want a change of scene, you could always make an application to college. You might do well in a new environment.'

'I'll think about it.'

'Get yourself off now, while there's still a bit of break time.'

Nim checked the corridor to see which way Michaela had gone. The fact that she hadn't waited for Nim wasn't a good sign. The obvious direction was outside. The teachers called it a playground but Michaela renamed it the 'bitch-pitch' – and everyone knew she was in charge. As Nim walked to the stairwell, hope of keeping this strange friendship alive drained away. Noticing new splatters of chewing gum on the treads, she avoided the blotches as she made her way down.

'Take a look at you, trip-trapping.' Michaela's voice plummeted from the landing.

'I'm not a goat.' Nim held her leg mid-stride as if deciding whether to continue down or turn around.

'Get yourself up here.' Michaela was bent over the railings, her hair trailing like hanging ivy.

'It's your turn to be red in the face now,' said Nim.

'Can't help it if my blood runs in the right direction.' Michaela flipped to an upright position as Nim approached and she fanned her face. A Year Seven boy stopped to watch what was going on.

'What you staring at?' snapped Michaela.

'Nothing.' The boy remained completely still, his gaze stretching across the space.

'What d'you want?' asked Michaela.

'He's not staring at you, Michaela.' Nim was used to the ridiculous antics of kids who knew no better.

'How d'you get a blackhead that big?' The boy's words splurged as if he'd been the first one to come up with the joke.

'Very funny.' Nim pressed a finger over the mole.

'Think you're smart, do you?' Michaela's eyes were ugly and she stamped the floor. 'Come here and say that.'

'You don't scare …' The boy's voice faltered.

'Fuck off, you little squirt.'

The boy turned and legged it along the corridor.

'Your blazer reaches your ankles,' Michaela called after him. 'Fucking penguin.'

He kept walking.

'Yeah, fuck off.' Nim's words tasted of freedom and power.

Michaela grabbed Nim's arms and they raced downstairs. Giving the fire exit a karate kick, Michaela released the bar and the doors swung open. The two descended the steps to an entourage of Michaela's mates. They passed through a haze of breath freshener and flowery perfume. At the bench, Michaela clicked her fingers, and the younger girls who'd started eating their packed lunches began to clear up and move away. Michaela was queen to her throne. There she sat, her hair bunched like a mane, as she surveyed the gathering crowd.

'Park your bum,' said Michaela.

Relieved, Nim copied Michaela's pose, her legs stretched out.

'Wish I had your legs,' said Michaela. 'Christ, they're much longer than mine.'

'Thanks.' Nim turned her ankles, basking in the compliment. She hoped Michaela wouldn't comment on her knees, which were always a cause for jibes.

'Shame they're so thin.'

Nim tucked her legs out of sight.

'No need to be coy,' said Michaela. 'Just because you need some meat on your bones. Jez likes a bit of bulk.'

The mention of his name sent a quiver through Nim. Sensing a blush might cover her face at any minute, Nim lowered her eyes.

'Don't get me wrong, he fancies you.'

'Oh.' The heat pumping her face was like a furnace.

'Thinks you're sweet the way you keep blushing.'

'That isn't the impression I'm trying to make.'

'Okay, let's say you're cute. Is that better?'

Nim nodded and smiled at Michaela.

'I'll fix it so you can meet him properly. Come to my house for a sleepover on Friday.'

'I'm not sure,' said Nim.

'Don't make excuses about swimming. You're due some time off, aren't you?'

'I guess,' said Nim. 'I'll let you know.'

'Cool,' said Michaela.

TWENTY-NINE

Nim followed Alice halfway along the bus. It was Alice's turn to sit beside the window and she launched onto the seat. Boys in the back row argued over places and the driver watched the mirror angled to observe anyone kicking off. He ignored the banter and the electric door made a shushing sound as it closed.

'Surprised you still want to sit with me.' Alice stuck her elbow into Nim's side.

'Watch out,' said Nim.

'I'm doing up my belt.'

A cloud of resentment descended. Nim was determined not to speak until Alice apologised. The stab of pain in her ribs magnified as her outrage grew. This was about Michaela; it was typical of Alice to get in a mood. She should know it was possible for a person to have other friends. Christ. She was being so immature. Nim shuffled on her seat, trying to get comfortable. Alice continued to ignore her until Nim could stand it no longer. 'Are you mad at me for something?'

Alice made a huffing noise and turned to stare out of the window. A little kid sitting in front pushed her face into the gap between the headrests. Her spearmint breath made Nim glance over, and she watched the gum swirl around the girl's open mouth.

'Mind you don't choke and die,' said Nim.

'I never swallow.' One more turn of the gum and she got the message. Flopping back, the girl restarted her chatter with the other kids.

After a couple of stops, the bus began to empty. Nim wished she could start a conversation but Alice sat there picking a hole in her tights. The ladder went from knee to ankle, then she started on the other leg.

'Shall I tell you what's wrong?' Alice talked to the window and her breath showed on the glass. 'You can't dump me just because you've got a new mate.'

'I thought as much!' Nim plucked Alice's sleeve but she wouldn't turn around. 'It's not like that. Come on, Alice. Give me a chance to explain.'

Alice tilted her head, showing her slit eyes. 'Go on.'

'You know I've got to sit next to Kala in Maths. Mrs Winchester put us together and there's no way I can get out of it.'

'Kala, is it now? Like you're best friends.'

Nim shrugged. 'Just because I'm mates with Michaela doesn't mean we can't be friends.'

'But you're joined at the hip.' Alice snorted. 'The way you carry on. It's like you love her or something. Are you a dyke just like your mum?'

'Don't start about my mum. You promised to keep it a secret.'

'Did I?' Alice made her face go blank. 'And not forgetting your poor, dead—'

'That's enough! Don't you dare mention Josh.'

Alice wasn't going to get away with saying stuff like that. Nim focused on the blur of bricks beyond the window and blotted Alice's face from her sight. 'You bitch.'

'Call me names,' Alice said. 'Think that's going to help?'

'Hoo-woo.' The girl's face was jammed between the seats again. 'You can't say bad things on the bus. I'll tell the driver.'

Nim grabbed her bag from the floor and threw it across the aisle. Her blood singed from anger and injustice. It wasn't like Nim had done anything wrong but she might've guessed it would be like this. Alice was a complete control freak. Diving onto a spare seat, she was glad to be alone. The stupid little kids stared and whispered. Nim stamped the floor and leered. The girl with all the talk opened her mouth.

'Fuck off, you little squirt.' One sentence and Nim shut her up.

The bust-up with Alice couldn't have come at a worse time. She'd been banking on the excuse of staying at Alice's as a cover for Michaela's sleepover. The driver cut the engine when they reached the last stop and warm air from the heating vents died. Nim remained in her seat as the others dragged out. She'd need to give Alice a good start. She didn't want to see her again on the way home. Not that Nim had to be embarrassed about her new friendship. Michaela was out there – she didn't put up with any shit and Nim didn't have to either.

At home, Mum had spent her day off pottering. She loved that word. Nim often suspected that this involved snooping on stuff in her room so it was worth the effort of hiding anything private. Mum seemed pleased that tidiness ran in the family.

'Leave off with your daydreaming.' Mum's voice coaxed. 'Give me a hand to shift the table. If we push it against the wall, it'll give a bit more space.'

'You're always moving furniture.'

'It's my hobby,' said Mum.

Nim helped to shove it over. 'I'm not sure it makes much difference.'

'Perhaps not, but you know what they say: a change is as good as a rest.'

'No one says that apart from you.'

Mum gave a quizzical glance.

'I'm teasing, you know.'

'Of course,' said Mum.

Nim took advantage of the relaxed atmosphere to pose a question. 'Can I go to a sleepover on Friday?'

'You and your sleepovers! I suppose it's Alice again. Don't you find her a bit clingy? She seems to want you around a lot.'

'Dad says old friends are the best.'

'Does he now.'

'So it's okay?' Nim wasn't about to distract Mum with the actual truth about staying at Michaela's. Mum would want to know all the details, and keeping the facts about Michaela from her was a kindness really, saving Mum from any worries.

'If you want,' said Mum. 'By the way, how is your father these days?'

'Back at work and seeing a solicitor.' Now Nim had permission for the sleepover, changing the subject was an easy way to deflect further questions.

'He'll be glad to be busy again,' said Mum. 'And making a will is the sensible thing to do.'

'You think he's making a will?'

'That's my guess.' Mum rummaged in a drawer and

took out a quilted table runner. 'Why else would he go to a solicitor?'

'You mean a will for when he dies?'

'To take care of his estate.' Mum spun the runner around and, watching, Nim began to feel dizzy.

'Don't say that.' The idea of Dad dying pierced then spread. Heat rushed to Nim's face and her skin became clammy. It was like she couldn't breathe, that she was wrapped in cling film, over her mouth, over her eyes. She sucked a breath and stumbled. Mum caught her arm, got her to sit in the armchair and went to fetch water. Nim listened to the rush from the tap and shook her head to get the strands of her fringe out of her eyes. Mum folded Nim's hand around the glass. Her voice was a burble as she encouraged Nim to drink. When her senses returned, Nim drew her legs together and pulled down her skirt, which had ridden up in the commotion.

'You've got a normal colour returning,' said Mum. 'Shall I take the glass?'

Nim passed it over and took a deep breath.

'Have you had a funny turn before?'

'No.' But then Dad dying had never seemed real before.

'Not even when your period's due?'

'No!' Talking about stuff like that was something to be avoided.

'Well. Your recovery is impressive. And you'll know what to do next time, if it happens again.'

'I guess.'

'Shall I give you a hand up?' Mum reached for her. 'To make sure you're steady on your feet.'

'Okay.'

Mum helped Nim out of the chair and wrapped her arm around her, drawing Nim into a hug. Nim noticed Mum's bony shoulder digging into her head but she didn't move. The proximity was strange yet reassuring. Mum pressed her face against Nim's forehead and the two took measured breaths.

'You mustn't worry about your dad. He's got stamina. I'm sure he'll live a good, long time.' Mum stepped away yet continued to hold Nim's hand, sandwiched between her own. 'Making a will is only a precaution.'

'I guess,' said Nim.

THIRTY

When the morning bell sounded, Mrs Winchester was on duty, so Nim made her way straight to the form room. She was careful to appear in class before the end of registration. The supply teacher gave a tut and marked her in.

Nim sat alone at a desk while Alice formed a group. A couple of boys sat at the edge, trying to get in with the girls. People were talking in especially quiet voices, but they'd better not be making Nim the subject of conversation. They were supposed to be studying Personal and Social Education during the extended form time on a Wednesday, but no one told the teacher. Actually, he wasn't bad looking, with shaved hair at the sides and a tumble of chestnut curls on top of his head. It wasn't just the girls eyeing him; the dirt-faced mob were looking to him for tips on appearance.

Nim didn't exactly know what Michaela was planning for the sleepover. From the sound of it, she wanted to fix Nim up with Jez. The idea sent a thrill zipping to her heart, although it was silly to expect it to work out. But if he did like her, well, Jez would be her first proper boyfriend. Nim 4 Jez. Their names went together well but that didn't stop her doubts. What would he see in Nim? Puzzling about the situation killed time and allowed Nim relief from the embarrassment of sitting alone. Not that she wanted to be part of Alice's clique. She could've moved closer to the group, but there was no point. It was better to be self-contained.

In double Geography, the lesson dragged. Staring at the chair legs of the row in front, Nim decided to keep her head down and avoid eye contact with the teacher. At the end of the lesson, Nim took her Geography file from her bag and stalked to the teacher's desk where she dropped it onto a pile. The draft essay was cobbled together with bits of information she'd found online.

'Sorry it's a bit late,' she said.

He raised an eyebrow. 'Better late than never.'

Leaving the building at break time, Nim found Michaela waiting by the picnic tables near the netball courts, curls of smoke playing around her lips.

'Try a fag,' she said. 'It'll keep you warm.'

'I thought you'd quit.'

Michaela took a long drag and Nim wished she'd never said anything. 'What's it to you?'

'Nothing ... I'm just not that cold.'

'Suit yourself.' Michaela paced along the boundary line. 'Aren't you coming?'

'Depends where you're going.'

'I'd give anything to be out of this shit house.'

Michaela dropped the cigarette and rubbed it over with her trainer. Nim approached and they linked arms. Together, they marched around the rectangular court. It was easy to exchange words without others hearing but Michaela always made it clear who she was talking about. A nod of the head or a squinted eye was all it took. When she'd done with bitching, Michaela pushed into a group of girls and nicked a packet of crisps from the ginger-haired one. She realised they were smoky bacon and tore the bag to sprinkle the contents over a Muslim kid who wore a scarf. The girl brushed away the flakes and turned her back. Nim released Michaela's arm as a slash of guilt sent heat rising through her.

'That'll teach her,' said Michaela.

'Teach her what?' asked Nim.

'Come to our country, she ought to eat our food.'

'Not everyone likes flavoured crisps – full of E-numbers.' Nim's attempt to divert the situation worked. Michaela threw back her head and sent her muddy eyes spinning. The girls who stood there watching began to laugh. Everyone became part of the joke when Michaela was messing about. The Muslim girl stepped away. It was good that she'd taken the cue to move on; it saved her from anything worse Michaela might've done. The tension in Nim's spine eased and it was okay to join in the laughter.

'I'm going for a piss.' Michaela pushed through the groups blocking her route and students scattered. Spotting Alice and her friends, Nim dodged to catch up and managed to direct Michaela around them. They formed a tight little circle but Alice wouldn't bend inwards like the others. Instead, she placed a hand over her mouth as if to announce she was gossiping.

'That's your mate, isn't it?' Michaela squared-up. 'She looks like a slag with her tits hanging out.'

'*Ignore her.*' Nim put as much disdain in her voice as she could manage. The last thing she wanted was the two of them in a fight.

'I'll let her off.' Michaela jabbed her finger in the air.

Alice puckered her nose.

'Take me on, would you?' said Michaela.

Alice pressed her lips together and, lowering her head, fell into the group, who closed ranks around her. A triumphant Michaela surveyed the gathering students. 'Let's get inside before the dross.'

When they reached the loos, Michaela beckoned Nim into the same cubicle. It was mad, the two of them squashed inside, jabbing knees and elbows because Michaela insisted on squatting to pee, saying she wasn't going to sit down and pick up crabs thanks to a bunch of slags. They changed places and Michaela held the bags. She began humming the *William Tell* Overture to disguise the splatter of Nim's wee. If she hadn't been on the toilet, Nim would've wet herself laughing.

Their paths divided on the first floor landing, Nim heading to the Arts block and Michaela going in the other direction. 'Are you okay coming to mine on Friday?' asked Michaela before they split.

'Course.' Nim made her fingers dance in a goodbye wave.

THIRTY-ONE

Nim checked her membership card and realised she'd have to go to the mid-week swim session or risk getting kicked out of the club. Not that it bothered her but Mum would moan about wasting money. Making the most of her hard-earned cash was always a priority for her mother, especially as a new catalogue had arrived with more ideas for home furnishings. There she was, embroidered cushions plumped around her in the armchair, staring at the pages, probably planning her next project.

'I'll get off to the pool,' said Nim.

Mum scribbled a few notes.

'I'm going swimming,' said Nim.

'Of course.' Mum didn't look up. 'I'll have supper ready when you get back.'

'Not too much stodge.'

Mum peeled off a Post-it to mark something on the page.

'Bye, then.' Nim circled around the table that had again been reorganised to look like an island in the middle of the floor. It was the sort of thing that drove Nim mad.

A chemical steam rose from the pool, making Nim's skin clammy. Around her, talk was interspersed with the trainers blasting their whistles. Nim curled her toes around the rim of the pool and drew her arms into a diving position. She clipped the water with a splash and plunged deeper than she'd intended. Her body became sleek and cool, her arms stirring as she came to the surface. With the silk of silence broken, she swung her head, measuring the space. In the next lane, swimmers ploughed, raking waves. It was time to make her stride and get into a rhythm. She had to complete at least sixty lengths or it wasn't worth turning up at all. Slicing the water, the practice left her gulping air, her chest heaving. She stopped at the shallow end and ripped off her goggles. She was one of the last in the pool. Nim launched onto the side, turning her hips to land in a sitting position.

The session supervisor tapped his watch. What was his problem? He couldn't even be bothered to call her name or say a few words. It wasn't Nim's fault it took her longer to do lengths than the others. Stuff the club; she wasn't interested in competing anymore. Swimming was a total waste of time when she'd never be in the winning lane. Ripping off her cap, she let her hair clump around her shoulders as she idled at the poolside.

'Haven't you got a home to go to?' he asked.

'You can stick your club – I've got better things to do.'

'Your dad might have a thing or two to say about that.'

'I don't give a shit – I'm not coming anymore.'

'Like that, is it? I'm locking up in five minutes. Best you be ready.'

Nim stretched her arms above her head as if she was in no hurry, but when the supervisor turned his back, she tore into the changing rooms and dressed. If she was quick, she might catch Ben coming out of the gym. But as soon as she saw Ben's expression, she regretted the rush to see him.

'I didn't expect you to be here,' he said. 'Don't you prefer hanging out in town?'

'This is my last session. I've decided to quit the club.'

'You're full of good ideas at the minute.'

'Don't judge me, Ben. I can make my own decisions.'

'And hanging out with Michaela is one of your better moves?'

'So, it's okay for you to be out on a Saturday night but not me?'

'That's different and you know it. I was coming back from a swimming meet. What the fuck were you doing?'

'I can look after myself,' said Nim. 'I'm entitled to a life.'

'What sort of life? They're losers and users.'

'How would you know?'

'Come on, Nim. I saw you. You could've ended up in a whole load of shit.'

'But, I didn't. Besides, I was helping a mate.'

'Yeah, I could see.' Ben smirked. 'So pissed she couldn't stand up. Is Michaela the kind of friend you need?'

'There's nothing wrong with her.' Nim was pumped with outrage. 'You don't know what it's like for me. You're just like the others from the grammar school – looking down your nose.'

'That's not fair,' said Ben.

Nim glowered at him, anger coursing through her veins. 'But it's true.'

'Sure.' He shrugged.

'Keep away from me, Ben.' Nim stuck her elbow into Ben's side and stepped past. 'One word of this to Dad and I'll never forgive you.'

THIRTY-TWO

Although Mum didn't realise Nim was sleeping over with Michaela and not Alice, the arrangement became convenient. It meant Mum needn't rush home to make dinner and she could, for once, go out with colleagues for a drink. If only she did that kind of thing more often, it would take the heat off Nim. As for her excuse about staying over with Alice, Mum would never bother checking, so the lie would hold. It was perfectly clear why Nim couldn't be upfront about Michaela. She was ballsy, loud and in your face, but that didn't make her a bad friend. It meant she wasn't easily accepted, certainly not by Nim's mother. Getting to know Michaela took time, and not everyone was prepared to make the investment. Nim imagined her mother scoffing at the mention of Michaela; she wouldn't even like the sound of her name. But, there wasn't much room for Mum to criticise, not when she'd landed her daughter with the name Imogen and then shortened it to Nim. Not that she minded the abbreviation – at least not until Michaela had thought it weird.

Everything was normal on Friday morning. Mum made porridge and cut a banana while Nim toasted a slice of bread. They sat together at the table, the news on the radio droning as Nim dipped crusts into honey before crunching them.

'I do wish you'd spread the honey. I bought that at the

farmer's market. It's orange blossom honey and cost a fair bit. If you used a knife the jar wouldn't end up filled with crumbs.'

'Next time.' Nim cleared her plate and filled her water bottle from the tap.

'I'll be back from work around five o'clock tomorrow. There's no need for you to rush home. You can please yourself how to spend Saturday.'

Nim tilted her head while the words registered. This was a change; Mum normally wanted everything pinned down. 'I don't need to go swimming this weekend.' Another lie executed without a jitter. 'The pool's being used for a water polo tournament.'

'That's fine.' Mum scraped her bowl, scooping and eating every last bit of porridge. 'A nice relaxing weekend.'

The strap of Nim's bag cut into her shoulder, the extra clothes and make-up accounting for the additional weight. She biffed a little kid with it as she turned around at the school entrance. Although she said sorry, her words were lost in the noise as others swarmed through the door. Nim scanned the trickle of latecomers heading down the path, but Michaela wasn't among them. She had to make it into school today, or else. Like a rising tide, heat ascended to Nim's ears and her heart thumped under her ribs.

Morning lessons became a wasteland of dashed hopes. If Michaela didn't make it into school, the sleepover would be off and Nim could do nothing about it. What she couldn't stand, more than anything else, was the thought that Michaela had let her down. And when she'd thought the worst of her new friend, the reasoning started: the bus was late, Michaela had overslept … She'd make it in for lunchtime, Nim was sure.

Circling the groups hanging out at break, Nim was gripped by an uncontrollable force that yanked her gaze towards the gate every few seconds. Her heart plummeted with disappointment when Michaela never appeared.

'Looking for Kala?' one of Michaela's lot asked, but Nim had a sense that she wasn't being friendly.

'D'you know where she is?'

'Might do.' She gave a mocking smile.

Nim stared at the scuff marks on her pumps and wished she had a new pair.

'You're in for a long wait,' said the girl.

Nim ran her fingers through her hair, making her elbows turn out like spikes. 'I guess there's no point being here.'

'Nope.'

In her Science lesson, Nim took a seat on a bench near the window. She was supposed to be watching a PowerPoint presentation about photosynthesis but Nim blocked out the teacher's talk while ideas about what had happened to Michaela curdled. Nim's eyes drifted again to the gate, but this time she was rewarded with a glimpse of her friend. Relief swelled. She should never have mistrusted Michaela. Of course she would be there. At the end of school, Michaela linked arms with Nim and tugged her along – the arrangement was going to hold. They were off to Michaela's place and she'd get a chance to meet Jez again.

There was no one at home when they reached the house. Michaela kicked off her flats and left them in the middle of the hallway. Although Nim did likewise, she thought better of leaving a mess, and paired up the shoes, lining them against the wall with the others. At Nim's house, wearing slippers was compulsory, but not here. Nim's toe had broken through the seam on her black tights.

'Snap.' Michaela waggled her foot beside Nim's but her nail showed a glint of shiny polish. Nim would remember to paint her toenails if she were invited again.

'Can I sit down?'

'Make yourself at home.' Michaela slumped on the sofa, letting the cushions wheeze. Her legs flopped sideways onto a rug. The pile was shaggy like it needed a good comb. Nim sniggered at the joke she knew wasn't good enough to share.

'What's wrong with you?'

'I've got a bit of a headache.'

'*Bit of a headache,*' Michaela imitated. 'Don't go soft on me now. Not when I've lined up an evening for you. Thrown my mum out and everything.'

'It's good we've got the place to ourselves.'

'You're easily pleased.'

Seven o'clock came. Freshly applied mascara made Michaela's eyelashes resemble ferns while Nim had been able to properly apply eyeliner. They both wore black: Nim in a scoop neck top and mini skirt while Michaela had on a slinky sleeveless dress. Jez arrived, armed with a litre bottle of red wine and a large packet of hand-cut crisps. He passed the bottle to Michaela and, to make things fair, he tossed the crisps at Nim. She was pleased to catch the packet without scrunching the contents. Nim didn't like red wine much and the admission made Michaela's temper flare.

'What a loser.' She poured wine into three glasses anyway. 'Get that down your throat.'

Nim took a sip, but the rusty taste skewered.

'Look at your face.' Michaela scathed. 'You're such a

lightweight. Need some lemonade in it, do you?'

'No.' Nim managed a decent swallow then downed the lot to prove she wasn't a kid.

'That's the way.'

'Come here, girls.' Jez stretched his arms wide and drew them both into a hug.

Held against his chest, Nim noticed a smattering of dark hairs showing under the fabric of his shirt, and a whiff of deodorant mingled with Michaela's strawberry breath. As they clung together, Michaela laughed then struggled free. All she wanted to do was down the wine.

'Look at you.' Michaela stumbled forward and dinged the mole on Nim's face. 'That almost flattened it.'

Nim turned away, crushed by memories of Josh doing exactly the same thing. It was like she'd been cast adrift on a rough sea, waves thundering. With no land in sight, she was forced to gulp air and breathe.

'You're ignoring me again,' said Michaela.

Through the pain and hurt, reminders of that bastard taking Josh brought Nim back to the moment. 'Don't pick on me like that.'

'You and your mates going to sort me out?'

'No.' Truth was she didn't have many friends left.

'I'm only kidding,' said Michaela. 'I've fixed up this evening for you. Wouldn't have done it for anyone else.'

Jez put an arm around Nim. 'Take no notice of Kala. She only opens her mouth to change feet.'

'Is that right?' Michaela stomped out of the room.

Jez stroked Nim's hair. 'It's okay. I think you're great.'

Michaela returned with a roll of toilet paper and a mirror. 'You've smudged your make-up.'

Nim took the mirror and dabbed under her eyes to remove blotches of mascara.

'Best thing for a bit of upset is a drinking game.' Michaela moved over to the coffee table and filled the three glasses to the brim. 'Come on now, on your knees.'

Jez limbered over and Nim lined up beside him. 'First one to down the lot by lifting the glass with only one finger from each hand is the winner.'

When the first bottle was finished, Michaela produced another and flopped on the sofa. Jez sat with one knee pointing east and the other going north. The seam on his jeans divided him in half, the bulge below his belt falling on the east side, nearest to Nim. He patted the cushions on either side of him and the girls sat. Michaela splayed her knees while Nim made a nook among the cushions. They were obedient foot servants. On TV, Kelly Clarkson did her stuff, lyrics filling the room. Michaela staggered up to dance, twirling around and chanting at her fingers curled into a microphone. When she stopped swaying, she drained the last drop of wine from her glass and Nim copied.

'Aren't you going to kiss him?' Michaela asked.

Jez stretched his legs out and smiled.

'You *have* snogged a boy before.'

'Course.' Nim tossed her head, letting her hair swing around her shoulders.

'I thought you were up for this.' Michaela yawned, her tongue showing a stain of wine. 'You're not gay, are you?'

'No.' Mention of the 'G' word sent Nim into action. She rocketed sideways, pouncing on Jez, causing him to topple. Swivelling, he pinned Nim against the armrest, his wine-tinged breath hot and heavy. She closed her eyes, and in the dark, her heart beat like it was bolting for freedom. While his tongue probed her mouth, she stayed calm. Instinctively she responded with tiny gasps.

In a glare of light, they separated.

'What the fuck,' Jez yelled.

'Getting the measure.' Michaela directed a reading lamp like a torch. 'I should be filming this as evidence. You can't say I don't keep my promises. Nim's ready, steady, go-go-go.'

Nim tried to bring the room into focus. The walls spun like a zoetrope. She slunk to the floor, held her head to stop it falling off her neck. Next minute, a cramp in her stomach had her rushing to the loo. She made it in time to aim the surge of vomit at the pan. Eyes watering, she sat cross-legged, waiting for a sense of orientation to return, but everything went blank.

Hemmed in, Nim woke up unable to move. She blinked, checking her surroundings. Swirls of Artex on the ceiling told her she was in Michaela's lounge. Her head was a dead weight that she could barely lift from the cushion. Light cut through a chink in the curtains, sending streaks of white across the carpet. Her shoulder was numb where Jez's head lay. His sticking-up hair pricked like a brush against her chin. He mumbled in his sleep, his dark lashes marking his closed eyes. He smelled of cigarettes. Straightening her top that had ridden up to her armpits, Nim was pleased she'd worn her best black bra with the satin trim. She'd get some chicken fillets one day and impress everyone with an enhanced cleavage. Her skirt was twisted and her whole toe was poking through the seam on her tights. She remained fully clothed. The realisation brought relief. There'd been nothing more than a snog and a grope … and a bit too much wine. Slumping back into the cocoon of Jez's body, she relished the idea of having a boyfriend.

THIRTY-THREE

As usual, she was to meet Jez on Friday. The date was special: their one and a half month anniversary of going out. Excitement fizzed in her stomach. She had talked to Michaela about what would make it really special. Of course, there was the one thing Michaela always recommended but that couldn't exactly happen on the porch of the cricket club pavilion in the middle of winter. Besides, there was ages to go before Nim turned sixteen and she didn't want Jez to end up in trouble.

'You're worrying for nothing.' Michaela tipped her head back to catch the last drop from a can of Coke. 'I've been having sex since I was fourteen. Virginity is something you're better off without. Aren't you curious, Nim? Don't you want to know what you're missing?'

'But it's never going to be like I imagine.'

'You don't know until you try.'

'It's not that,' said Nim. 'It's more to do with sleeping in a proper bed, rose petals on the sheets, that sort of thing. I want my first time to be romantic.'

'Doing it the first time *is* romantic.'

Six o'clock at the park gates was their rendezvous. She'd taken to staying over Friday nights at her dad's, and the excuse of an evening at the youth centre gave Nim the chance to hook up with Jez. He couldn't offer to take her back to his place – he said his landlady would go mental. She'd call the authorities if Nim turned up in her school uniform. It seemed their relationship was stuffed until Nim turned sixteen and then she'd front-up her parents. Even her mother would be unable to object once she'd reached the age of consent. It was a barrier and, at the same time, protection. Nim took advice from the problem pages seriously. If Jez was all he claimed, he'd wait for her, no matter the contempt from Michaela.

That Friday, Nim's bag chinked with glass holders that she'd brought along to stop the tea lights from being blown out by the wind. She wanted to make the pavilion pretty, hoping Jez would bring the picnic blanket as he'd done the last time they met. Some wine would be lovely and a glass, rather than swigging from the bottle.

When Jez took off his helmet, his hair was flattened. She didn't mind that it wasn't a cool look. She'd been waiting in the telephone box to avoid the wind. The stink of piss made her nostrils burn, but in the light she checked her face. Jez preferred make-up to be natural so she only used a dab of foundation to cover her mole. She finished with a little lip gloss and a coat of mascara on her lashes. As a greeting, he hung an arm across her shoulders and pulled her to his chest. She smelled the leather of his jacket, damp and earthy. She was hungry for him, wanted to devour him with kisses, but Jez simply brushed the top of her head with his lips. Gripping Nim's shoulder, he guided her towards the bent railings that had become their entry since the park gates were locked. Her foot sank into the flowerbed. She straightened and darted towards the path.

Rather than watch Jez struggle through the gap, Nim

walked to the pavilion. Rifling through her bag, she found the tea lights and holders. Several matches rasped and died before she got the hang of lighting the wicks. As he passed the line of flickering flames, Jez's face became illuminated. Nim just wanted to nuzzle against his neck. The floorboards groaned as he shifted his weight, and the shutters over the windows tapped.

'There's my Nim.' Jez unzipped his jacket and drew out a bottle of wine, then a glass with a stem. 'I remembered.'

Nim smiled. He looked ridiculous with the picnic blanket slung around his shoulders like a poncho. She gripped the end and unfurled it, arranging the rug in a corner where they usually nested. Jez sat and leaned back against the wall while Nim curled up beside him. She heard the scour of metal against glass as he opened the wine, and the glugs as he drank from the neck.

'Give me some.' She passed the glass.

'Here.' He filled it and watched her take a few sips. 'Down it in one, it's the only way to keep warm.'

'You're probably right.' She finished the lot and wiped her mouth with the back of her hand.

'Time for a refill.' Jez topped up her glass, then turned the bottle against his lips and swallowed.

'Cheers.' She took a couple of mouthfuls before balancing the glass on a wonky floorboard. 'I'll leave some for later.'

The glow from the wine dulled the period pains in her lower back. She wanted to possess Jez, make him groan about ball ache, get confirmation that he desired her. She reached for his jaw. His stubble grazed her palm as she clasped his face. Limbering closer, she stretched her neck to reach his mouth and the two were joined. The kisses were hard as they pressed against each other; then, like a last gasp, Jez broke free to kiss her neck and her collarbones. She let the rumblings of a moan escape before she pulled away.

'Not again.' He thumped his chest to disguise the panting.

'Need to finish my drink.' She eyed him over the rim of her glass, gave a smile of satisfaction.

'Fuck you.' His arm caught the bottle, sending it rolling across the floor and the last of the wine slurped out.

'Have a swig of mine.' Nim offered the glass.

Jez snatched it and guzzled. 'You can't keep doing this.'

'But the problem is ...' Her words fizzled as Jez reached for her hand and pressed it against the bulge in his jeans.

'See what you've done?'

Nim knew what would happen next, a repeat of every week they'd been meeting. Jez groaned and reached for the cigarettes inside his jacket. She watched him light up, admiring the orange glow, and waited for the wisp of smoke to escape his lips. Ideas for how to begin a conversation bolted through her head. 'How was your day?' She picked at a tag of skin around her thumbnail, waiting for him to reply.

'Listen.' He stubbed out the half-smoked cigarette and pressed the end behind his ear. A gust of wind extinguished the candles. She wanted to relight them but he caught her arm. Pulling her, Nim fell against him. He slid beneath her, adjusting Nim's legs so that she lay astride him. Easy as turning an egg, he flipped Nim over and grappled with her tights. Christ. They were down to her knees.

'I've got my period.' She gripped the trim of her underwear.

'No need for lubrication, then.'

Jez's arm pinned her down while he ripped open the foil of a condom with his teeth. He fought his way inside and shunted against her. Pain tore through her body. Held tightly, she squirmed but couldn't break free. Fear paralysed her limbs. The smell of him made her wretch. Inside her mind a switch flicked, then pictures of bright tulip petals filled her head and she created an arrangement with purple and pink heads. She wondered why she hadn't used the yellow ones. A glob of his spit splattered onto Nim's chin and Jez rolled onto his back. He found the stub of cigarette behind his ear and relit it.

THIRTY-FOUR

Tripping on a paving slab, Nim steadied herself against a garden fence. Already the houses near the park showed signs of Christmas with neon Santas beaming through the windows. In her pocket she found a serviette from KFC, one that hadn't been used when she and Michaela had sparred with chips. She wiped her eyes and stared at the smears of make-up on the tissue. Grappling in her bag, she found her mobile and using fingers stiff with cold she brought up Michaela's number. Her beating heart made her whole body judder as she waited for an answer. Christ, she was an idiot for not realising what Jez was up to.

Michaela answered in a tone she didn't recognise and this brought her tears streaming again. All Nim could do was mumble while the silence from Michaela's end registered. Taking deep breaths, Nim became still.

'Get a grip,' said Michaela. 'I can guess what's happened. You should be happy, not blubbing down the phone.'

'What d'you mean?'

'You can't string Jez along forever.'

'But I didn't …'

'Course you did. And you've been gagging for it all these weeks.'

'No. No. That's not right.'

'Jez popped your cherry just like you wanted.'

Nim's mobile fell from her hand and crashed onto the ground. The babble of Michaela's laughter disconnected. Finally she understood why Michaela had wanted her as a friend.

Nim couldn't face going to Dad's place, not with him being cheery at the start of the weekend. She wasn't strong enough to pretend nothing had happened, that it was some sort of joke. The idea of breaking down in front of Dad was more than she could stand. She didn't want Dad smothering her with hugs, she couldn't stand it. Instead she decided to take the long walk back to her place, to the home she shared with Mum.

After sliding her key into the lock, Nim entered the hallway. 'It's only me.' Her voice wavered and Nim sunk her shoulders, trying to control her limbs as they jangled. 'Didn't feel like going to the youth centre tonight.'

Mum hovered in the doorway of the lounge, her bare feet showing that she wasn't observing the rule about slippers. 'Did you get a lift home? You look a bit peaky. Are you okay?'

'Bad period pains.'

'Have you eaten? Have you told your dad you're here?'

'I sent him a text.' Nim clung to her bag, pressing it against her stomach. 'I'm going to bed.'

'Have you taken paracetamol?'

Nim barged past. 'No.'

'I'll bring you up a couple.'

'Thanks.' Nim stared at the carpet treads as she made her way upstairs.

Nim wouldn't get up the next day, and when Sunday came

this threw Mum into a frenzy. Her interrogations made it clear she believed there was more to Nim's retreat to her room than she was letting on. Perhaps Nim had a fever; Mum pressed her hand against Nim's forehead, which was seriously annoying. It wasn't as if she was a little kid needing a dose of Calpol. Nim rolled over and faced the wall but Mum didn't get the message. She pulled up the chair from Nim's desk and sat at her side. When the back rubbing started, it was more than Nim could stand.

'I'll only get better if you quit fussing,' said Nim.

'There must be a thermometer somewhere,' said Mum. 'I'll have a search for it.'

'Don't bother,' said Nim.

'Let me get you some soup. You could manage a few mouthfuls, surely?'

'No.' Nim remembered the time when Mum had pestered Josh into eating a bowl of tomato soup when he had an upset stomach. The plastered mess on his bedroom wall and carpet made redecorating necessary. Would she never learn?

'I've followed a recipe from the Sunday supplement. It's vegetarian and very wholesome. I can leave it in chunks or blend it to a smooth consistency. Which would you prefer?'

'Why don't you ever listen to me? I don't want anything to eat.'

'I thought I could tempt you with something delicious. It's got several cloves of garlic in it. I know you like that.'

'Please, Mum. I want to be on my own.'

'But you'll fade away without any nourishment. Your dad's been on the landline, too. Wants to know why you're not answering his texts and whether you're okay.'

'Give me a break – I've turned my phone off. I don't

want to talk to anyone.'

'I'll let you rest for a while. Don't mind me if I sit here and wait for you to drop off like I used to do when you were little.'

Nim closed her eyes and pulled the duvet over her head. Her breath collected in the folds and made the space clammy. Why was it difficult to understand that she needed time to herself? Irritation stung. Clearly her mother was staying put, judging from the way the chair legs creaked. As soon as she got bored with watching the lump under the duvet, she would go downstairs. A bit of room to breathe wasn't too much to ask.

Rage licked Nim's insides, making the heat burn. If she didn't have a temperature before, she certainly did now. Flinging back the covers, she jumped from the bed, making Mum startle.

'I'm going for a shower,' said Nim.

'Good idea – that'll freshen you up.'

'I'm not going for that reason. Seems like the bathroom's the only place I'll get any privacy.'

'Don't be like that, Nim. I'm only concerned for your wellbeing.'

The shower brought a measure of calmness that Nim craved. If only she could wash away the memory of Jez as easily: his open mouth hanging slack and wide, his breath filling her nostrils. Rewinding events, she regretted the silly smirk she pulled, tempting him. The way she tried to reel him in, keep him under her control. Yet he'd turned things around absolutely. And now here she was, not one friend to share the horrible story with. In truth, she didn't want to admit Michaela was part of Jez's plan. But one thing was for sure – she hadn't agreed to have sex. It wasn't her fault.

When she returned to her room, Mum had set a tray on the desk. Soup steamed from a hand-thrown bowl that Mum had bought at a charity auction. A smell of onions and carrots drifted as Nim stirred.

'Oh good.' Mum stood, holding a plate. 'I've cut you a slice of fresh bread to go with it. Get that inside you, and you'll be fit for school in the morning. I was beginning to think I'd need to take a day's holiday from work to look after you.' The door frame became like the mounting on a picture that captured Mum in full length. She looked the part of an overbearing parent.

'Leave me alone, for fuck's sake! I can't breathe with you hanging around, watching me. I'm not compensation for Josh. If you'd paid more attention to him maybe none of this would have happened.'

Shocked by the words that flew from her mouth, Nim's stare made her eyeballs ache. She watched her mother fold over. The plate slipped from Mum's clutch and clattered down the stairs, the bread gummed to the carpet. Mum's face was puckered like the crinkled blooms on a dying shrub. 'Don't treat me like this, Nim. You can't blame me.'

'Why not? Everything's your fault.' The words scorched Nim's tongue as she watched her mother crumple and stagger away.

Nim sat on the bed and hugged her legs. Anger and pity rubbed together, leaving her stained with regret. Mum might have been asking for it, but actually seeing her there, shrunken, was not a memory to savour. She might drive Nim mad half the time, but she was still her mother. Pressing her head against her knees, Nim curled tight like a bug. If she'd had wings, she'd willingly fly right out of there. Christ. There was so much going on without Mum downing tools as well. Nim knocked her knuckles against her head, tapping a beat she hoped would shape her thoughts. There was nothing for it. She would have to apologise.

Taking the stairs, she avoided the corner step that creaked and waited outside Mum's door. The sound of her sobbing slid into the hallway and made Nim feel weak. How come she had the power to reduce her mum to a crumbling wreck and yet she couldn't keep Jez from doing what he did? She never wanted him to. The thoughts bolstered her resolve. They'd not get the better of her. Nim shook her head. Not Mum, not Jez, not Michaela. Turning around, she retraced her steps. She edged along the landing and the sound of Mum's crying diminished. Unwilling to return to her room, she lingered outside Josh's door, then entered.

She ran her hand over the emulsion as she paced alongside the walls and stopped in front of the wardrobe. Inside was Mum's personal haberdashery. Nim checked the piles of cloth and turned to the sewing box where a length of cord dangled. The golden colour matched the trim on the cushions in the lounge and must have been left over from Mum's last project.

Nim laced the cord tight around her fingers until her flesh bulged and the pain became too much. Loosening the string, a pattern of red lines marked her skin. She felt like slicing into her flesh and gaining release by shedding blood, but she was too much of a coward. Instead, she tied the cord into a loop and let it hang across her palm like a rainbow string. She remembered the pattern of turning and twisting and pulling string. The parallel lines of the string figure crossed her knuckles. Releasing the cord from her thumb, she tugged on the loose line to make the string figure vanish. Josh called the figure a worm and liked to imagine it as bait for a fish. But the string figure could also be a train disappearing into a tunnel or a mouse racing to its hole. But how would it reappear? If the string figure was Nim, how would she change?

THIRTY-FIVE

Nim stood away from the others who crowded at the bus stop. A boy imitating the head teacher told a couple of girls to unroll the waistbands of their skirts. The rule said two centimetres above the knee was an appropriate length. A couple of Year Seven girls began a game that saw them wriggle and turn. Nim absorbed the rhythm of their clapping hands and tried to imagine she was somewhere else. She stood with her foot tucked around her ankle, a way to hold herself together. Straightening her spine, she jutted her chin forward and ignored the boy who rubbed a finger under his nose and said she was stuck-up.

Last off the bus, she walked the path from the school gates. She stared at the sky, skimming the heads of those grouped around. Although her eyes were brimming, she sucked back tears and made her neck long like a flower stem. She ignored the shouts and tuned into the buzz of the crowd as she made for the entrance. In her peripheral vision, she saw a mound of dark hair like a daub in the distance. Michaela advanced, grabbed Nim's arm and spun her around. Nim bit her lip until she tasted blood. Michaela's eyebrows were like gulls wheeling and her gabbing voice filled the space between them. Finally, Nim tuned into the repeated phrase. Michaela kept saying, 'Nimday! Nimday!' Realising what she was on about, Nim stepped away but the chorus became louder. There was Michaela swinging her arms to conduct her mates in the chant.

'Don't turn your back on me,' Michaela shouted.

The voices grew quiet as Nim stiffened.

'We know what you've been up to.'

Nim tried to walk away but it felt like her foot had been stapled to the ground.

'You can't deny it.'

Hanging her head, Nim made her toes wiggle inside her pumps.

'Nim's finally lost her V-plates,' Michaela announced. 'And we've renamed today as Nimday in her honour.'

Laughter erupted and rippled to the stragglers at the gate. Nim had rehearsed again and again what she would say to Michaela, but the lines ribboned in her throat as her mind frothed with embarrassment and hate.

'Jez has always wanted to pop a cherry.' Michaela sneered. 'Pleased I was able to help.'

Nim's breath failed and she began to cough.

'Happy Nimday!' said Michaela. 'Give us a speech.'

Nim swallowed. Clearing her throat, she replied in a steady voice, 'You've got it wrong. My name is Imogen.'

PART THREE

Jacob's Ladder
Eight years later

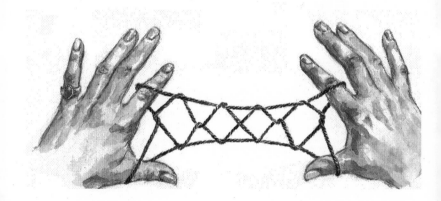

THIRTY-SIX

Where the path narrows, Imogen lingers watching the Thames. Waves of slate and mottled brown weave together like twine. It's low tide and the river has shrunk, making a beach. Imogen leans against the railing and a glimpse of winter sun rewards her for leaving the office at lunchtime. A woman stands by the water's edge, and in the shallows there is a boy in wellington boots.

'That nipper's the same as my grandson. He loves the water.'

Imogen glances at the man who's stopped beside her. His tartan scarf is bright against his paper-white face.

'He's like my brother, too.' Imogen's voice trails as an image of Josh appears. He's four years old and wearing *Thomas the Tank Engine* trunks. She remembers his sticky fingers patting her arm during a last hug, back when she was a girl called Nim.

'My son's taken him to Australia,' says the man. 'I talk to him on Skype every week.'

'That's a good way of staying in touch.'

'You're right.' The man's smile creases his cheeks and then he turns to watch the boy. 'Take a look at him now.'

The boy hunches his shoulders, his clothes are wet and muddy.

'Where's his mother gone?' The words catch in Imogen's throat like bile. 'He's not safe.'

She rushes towards the steps and takes them two at a time. Her heart pounds as she makes for the water but the ground is claggy and sucks her boots.

'Hang on,' the man's voice booms. 'His mother's back.'

Imogen watches the woman launch a towel over the child, covering him. She pulls the boy close, rubbing his hair and tickling him until he collapses with laughter. Imogen tries to move but finds she's stuck. She throws out her arms for balance and grabs the strap of her handbag as it falls from her shoulder. Wrenching a foot free, muck splatters her coat. A stink from the disturbed ground rises. She's plastered with mud and dreads to think what the gossips at work will say. Nothing ever goes right, even when she's trying to be helpful.

'Do you want a hand?' the man shouts.

Imogen shakes her head and, stumbling through the boulders, finds a path back. She slumps on a bench and the man sits beside her. Why can't he leave her alone? It's too humiliating – she's been an idiot and now she's left with a woollen coat in need of dry-cleaning and a pair of ruined boots.

'Never mind,' he says. 'You only wanted to make sure the boy was safe.'

'He was so alone.' The admission springs from her mouth as if she has no control over her speech. Her words make the memories jostle. There's Josh licking a cone, melted ice cream sliding over his fingers. There he is again, scratches on his legs from hiding in the bushes. Imogen holds her face between her hands.

'Don't be too hard on yourself,' says the man.

The words prick and tremors run up her arms. A vein in her neck pulses. Heat rises to her face and panic spreads. It's as if she's been swallowed up, consumed by something she has no control over. Her heartbeat pounds, making her whole body shake. What the fuck is happening? She gasps for breath. It's oxygen she needs.

'Are you okay?' The man grips Imogen's arm.

She twists her fingers, eyes smarting, and opens her mouth. No words come but her mind scrambles and she locates answers that simply can't be spoken. A gurgle escapes from the back of her throat.

'Put your head down.' The man presses the back of Imogen's neck, making her hair flop between her legs. She's a rag doll looking up her own skirt, and her tights are dark around her crotch. Next minute he's made her sit up straight and he's shoving a brown paper bag to her lips.

'Breathe into this,' he says.

Imogen does as she is told. Her eyes fix upon the sandwich in its cling film wrapping that he's slung on the bench. The man's not going to want his lunch returned to the bag with all her germs inside.

'That's right,' he says. 'Keep breathing. Nice and slow.'

The crinkled trim of paper itches her nose as Imogen watches the bag fill up with her breath and then collapse again. Minutes pass, and a bead of sweat trickles along her hairline. The man pulls a bottle of water from his pocket and offers it. Imogen shakes her head. She's not obliged to accept, but she needs to respond somehow. 'I couldn't breathe. It felt like I was suffocating. It was horrible.'

'Good job I remembered my first aid training.' He rolls the paper bag into a ball and chucks it into a bin. 'Can I call someone for you? A boyfriend or family member?'

'My dad's dead.' Tears run down her cheeks and drop from her chin. 'It was a heart attack – happened over a year ago. I should be used to the loss by now.'

'I'm sorry.' He watches the passers-by like he's ready to join the flow of people, embarrassed to be with a woman who can't stop crying. 'Best you get to the doctor. Things like that can run in families.'

'I know.'

'I'm sure you'll be alright, though. You're young.' The man grips her shoulder. 'You look after yourself.'

'I will.'

He gives a nod and walks away. Imogen watches him blend into the crowd.

Staring at the gunge on her coat, Imogen considers the options. The man is probably right. She taps the heels on her boots together but the clumps of mud cling. There's no way she can return from her lunch hour looking like she's emerged from a swamp. Ideas flutter, then the thought of walking away dominates. And it's not just the graduate scheme she wants to leave; she needs freedom from a life littered with untimely deaths.

THIRTY-SEVEN

Imogen walks home from the doctor's surgery with drizzle dampening her face. Outside the Tube station, commuters pour onto the pavement, but still the Romanian woman who sells *The Big Issue* finds her. It's worth the purchase price simply for the greeting; there's no one else who calls Imogen 'darling'. The security light shines a lemon beam onto the tarmac as Imogen approaches the garden flat. Inside, she slings her coat onto a hook and walks into the bedroom/lounge. Propping the prescription beside the telephone, she slings her shoes under the bed and presses her feet into fleecy slippers.

Underneath yesterday's newspaper, Imogen finds the remote. She flicks through the TV channels, but there's nothing to catch her attention and she returns the room to silence. The clock shows there is time to fill until her mother arrives. Although Imogen has put off inviting her, when she does make an offer, Mum can only spare a little while. Nothing about communicating is simple, not in a family wrought with disaster. Imogen throws back her head and stares at the ceiling. A crack in the plaster runs all the way to the bathroom door, and she drags her limbs to investigate. It can't be anything serious, or it would've shown up in the survey.

Tiles in the bathroom cover any hint of damage, and the radiator pumps too much heat into the space that must once have been a cupboard under the stairs. Imogen wipes the mirror and stares at her reflection. Leaning close, she checks the tiny white scar like a feather on her cheek, a sign of her cowardice. She digs her finger into a pot of foundation and smears colour over, making the mark disappear.

Tapping on the front door comes in a familiar rhythm. If talking about the past was as easy as playing a tune with the door knocker, there wouldn't be a problem. Had Mum been more available, more like an ordinary mother, then the tension stiffening Imogen's shoulders would fade. She walks to the hallway and raises her hand to the lock. The trouble is they're both inexperienced in confiding or sharing. Under the cover of their relationship, anxieties bubble like tar. Imogen pastes a smile onto her face and swings the door open. Her mother waits under the porch where the outside lamp shines in a circle.

'Hello, Mum.' Imogen stares at the pot plant her mother holds in its cellophane wrapping. 'It's good of you to come.'

'I was in the area anyway. Besides, I've been wanting to see your new place.' Mum steps inside and passes the plant to Imogen.

'Thanks.' Imogen knows it's a cyclamen from the upswept petals.

'I've a ticket for the Arts Centre – the play's received splendid reviews. But you're more interested in films, aren't you? Blockbusters and the Hollywood brigade.'

'Even the odd foreign-language film.'

Mum undoes the buttons on her jacket as she enters. She clearly isn't interested in discussing the merits of international films and Imogen lets the conversation drop. A silence drags, like it always does. It's not easy finding a route through their shared history. Mum takes her time in formulating the next sentence, scrutinising the terracotta walls and the furniture for inspiration. 'A coat of paint would brighten the place up.'

'That's my next job. I've got to choose a colour.' Imogen's not going to opt for whitewashing, as Mum did, covering Josh's existence with a layer of emulsion as soon as her brother no longer needed a space to sleep. Even Imogen's room had been reorganised while she was at university, so it's just as well she has her own flat.

Mum perches on the edge of the bed, picks up the prescription and squints to read it. 'Are you ill? Is that why you want to see me?'

'That's part of the problem.' Imogen takes the paper and drops it into a drawer.

'If you're not well, Nim, you should always tell me.'

'I wish you'd use my real name.'

'Of course, Imogen.' Mum tilts her head and catches Imogen's gaze. 'What's wrong?'

Headlights from a car turning in the road spill into the room and distract Imogen. She holds her hand to her forehead and the ring on her little finger gouges her skin. She struggles to find the words. 'I'm in a mess, Mum. I don't know what to do.'

'There's always a solution – whatever's the matter. You've just got to find a way forward.'

'Sure.' Imogen slumps on the bed and stares at a stain on the carpet. Mum moves a little closer, making the duvet clump between them.

'It can't be that bad.' Mum rests her hand on Imogen's

shoulder for a second, then her fingers slide away. 'Look at all the things that are going right for you: a graduate job with a future, owning your first property. There aren't many twenty-three-year-olds in your position.'

'Saying that doesn't help.' Imogen swallows. 'You don't know how awful things have been. I had a panic attack – it was so bad I thought I was going to end up with heart failure like Dad.'

'Don't be silly,' Mum coos. Her fuchsia lipstick has seeped into the cracks on her lips. 'Your genes come from my side of the family. We're the healthy ones.'

Imogen folds her arms tight across her chest. She traces the knobbles of her elbows while she organises the things she needs to say. Lines of dialogue race through her mind until she settles on the words. 'My doctor says Dad's death has triggered feelings of unresolved grief over the loss of Josh.'

'These medical types,' Mum huffs. 'Why can't they leave well alone? I mean, what's the point in dragging up the past?'

'I want to talk to you about Josh.'

'There's nothing new to say.' Mum tucks a loose strand of grey hair behind her ear. 'How about a cup of tea? Shall I make a pot?'

'I'll do it.'

In the galley kitchen Imogen searches for the unopened packet of pure peppermint, bought with Mum in mind. She tears the wrapping and rips open the box. Mum can't stand hearing his name; getting her to talk about Josh was never going to be easy. Imogen lets the teabag infuse for the required three minutes. She wouldn't feel so alone if Dad were still around. He liked sharing stories about Josh. Images and voices merge as Imogen remembers Josh using Dad's leg like a train track, pushing his Thomas the Tank Engine in time with the tune he hummed. Tilting her head as the pictures evaporate, Imogen senses the warmth of the scene and smiles. Returning to the moment, she hoicks the teabag from the mug and takes the drinks to find her mother sitting in the armchair.

'There's not much storage space, is there?' Mum crosses her legs and adjusts the hem of her skirt to cover her knees.

'There's plenty for one person.' Imogen passes the tea.

'Thank you.' Mum lines up the mug with the edge of the coffee table.

Imogen scans the room, noticing how the pillows are piled on one side of the bed, as if to reinforce the fact that she sleeps alone. She should have cleared up before Mum arrived. A cobweb flounces from the wall and coffee rings mark the table like an Olympic flag.

'Ignoring what happened to Josh doesn't make the pain go away,' says Imogen.

Mum picks a thread from her skirt and drops it onto the floor. 'I wouldn't call it ignoring. Let's just say I don't like to dwell upon things. Keeping busy works for me.'

'I'm different. Look at me! I'm living a half-life.'

Mum delves into her handbag, pulls out her chequebook and pen then lands them on the table. 'I want to make a contribution to celebrate the purchase of your new home. I know you've had thousands from your father's estate but I want to do my bit.'

'I don't need money. It's getting my head straight that's the problem. There's so much sloshing around, I don't know what to think anymore.'

'Perhaps if you focused on your job?'

'I'm not going into work again until I feel better.'

'Is that wise?'

Imogen paces around the bed and pummels a pillow. Once it's plumped, she places it against the headboard. 'At least I can still do a bit of housework.'

'That's a start.' Mum blows across her tea and takes a few short sips. 'I should leave the tea to cool for a bit longer.'

'There must be something you can say about Josh.' Imogen stares at her mother. 'Help me.'

Mum clicks the end of her ballpoint and begins writing. She rips the cheque free and flaps it in front of Imogen. 'Here you are.'

Imogen glances at the three figures. 'Thanks.'

'If you don't want to spend the money on the flat, how about a little holiday?'

'Back to France?'

'No, Imogen, I'm not suggesting that.' Mum zips her bag shut and tucks it under her arm. 'You'll find nothing to help you there.'

'Maybe. Maybe not.' Imogen turns her wrist in a circle, making her bones click. 'Going back may bring me some peace of mind.'

'I doubt it.' Mum sighs and looks at her watch. 'I've got to go. Will you ring me at the weekend, Imogen? I can tell you about the show.'

Mum gives Imogen a perfunctory kiss as she leaves. The pressure on Imogen's cheek remains long after the front door is closed. It was a mistake inviting her round but she'd dropped the seed of an idea. Imogen checks the chest of drawers and removes a cable jumper and a pair of clean cords. In a bag, she organises the clothes that will keep her warm during the

February gloom. She riffles through a shoebox of papers to find her passport and skims the empty pages. Going abroad is usually something to look forward to but this is no holiday. Imogen falls onto the bed exhausted and relieved that she's finally made a decision. It is to Rodez that she'll travel.

THIRTY-EIGHT

Imogen arrives on market day. The bus from the airport drops her at the town and she stands on the corner of the street, cars veering as she wrings recognition from the place she's tried to blot out. The greys merge into a blank screen like there's a programme on TV about to start. Imogen follows a man carting a massive suitcase. His wife paces beside him, one hand on the shoulder of her boy. How old is he? Eight? Nine? He should be at school, but instead he swings his scooter onto the pavement and pushes off.

'Attends!' the man calls after him.

'Wait,' Imogen translates, and an image dances on her retina but the picture disintegrates as the whimpering gets louder. It's Josh's voice and there's no way to comfort him. Her heart thuds and a tide of heat makes her tremble. Edging away from the roadside, she leans against the wall, her limbs weak. She takes great gulps of breath while tears seep from the corners of her eyes. Finding the pills in her handbag, she swallows one back. Closing her eyes, she waits for the Xanax to do its work.

With the promise of approaching calm, Imogen heads towards the town square where stalls dressed with gingham trim are arranged in a horseshoe. In the middle is a hotchpotch of sellers who display their goods on groundsheets. An African man wearing kente cloth presides over a row of leather belts, and in his basket are some carved heads of tribesmen and women, the wood stained dark to give the impression of quality. He holds a tray of disposable lighters and presses Imogen to take one. She shakes her head and pushes her hands into her pockets. Next to him a woman sorts a pile of clothing, displaying the best items on hangers. Among the throng of food stalls the smell of fishy paella drifts from a giant pan where the cook turns rice with a paddle. At the corner of the square there is a stall selling children's toys. Mounted at the back are personalised clocks. Flowers with heart-shaped petals for Amelie, a giraffe with its neck bent double for Claude, an engine with steam pouring from the funnel for Maxime. *Maxime.* The name makes her blood rush and she's blushing at the thought of him. She turns, her arm flailing, and almost topples over a stand of rainbow strings. They're bright like an exotic wig, and she can't resist the feel of the threads slipping through her fingers. She imagines hooking the string and twisting it to make different figures.

'You like?' the stallholder asks, showing his nicotine-stained teeth.

'Yes.'

'How many you want?'

'No. I don't.'

He makes a clicking noise with his tongue. Embarrassed, she scrambles to find her purse. 'Okay. Give me one.'

He loops the string into a bow and ties a knot. Imogen passes over the money and slips the string into her pocket.

She continues through the main thoroughfare, searching for a place to stay. According to TripAdvisor there's a clean and comfortable place nearby. The gravel crunches as Imogen goes through a courtyard towards the hotel entrance. The pebbledash walls have been painted white and the window frames and shutters gleam yellow. Pushing the glazed front door, Imogen steps into the reception. There's a desk with a bell that tinkles when she presses the button.

'Bonjour, Mademoiselle.' A woman with dark hair combed into a bun approaches. Streaks of grey show around her temples and a lavender fragrance drifts in the air.

'Bonjour.' Imogen has found the words she needs on Google Translate and she reads from her smartphone. 'Une chambre pour une personne, s'il vous plait.'

'For how many nights?'

'Three or four.' Imogen smiles, relieved she doesn't have to struggle with the language. Madame presents a form for completion.

'Fine.' Madame turns her attention to the computer screen on the desk. 'I'll give you room five. It's upstairs on the left.' She passes the key over in exchange for the paperwork.

'One minute.' She taps the registration card against the desk. 'Your name's Mashard, that is right?'

Imogen hesitates, wondering at the frown spreading across the woman's forehead. Admitting to her name becomes something strange. A tingle of heat makes her nervous. This is ridiculous. 'Yes, I'm Imogen Mashard.'

'There was a case some years ago. It was very sad. D'you know about it?'

'I do.' Nerves make her stare squarely at the woman, a bid of defiance.

'You have the same name as the boy.'

Anxiety spreads and heat burns her cheeks. She's seen

every newspaper article, remembers clips from the television and radio interviews. 'There was a lot of coverage. You couldn't avoid hearing about it.'

'Some businesses in town have never recovered. Not here at this hotel, but other places.'

'You have loyal clients, Madame.' Imogen picks up her bag. 'Which way do I go?'

Imogen's heart thunders as she enters the bedroom. This is a mad idea; it's crazy to think something can be gained from returning. Anger makes her weak and she sinks onto the mattress. She closes her eyes, inviting sleep to provide respite, but she's too agitated. Imogen punches her fist against the mattress, sits up and examines the pastel walls. It's a functional space. A clock marks the passing seconds, registering the time that slithers away.

Gathering her wits, Imogen finds her make-up bag and heads for the bathroom. There's a diminutive shower and a sink tucked under the eaves. Angling her face close to the mirror, Imogen stares at her reflection. The hazel flashes in her eyes are a reminder of Dad. At least he saw her graduate. That was his aim, according to Sally Jenkins, the solicitor who always wore a fitted black suit. Imogen's shoulders stiffen as she remembers the formalities of probate. Strange that he chose a solicitor to confide in. Stranger still for Imogen to be in the office, talking to the woman she once suspected of being his secret girlfriend. Crazy thoughts planted by Michaela. Best thing Imogen ever did was go to college and leave the chaos and Nim behind. Yet, being in France means that she has to reconnect, retrace the steps of her younger self. Imogen refreshes the burgundy gloss on her lips and adopts an appearance of confidence. She can do this, she really can.

Beside the window there's a chair and a little table where leaflets about local attractions are arranged. Imogen flicks through the brochures to see if one of them mentions la plage. Her search is unrewarded. According to Madame with the lavender fragrance, the town remembers Josh, but there's no information about where Imogen wants to go. There's something terrifying and irresistible about this urge to return to the place she last saw Josh. She supposes this visit is like a reconstruction intended to unleash memories that will set her free. That's the hope. She can't wade through treacle any longer. The physical act of being there, the sensory reality of the place, that's what she's after.

THIRTY-NINE

The next morning is fresh. Imogen crosses the road to the town square, but today the space is empty. Without the market, puddles gouge the ground and Imogen follows a path around the edge. Shops line the pavement and she's drawn to the estate agent's window. It's as if buying her flat in Tooting has made Imogen addicted to searching for a dream home. A girl at the far desk answers the telephone while the guy nearest the window sits in front of a computer screen. His eyes are fixed but his hair falls about his chin in loose curls. Something about the way he holds his head is familiar.

A lorry revs in a parking bay, making exhaust fumes swell. Imogen grinds her teeth at the untimely interruption. The cab slews into the road, dragging its load behind. She watches the vehicle trail past, then her eyes fall upon a shop that appears from a distance to be a car rental place. She'll need wheels to get out to la plage and a good map with directions. The shop window shows a display of jeeps; not the sort of car Imogen wants. A tiny hatchback is more her style. She enters and a doorbell chimes as she crosses the mat. At the counter, a girl in a pressed shirt sings, 'Bonjour.' A badge shows her name is Véronique. Very continental. She smiles as Imogen approaches.

'Do you have a small car?' Imogen abandons any attempt

to try a few words of French.

'Small car,' the girl repeats making the English sound like another language.

'I don't feel very confident with a big motor.'

'Big motor.'

'No. A small motor, a small car.'

'Oooh.' The girl pouts.

'A Citroen or a Peugeot, maybe?' Imogen tries to put emphasis on the right syllables, an attempt at improved communication.

'Ahhh.' The girl raises her eyebrows so they show above her metal-rimmed spectacles.

'Just for a few days,' says Imogen. 'I only need a car for a few days.'

The girl shrugs and rattles off a line of French. She points to the display of vehicles and opens a folder which contains pictures of farm equipment. Now it's Imogen's turn to shrug and shake her head. She's come to the wrong place. As if a tractor would be any good! There must be somewhere else in town to hire a car.

Wind funnels along the street, making Imogen wish she'd brought her gloves. Tucking her hand into her pocket, she finds the slip of paper on which Madame sketched a map to the library. That's where she should be going. The purpose of this trip is to pin down some facts, and where better to find information? Not that she revealed her intentions to Madame, especially not when she queried Imogen's name. The layer of hostility from Madame was unexpected. Poor little Josh – he never did any harm.

Imogen studies the pencil lines and the tiny writing that she can hardly read. She needs to find an information office and a proper map. Returning the paper to her pocket, her fingers catch on a knot of string. She draws out the loop of rainbow thread and stretches the string around her hands. The stallholder clearly had a dislike of English people who failed to make a purchase. She recognises her people-pleasing behaviour, buying something, anything, to stop him from dismissing her. The string is silky; colours of orange, yellow and green merge. She can't be the only person who ends up buying stuff that's of no use. Lacing the string around her hands, Imogen picks up the curves with her middle fingers and admires the cradle. She laughs, mad as she is for standing there with a string tying her up. Letting it drop, memories of Dee saturate her mind. She's filled with a sense of … what? Camaraderie. She listens for Dee's bellowing laughter and waits for the tickle and poke routine that left Nim breathless. Imogen clasps her side, conscious of an ache that occurs whenever she laughs too much. Dee was responsible for the jokes and fun at Le Camping. Mum was a different person when Dee was around.

Rain starts to fall, bouncing on the pavement, and Imogen scans the street for shelter. Outside the estate agent's office there's a large porch. She rushes over and gets under cover before the deluge begins. Imogen tidies her fringe, organising the damp strands to lie evenly. Behind her, she hears the door open and a voice calls, 'Mademoiselle.' Imogen turns. He stands in the doorway wearing a jacket but his shirt is open at the neck. She squints, focusing on his jaw, the way he holds his head. When he smiles, a star-shaped dimple shows. Excitement and anticipation lace together. Another look at the shape of his face, his bovine eyes, and she's sure it's him. She holds her breath while memories flash and tangle.

Gail Aldwin

'Mademoiselle, voulez-vous attendre à l'intérieur?' He gestures for Imogen to wait inside, and as she passes, his lips turn into an 'O' and he raises his eyebrows. That's exactly how she remembers Maxime. He does a little bow and directs her to the chairs lined up against the wall like it's a waiting room. She sits, wondering if he's recognised her as well. The heat rising to her neck is released as she unfurls her scarf. Wondering what to do, what to say, she turns out her bag looking for her mobile. Studying the photo on her phone screen buys a little time, but shots of party nights out with university friends are a thing of the past. Imogen spies him glancing in her direction, tries not to notice his eyes resting on her. Is it really him? Is he wondering the same thing? Is it really her?

In Imogen's mind's eye she sees Maxime wearing a baseball cap and carrying his skateboard. Back then, she couldn't help but stare at him, and now it seems the same pull exists. She presses her lips together to stop girlish giggles from spawning. He sits, attending to his work. The nameplate on his desk is confirmation. This is Maxime. The computer screen obscures his face like he's a model in a cubist painting. His fingers are busy on the keyboard. Imogen hangs onto the silence between bursts of tapping and waits to catch his gaze. When he turns to collect pages spilling from the printer, Imogen's impatience builds. She feels like she'll boil over if she has to wait for him to speak first. Instead, she makes an approach, sidling to the desk, a question forming in her mind. When she stands opposite him, all she can manage is a line of schoolgirl French. 'Vous parlez anglais?'

'Of course.' He smiles, tiny creases mark the corners of his eyes. 'You want to buy a property?'

He's teasing. His tongue darts between his teeth, an acknowledgement.

Imogen plays along. 'I've spent my money on a flat in London.'

'A holiday home, then?'

'I can't afford a caravan, not even one at Le Camping.'

Maxime blinks. 'Of course. I know you.'

'It was a long time ago, but I remember you, too.' She tilts her head to the side. 'I was called Nim back then.'

'Nim and Josh,' he says. 'It was sad, what happened to your brother.'

'Indeed.' She hangs her head. Straightening, she flicks her hair over her shoulder. 'I go by the name of Imogen these days.'

Maxime gets up, and with two paces he stands beside her. His eyelashes are as long and as straight as ever. 'Welcome back.' He leans over to start the kissing routine, one on each side. His breath is hot against her neck. There's a little pause while their eyes meet and then a last kiss. 'Imogen is a good name.'

'Thank you.'

'Of course, to buy a caravan at Le Camping there are problems. The place is closed. Only cows there now.'

'That can't be right.' After coming this far, it's not what she wants to hear. 'But in the summer, people go there in the summer, don't they?'

'Not enough to keep the business going. It's finished.'

'Oh no!' The whole point of retuning was to see it again.

The telephone rings and he picks up the handset; his talk is a jumble of words that Imogen can't understand. It sounds like a conversation with a friend, but when he scribbles on a

255

pad, she thinks not. Outside the rain has turned to drizzle, and where the clouds tear apart, a slash of blue shows.

'More rain is coming.' Maxime nods his head towards the distant clouds and returns the handset to the cradle. 'Can you wait while I finish? We can go for a coffee and talk.'

Imogen's mobile peeps and she checks for texts. There's one from work. It's Fiona, the only girl she likes on the graduate scheme. The rest are overconfident and loud. Imogen doesn't fit in, no matter how she tries to be part of the group. *How are you feeling?* Fiona asks. Clearly word has got around that Imogen's taken sick leave. Although she'd like to compose an enigmatic reply about a French bon-bon named Maxime, she simply says she's having a rest.

'Come.' Maxime takes a golfing umbrella from the stand and guides Imogen out of the office. 'Let's go to the café.'

Imogen watches Maxime press his elbows against the counter and he rocks forward as he places the order. He could be swinging on the gate at the playground, making the hinges groan. He glances upwards and his hair sways. She remembers how things were when she was a girl. The way they communicated through gestures more than language. How she watched him then, the way he slunk towards her with a grin on his face. At la plage, the danger and thrill of the rope swing.

Memories of the river make her heart beat like a hammer as dread of the place creeps over her. Getting to grips with the past is a work in progress. Imogen clears her mind by studying the weave on Maxime's jacket. He takes out his wallet, and a vent at the back shows a scarlet lining. He carries a cup in each hand and she admires his balance.

When the coffee has been drunk, Imogen is still prattling about her job at Mezzo Hotels. She makes it sound glamorous. It's obviously an exaggeration and she wonders why he hasn't suggested another topic of conversation. He holds the spoon between his fingers. His nails are manicured and show half-moons. Perhaps he likes the way she chatters, but it's her nerves that keep her talking.

'Let me tell you something.' Finally he speaks. 'It's a good idea to see the chateau. The view from there is spectacular.'

'C'est magnifique?' Imogen shakes her head as she recognises Dee's words. 'I'm being stupid. Ignore me.'

'But you are right. The architecture is fabulous.'

'If there's time, a visit would be nice, but my priority is different.'

'What's that?'

She hesitates. A hollow feeling in her stomach warns Imogen to keep quiet, but she has to say something. 'It's about remembering that summer. Back when I knew you.' She blurts the words. 'I keep thinking about Josh. That sense of something not being right has never left me.'

'And how is it, now you are here?'

'I don't know.' Imogen plaits her fingers. 'I just want to get things straight.'

Maxime strokes his chin, appears to be digesting her words. She's pained by the silence and she's conscious of her neck flaring with heat. Blood bolting through her veins warns of an anxiety attack. Embarrassed, she flicks her head from side to side, searching for the loo. 'Excuse me.' Imogen rushes away and slams the door shut behind her. She rests her face against the tiled wall, absorbing the still, cool whiteness and becomes calm.

Brushing her hair, Imogen coaxes the straight ends to turn under. There's no way she wants to continue her conversation with Maxime. It's too embarrassing. Hopefully, he will have gone, got tired of waiting for the girl hiding in the toilet and left. Imogen washes her hands. The soap makes few bubbles and the towel dispenser releases one sheet. Nothing is going right. She pushes the door and peeks into the café. At the table, Maxime waits with his back to her. He scores points for patience.

Returning to her place, Imogen sits.

'I try to think,' he says.

'I haven't made it easy. I should explain. I want to know more about what happened when Josh went missing. Not that it will change stuff, I just want to understand it better.'

'A little boy dies. Everyone thinks how terrible it is. The whole town suffers. It is too sad.'

'You're telling me.' Imogen traces the grooves on the wooden table. 'My mother thinks I'm wrong to go poking about in the past.'

'Things don't change but perhaps you feel better.'

'Exactly.' Imogen releases a breath that whistles through her lips. Thank God he understands. 'My plan is to search for information at the library. See if I can find anything different from what's available on the Internet.'

'You think there is more to know?'

'Maybe there are local reports or articles.' Imogen stares at Maxime through the strands of her fringe. 'To be honest, I'm not sure, but I'm looking for reassurance.'

'About what?'

Imogen's mind is filled with an image of la plage as it was that first time they visited. The water was still and the trees were a bower into another world. She blinks to disrupt the picture. 'I want to know how it finished.'

Maxime reaches for Imogen's hand. Her skin is fair against his faded tan. 'You want to know he died cleanly? If you can say that in English. Is that what you want?'

'To know he died cleanly. Yes. To know that.' The words are raw on her tongue but Maxime's eyes offer comfort. 'Although he was always grubby.'

'He liked playing in the dirt. The best kids always do.'

'Yes.'

A moment of silence nurtures her.

'So, the library is a good place to begin, but you'll need me to translate.' Maxime checks his watch. 'I have a meeting now, but I can walk with you. Do you stay at a hotel in town?'

'Yes, the one with yellow shutters.'

'I know it.'

Outside, Imogen nestles under the umbrella with Maxime. Splashes of rainwater make her leather shoes dark. When Maxime crashes the umbrella against a wall, water jettisons on his head, flattening his hair.

'Never mind.' Imogen admires the boy who plunged into the river, eyebrows dancing as he surfaces.

'I must look ridiculous.' Maxime runs his fingers through his hair, making furrows. 'Come on.'

He cups her elbow and they walk together, hurrying to reach the hotel and get out of the wet. In the lobby, they exchange mobile numbers so that Maxime can text with details about going to the library. He gives her the French three-kiss routine and then he's gone. With the promise of Maxime's help, she is sure to find out what happened to Josh.

FORTY

Imogen enters the lounge. It's a large room with chairs arranged around low tables. The fireplace is stuffed with a display of dried flowers that have lost their colour. It would make good kindling for a fire but getting one organised would be too much trouble for Madame. Imogen finds a sofa in the corner and wonders if this was the place where Dad stayed. It would have been busy in the middle of summer. Dad complained about the expense but he'd probably stuffed loads of pastries at breakfast to make up for it. He would also buy a baguette from the campsite shop for his lunch and take bites straight from a chunk of cheese. Dear old Dad.

French magazines spread in a line don't interest Imogen. Instead she scrolls through Facebook posts on her phone. If things had been different, she might have posted a photo of the town, let her friends know of her impromptu decision to head off. She likes to surprise, but knows it's better to stay quiet about her jaunt overseas. God knows what her manager would think about her slacking off work. Voices drift from the reception area. Madame is tidying papers on the desk. She nods at Imogen and calls over, 'Did you find the library?'

'The weather was too bad.' Imogen doesn't want to speak to the woman but then thinks better of it. 'I'll go another day.'

'I see.' Madame's response is clipped.

Imogen checks the time. She's not expecting contact from Maxime until later, but she's restless with the library trip delayed. It's crazy to be stuck in the hotel, wasting time. The need to be active niggles, and from somewhere in the depths an idea swoops. Since Maxime has stayed local, maybe Pierre has as well. He might've risen through the police ranks, shaved that moustache and deepened a few more wrinkles, but he would be willing to help, Imogen is sure. She fixes her mind on the police station, remembers the exterior walls shaped like the bow of a boat and the salmon pink paint. She has to go there. Thinking better of asking Madame for directions, she reaches for her phone.

The building sits at a junction of two roads, several blocks from the hotel. At the entrance, Imogen takes a nervous step that turns her ankle and makes her topple across the tiled floor. Her elbow bangs the wall, and she collides into the counter.

'Ow.' Imogen rubs her knee and then her elbow. The pain makes her want to dash about the place. 'Ow, ow ow.'

'Je peux vous aider?' An officer jumps to his feet.

'I'm okay.' Imogen holds onto the wall.

'Je peux vous aider?' The officer repeats as he approaches.

'I'm alright.' Imogen straightens.

The man drags a chair and the legs grate against the floor. He waves his arms, gesturing for Imogen to sit, and she obliges. He bends closer, making their eyes level. His hairline recedes and his breath smells of roll-ups.

'I'm okay.' Although her knee aches, she isn't going to check for damage by stripping off her jeans. Instead, she turns back the sleeve on her jumper, revealing a red lump. At least there's no blood. Imogen covers her arm, hoping she won't be stuck with bruises that will make her resemble a Friesian cow.

'Bien,' he says.

Imogen struggles to find words in French. Her mind whirs as ideas ignite and dissipate. She nurses her sore arm. If sliding across the floor like a novice ice skater wasn't bad enough, now she can't utter a sentence. Taking her smartphone, she taps into a translation website. She forms a question about a policeman called Pierre who has an English mother. As she types, Imogen scours her brain for more relevant information but nothing comes to mind. The officer reads from the screen and shakes his head. This is a mad idea. There must be millions of Pierres in France. Imogen is tempted to leave while she still has some dignity but she tries again. This time she writes Josh's name. The man looks at the screen, scowls, then takes the phone and writes a reply. The translation reads: 'Are you a journalist?'

'No.' Imogen snatches the mobile. Words split her brain, questions about the case formulate and her fingers get busy. When she reads the screen, the message is confused. There's no easy way of explaining what she's trying to do, what she wants, what the hell she's doing there. She deletes the lot. Instead she writes: 'Is there anyone here who speaks English?' She presses the translate button and passes the handset. He reads, shrugs and begins tapping a message. When the mobile is returned, she is asked to leave. No one will speak to a journalist.

'You've got it wrong. I'm his sister.'

The officer folds his arms.

'Pierre.' The name slips from Imogen's lips. 'A man called Pierre?'

'Non.'

Imogen gives a nod. There's no point in continuing. She's made a fool of herself and the simplest thing to do is leave. As if anyone in this town wants to help.

FORTY-ONE

There's no greeting from Madame in the morning; she's busy on the telephone. While Imogen waits for Madame to finish her conversation, she browses the display of postcards on a rack. There's one of the town hall, another of a chateau on a hill in the evening light, and a drawn map of the region. She wonders whether to buy one and send it to Mum but thinks better of the idea. With all the years Mum's spent trying to forget the place, she won't thank Imogen for the reminder. Better to send a text, stay in touch that way.

When Madame finishes the conversations with an 'au revoir', she clicks the receiver back into place.

'Thank you for bringing breakfast to my room,' says Imogen.

'There is a problem.' Madame writes on a pad, pressing so hard that words across the page are slow to form. Imogen tries to read the upside-down handwriting but the attempt is futile. A written page of French doesn't make the language more accessible. 'Your room is needed for another booking. You will have to leave the hotel tomorrow.'

'I thought …' Queries clatter inside Imogen's head. 'I don't mind moving to a different room.'

'Not possible.'

'But the place is deserted!' says Imogen.

'Check out time is ten o'clock.' Madame continues writing, and when she's finished, she underscores the digits that appear at the foot of the page. 'You can find another place, Mademoiselle Mashard.' She spits Imogen's last name, giving the clue.

'I can't believe this!' Anger knots Imogen's throat, making her voice loud and high. 'You want me to leave because my brother died? Is that it?'

'Not especially.' Madame turns the ends of her lips downwards and shakes her head. 'Too much damage was done to this town. The court case, the publicity – I won't be part of it.'

'If that's how you feel, I'll leave right now.'

'As you like,' says Madame. 'I'll prepare your bill.'

Imogen seethes as she hands over the money.

With her bag slung over her shoulder, Imogen steps onto the pavement. Mist has turned the day grey and the air is damp. She's never been thrown out of a hotel before and it's not as if she's done anything wrong. Anger converts to helplessness. She carries what happened to Josh along with her luggage as she trudges along the road.

Spotlights in the estate agent's window glow, inviting her to approach. Imogen squints, trying to see if Maxime sits at the computer behind the window display. There's no harm in asking a friend for a favour. With her mind made up, Imogen crosses the square. She sees him and there's a smile on his face. As she makes it to the entrance, he's there holding the door open and he greets her with the kissing routine.

'What can I do for you, Imogen?' he asks.

'Bit of a disaster.' She suddenly feels presumptuous, like

she shouldn't be disturbing him. But, she's away from home and could do with a hand.

'What happened?'

Something about his voice makes Imogen abandon the rant that's been forming. She's robbed of all thought and stands there, vulnerable. Maxime ushers Imogen through to the back office, where filing cabinets line the walls and there's a small kitchen area. He offers her a glass of water but she shakes her head and falls against him. Resting her head in the crook of his neck, she feels his arm heavy on her shoulder.

'I've been thrown out of the hotel!'

'What do you mean? Why?'

'The owner says I can't stay there any longer. That she needs the room. It's perfectly ridiculous, there must be loads of spare beds.'

'It doesn't matter. I can help you find another place.'

'That's not the point. She hates me because … It's too crazy. I'm not responsible for the downfall of the entire town.'

'In a place like this, people don't forget. They say the women, they liked each other too much to watch the children.'

'Lesbians can't be proper parents, eh?'

'I don't know. People say things. Maybe they think the English aren't good parents. It's impossible to know for sure.'

'Is that what you thought at the time?'

'I was too young to know,' says Maxime.

'You must've thought something.'

'It was terrible.'

'Yeah.' Imogen curls stray hairs behind her ear and drops her gaze to stare at Maxime's loafers. Laced with a tight double knot, they're different from the trainers he wore as a boy. The ones he could slip on his feet without bothering to tie up. He was always in a rush to be off somewhere, racing to hang out with his mates. That's the problem with peer pressure: the popular kids have the others running about. Imogen should know. Look at the mess she got into with Michaela and Jez. Turning her head, Imogen studies Maxime's profile: straight nose and lips that seem to be permanently tweaked into a smile. It was a strange sort of comfort to be standing with Maxime. Ten-year-old Nim would be thrilled at their proximity. 'Can't I stay with you? I don't want to find another hotel. I wouldn't be any trouble, honestly. Give me a sofa and I'll be fine.'

'It isn't possible. The house is not right. Too much dirt. I will find you a nice place to stay.'

'But it'll be the same wherever I go. As soon as they know my name, they won't want me.'

'Not everyone is like Madame. There are good people in this town. Trust me, Imogen.' Maxime lifts her chin. 'I will help you.'

They walk side by side. Imogen resists the urge to link arms and instead watches her feet move over the paving stones. The hotel he recommends is near the park. Maxime does all the talking so check-in goes without a hitch. She takes a third-floor room with a view over the gardens. It would be lovely in summer with flowers planted but the weather makes the outlook hazy. She loves the Wedgwood blue walls patterned with fleur-de-lys and the bedstead with its deep mattress. She slings her handbag over the metal frame. There'll be no problem getting to sleep, even if she has to be alone.

'It's a lovely room. Much better than anything Madame could have offered.'

'Madame can sit on a pin.' He laughs and makes the sound of a balloon flying across the room.

'Too right.' Imogen smiles.

'Would you like dinner tonight?'

'That would be very nice,' says Imogen.

'There's a brasserie next to this hotel. Meet me there at eight o'clock.'

FORTY-TWO

Maxime stands under a street lamp outside the restaurant. A scarf is wrapped around his neck and his hair flies in the wind. As soon as Imogen's close, he's ready with the kisses. It means nothing, she tells herself, it's simply a polite greeting: a kiss on each side and one for luck. He pushes the door open so that Imogen can enter first, but she gets in a dither about what to do next and he's there again, holding her elbow, showing her the way. The table is laid and there are two ceramic jugs with wine and water ready for pouring. Maxime does the honours and lifts the glass of red. He waits for Imogen to mirror his actions, all set to toast.

'Thank you for helping me.' Imogen gets the words in first.

'That's easy,' he says.

'And you've found us a place to eat.'

'It was a cellar once. You can tell from the arches.'

A waitress comes to take the order. There's a choice of three starters and three mains. She goes for soup followed by duck, knowing it's a local speciality.

'You've chosen well,' says Maxime. 'You get the best confit du canard here.'

'So why have you gone for fish?'

'A change.' He smiles, making the dimple show, and glances at his watch.

'Have you got to be somewhere?' Does he have a girlfriend, or even a wife?

'Someone is calling by my house.' He presses his lips together like he's holding back a secret. 'We have time.'

'Okay.' Best not to ask too many questions.

'Tell me, Imogen, why are you called that now?'

She holds his gaze, could stare at him for hours, anything to avoid answering the question. 'It's not very interesting.'

'Nim is the name of a pretty girl. Very énigmatique. But now you are Imogen.'

'I went to college with a clean slate and a new name. It was one way to dust off my school days.'

'You left Nim behind.'

'Imogen suits me better.' She holds a hand behind her head and takes a photographic pose. 'Classy, sophisticated.'

Maxime gives a smile and the dimple pricks his cheek. There was a time when they were two of a pair, she with the mole on her face and he with the dimple. Now all she has is a tiny patch of scar tissue. She shakes her head, bringing her back to the moment.

'Enough of me,' she says. 'How did your English become so good?'

'I spent time in Australia.' He talks from the side of his mouth: 'G'day, mate.'

Imogen can't help laughing. 'Why did you come back?'

'Many reasons.'

A crash from the other side of the restaurant, plates smashing, makes Maxime look around. There's a group at the bar and a man with flattened hair shouts over a greeting.

Maxime pushes back his chair and stands. 'There's someone I know. I won't be long.'

Imogen rests her chin on the heel of her palm and watches him walk away. Greetings in French tumble and there's shoulder slapping with someone she can't see properly as he's hidden behind a column that divides the restaurant. She takes the napkin, turns it into a triangle and drops it onto her lap. It wasn't necessary to share the real story about her name change with Maxime. No need to mention Michaela and the price paid for trusting the wrong person. Imogen ruffles the edge of the napkin, letting her fingertips run over the stitching. Dear old Dad, he learned about the whole charade from Ben, and that scuppered another friendship. That was how it went.

The soup arrives and Imogen stares into the bowl while steam drifts. She looks around for Maxime and spots him making his way over.

'I'm sorry you have to wait.' He sits. 'My cousin sends good wishes.'

'That's who you were talking with?' So he does have family nearby.

'Yes.' Maxime nods towards her bowl. 'You start.'

The soup runs hot down Imogen's throat and she gives it a stir before trying again. 'What does he do, your cousin?'

'He works at a vineyard outside of town. I can take you there tomorrow. You must try the red wine, it's won prizes.'

'Shouldn't we be going to the library?'

'There's time for that. Come on, Imogen. Let's have some fun.' He tilts his head, coaxing her to agree.

'So much for concentrating on what needs doing.'

'You're in France. Tasting wine is compulsory.'

Imogen hesitates, staring at her soup for inspiration. Lentils float, making a dot-to-dot pattern. 'I guess that's just the sort of thing to keep a tourist occupied.' Imogen drops her spoon and it clanks on the edge of the bowl. 'But I'm not on holiday, Maxime.'

'It will give us time. We have a lot of catching up to do and it will help for when the hard work comes. Reading about your brother is not going to be easy.'

'Tell me about it.' Imogen cups her face between her hands. 'And I want to go to la plage.'

'Everything. We'll do everything.'

Imogen doubts that spending time in the French countryside will make any difference to how she feels, but one day isn't going to hurt. 'Wine tasting will be nice.'

FORTY-THREE

Imogen shifts her position on the ribbed passenger seat. The Renault is ancient and when Maxime slams his door shut, the car vibrates. Imogen clinks the seat belt into the buckle.

'Cars like this have character,' says Imogen.

'I drive a different car for work, a new one.' Maxime shows his dimple. 'I think you like this better. It's very French.'

'It has charm,' she says.

Maxime stops at the junction. He watches cars until a gap appears. 'We're on our way.'

'Tell me about your life, Maxime.'

'I have a sister, she lives in Rouen, and two nephews.'

There's a start. 'How old?'

'She's twenty-nine.'

'I meant your nephews.'

'Six or seven and …' Maxime raises his eyebrows. 'Four, perhaps.'

'I take it you don't see much of them.'

'They visit in summer.'

'Oh, good,' Imogen gushes.

'Good?' he asks.

'Good that you have family around. I don't like to think of you as being alone.'

'It's not simple,' says Maxime.

'What does that mean?' She regrets asking the question as soon as the words leave her lips. It's as if she's prying, like she doesn't trust him.

'Life is hard.' Maxime takes a road that goes through fields striped with vines. The branches stretch out as if they're holding hands. A great belly of winter sky rises over the land. The gearbox crunches as Maxime manipulates the stick. He smiles and glances over. Her fingers twitch. She wants to rest her hand on his leg, grip his thigh.

'Have you got a girlfriend?' She shrinks, not wanting to hear the answer.

'No.' Maxime's reply is instant.

Imogen ponders. She's surprised and disbelieving at his answer. 'I only ask because you don't talk about yourself much. D'you have secrets?' she teases.

'Not secrets, but I am private.'

Maxime swings into a drive and follows the dirt road. At the end, there is a modern building with a square pyramid for a roof. Maxime turns the car in a circle and parks. They find a side door and go down into the cellar. At the far wall there are huge barrels lined up. Electric bulbs shine pools of light and a candelabra lamp glows. Opened bottles are arranged on a table, each tied with a tag that displays the price. The wine seems remarkably cheap to Imogen, a few euros for a bottle with a pretty label that shows a pen and ink drawing of the house.

'You try one.' Maxime fills a glass with red wine and passes it to Imogen. He watches while she drinks.

'Very smooth.' She holds the stem and swirls the remaining wine inside the glass. Turning her head and letting her hair fall around her shoulders, she feels relaxed. 'Where is everyone?'

'I don't know.' He pours more Merlot.

'Aren't you going to have some?' Imogen holds the wine glass to the light, acting as if she knows something about wine.

'Give me a taste.' He reaches for the glass and takes a sip like he's sucking through a straw.

'Is that how the experts do it?' Imogen laughs.

'I know a little. My cousin taught me.'

'Oh, yes. He works here, doesn't he?'

'Yeah, but sales are quiet in winter. Only a few visitors. I'll take two bottles and pay Anton when I see him again.'

Anton. The name makes Imogen stiffen. It can't be the same person. An image of the gangly youth comes to mind, his top lip curling. 'You're not talking about *the* Anton, are you?'

'You remember him?'

Imogen bows her head, speaks to the floor. 'I never knew he was your cousin.'

'It is incredible the way he has turned his life around,' says Maxime.

Imogen doesn't give a shit about Anton's life or Anton's future. The flavour of wine in Imogen's mouth turns to metal. 'I can't believe you've brought me here.'

'Anton thought you would like the wine,' says Maxime.

She clutches the table to keep her balance as a sick feeling swamps her. She reconstructs a scene from la plage, sees Anton charging through the field of wheat, his figure blurry in the afternoon sun. This could be the missing link, the answer to why Josh keeps coming to mind. Perhaps he followed Anton and that's why Josh became lost and vulnerable. Imogen blinks back tears.

'Are you okay, Imogen?'

'I don't feel well.'

'What's the matter?' His look is one of concern.

'I need to get out of here.' Imogen rushes to the exit. Her eyes sting as she enters the daylight. Maxime follows, the bottles he carries clinking together.

'Wait for me,' he says.

She stops walking when she reaches his car and leans against the bodywork.

'Why did you bring me here? You must know I don't want anything to do with Anton! Why didn't this town turn on him like they've turned on me?'

'Don't be angry,' says Maxime. 'He was a crazy boy. He drank too much whisky but he's okay now. It was clear in the end. He had nothing to do with what happened to Josh.'

'I'm not so sure.'

'There's no need to doubt Anton. I can stand for him.'

'I've had enough today, Maxime. Please take me home.'

Silence fills the journey. The fields are a blur of brown-grey earth. There's nothing special about this place. It holds the pain and sorrow of her childhood. Imogen's neck is tense. She doesn't want to look at Maxime, doesn't want to acknowledge his presence. Concentration is what's required. She needs to go back to London with answers. Resolve the issues that have caused the panic to descend. When the car draws to a stop, Imogen cranks the door handle but it refuses to budge. Maxime leans across and releases it. She notices the way his curls fall. She hesitates.

'Don't be angry with me,' he says.

'It was Anton who watched when we kissed. You didn't think I knew about that, did you? And then with Josh.'

'It happened a long time ago.'

'You were his puppet then and things haven't changed. Anton's still pulling your strings.'

'It's not like that, Imogen.'

'I think it is.' Getting out of the car, Imogen is tempted to slam the door shut but Maxime is at her side.

'Don't go.' He takes her hand, slides his fingers between hers, locking them together. She wants to change her mind, have Maxime persuade her. To really believe that their history has brought them to a place where they can start over. It might have been possible, if memories didn't hang over them.

'It's no use.' Imogen breaks free. 'I need to be on my own.'

Imogen lies on the bed and studies the pattern of fleur-de-lys on the walls. In the corner the prints bunch together, spoiling the effect. She turns on her side and grips the duvet, kneading the fabric. Everything gets ruined. Her thoughts cluster around Maxime. She tries to block out the argument, but the reproaches continue until she can't stand it any more. She begins to wish she'd never embarked on this trip to France. Imogen puts on her jacket. It's too late to find the library, too dark to contemplate going to la plage. She should try to accomplish something. The least she can do is walk around the town, have a drink in a bar, anything to stop the thoughts from circling.

Houses on the street are joined together like bread rolls on a baking sheet. At the junction, Imogen comes to a row of shops. A flash of green neon identifies a pharmacy, and through the glass frontage, Imogen sees the sanitised interior. Further along she passes a bar with the double doors open. Men stand around upturned barrels, and a pinball machine pummels a tune. It's not the sort of place she has in mind. Next there's an establishment with lace curtains. It looks more like a tea shop than a bar. She goes inside. No one but the staff will notice her in the corner.

Imogen drapes her jacket over the back of her chair. In

her handbag she has a paperback, useful for times like this. She can disappear into the pages, pretend she's not alone. The waiter approaches. He wears a leather waistcoat over a check shirt.

'Que voulez-vous boire?'

'Un verre de vin blanc, s'il vous plait.' She says the words mechanically, memorised from a translation website.

'Okay.' He wipes the table with a cloth and strikes a cigarette lighter to make the candle glow. There's no need to create a romantic ambience when she sits alone but the additional light makes it easier to follow the lines of the story. Not that she's actually reading. The words flow without registering. The book is merely something to hide behind.

The waiter carries a tray with a carafe and a single glass. He pours and leaves the carafe on the table, slipping the bill alongside. She knows she should stop drinking once she's downed the first glass but she refills. The anaesthetic quality of alcohol is what she needs: relief from the row with Maxime, distance from Anton, and a break from researching Josh. When she upturns the carafe and only a few drops fall from the lip, it's like an accident has happened. She's become giddy and light. The waiter watches, as if expecting another order.

'D'you know about the English boy who died in this town?' Imogen asks the question believing he won't understand.

The man inches over and collects the carafe. 'The boy die, the town die, too.' He points to the glass. 'You want more?'

'No.' She meets his lizard eyes. 'Why? Why did it happen?'

'English mother.' He rubs his chin. 'She don't ... She no good.'

'You're wrong.' It's a long time since Imogen has defended her mother.

The man shrugs and slopes away. Imogen ferrets in her bag for money. A car parked in the road outside blasts an ABBA chorus and she hooks into the tune until a slamming door daubs the place with quiet. Flicking to a memory from the campsite, Imogen sees Dee strutting about the deck of the caravan. She holds a Coke bottle in her hand as a microphone and belts out the lyrics to 'Dancing Queen'. On the deckchair, Mum laughs so much she holds her stomach and Ella shuffles onto the stage like a backing singer. Josh is the statue of a warrior, his digging stick to root out ants motionless in his hands. He stands amazed, watching the performance as Dee swaggers. With her face in profile one minute, Dee's ski-jump nose shows and beads of sweat drop from her chin. Next minute she's facing the front and her curls bounce as she nods and shakes her head.

'Stop,' squeals Mum. 'I can't breathe.'

'Your turn next, Jenny!'

'Go on, Mum!' says Josh.

'I can't sing for toffee,' says Mum. 'You skedaddle, Josh. There's time to dig up dinosaur bones before dinner. Nim can help. I'll give you children a call when everything's ready.'

The girls follow Josh into the woods. There's a sawn-off tree trunk that marks their camp and Ella sets about making fairy perfume by crushing leaves. Nim's sure it'll never make a pleasant smell but there's no harm in joining in. Using his stick to dig the ground, Josh is off. Nim plucks a few daisy heads and arranges them on the trunk but Ella ignores the pile and continues squelching leaves, mincing them between a couple of flints.

'I want to make a fire,' says Ella. 'I need to boil everything up for a potion.'

'Here's some wood.' Josh aims his stick and throws it like a spear. It doesn't fly through the air but clonks onto the ground. 'That stick's gay.'

'Don't say that,' says Nim. 'Children in my class lose house points if they ever use that word. You don't want to get into trouble, Josh.'

'My mum's gay,' says Ella. 'I think she loves your mum.'

'What?' Josh turns and stares. Through the bushes it's possible to see the mums. Dee stands at the picnic table laying out plates, and Mum's at her side filling beakers with squash. Their voices carry with the breeze that makes leaves twirl on their stalks. 'Is it okay to be gay?'

'Yeah,' says Ella. 'You can't choose who you fall in love with.'

Imogen remembers the scene: it was the moment she understood. Of course Mum loved Dee. It had been obvious all along. And now, because of that love, these people blame her mother for businesses that have gone belly up. Josh is squeezed out of the picture. They're more concerned with making money than the human cost of loss. The barman's a bloody racist, a homophobe, a complete idiot. Outrage wells and Imogen is surprised at the vitriol. She brushes past the waiter, tosses a note onto the tray and escapes into the night where the cold claws and the chill makes her thoughts sharp. These people and their lack of empathy! Everyone in the town is the same. Everyone except Maxime. She's been stupid, falling out with the one person who has been offering her support. What can she achieve without his help? Imogen decides to call him, try to make amends. She sees on her mobile that it's gone eleven o'clock, but it's not an unreasonable time to call.

'Allo.' He answers.

Imogen savours his voice.

'Qui est à l'appareil?'

Why is he speaking French? His mobile must show it's Imogen calling. Or he's deleted her number.

'Allo.' His voice has an edge of impatience.

'Hello, Maxime.' His name remains on her lips while she hopes her words are welcome. 'It's Imogen.'

'Wait a minute.' The background buzz of the television becomes silent, then he speaks. 'I'm here.'

'Sorry, Maxime. I'm famous for rushing in and mucking things up.'

'Mucking up?'

'Making a mistake.'

'Okay,' says Maxime. 'What can I do?'

'Let's start again.'

'Is that possible? If you are angry with Anton, you're angry with me.'

'I'm not sure angry is the right word. I'm confused. I want to find some clarity. Be able to understand what's at the bottom of everything I'm feeling.'

'We can't talk about this on the phone. Where are you, Imogen? Shall I come to your hotel?'

Imogen's heart quickens. 'Let's meet in the lobby in half an hour.'

FORTY-FIVE

Imogen waits on the button-pin sofa with the high back. It's not exactly comfortable, but then meeting in the reception is hardly ideal. The office space behind the counter is dark, although light seeps from the lounge. Imogen twirls the ring with a turquoise stone around her little finger. She allows a slideshow of images to glare and then fade. Dee's face with her chipmunk cheeks makes Imogen smile. Perhaps, when she gets home, she'll look Dee up. It won't be that hard to track her down.

His footsteps are light and with three paces he is beside Imogen. Their thighs brush as he sits. Taking her hand, Maxime threads his fingers through hers and Imogen listens to his breathing.

'Have you been running?' she asks.

'I can't stay long,' he says. 'But I need to say something.'

'Go ahead.' Imogen stares at the tiled floor, noticing where the worn edges make a wispy pattern. He doesn't speak. She adjusts her chin, so that their eyes are level. 'I'm listening.'

'I was thinking and now the words have gone.'

'Just say it.' Cramp in her belly indicates she's expecting the worst kind of news. She taps the toes of her shoes together, marking time.

'I'm sorry,' he says.

'Sorry?'

'For what happened to Josh.'

'That makes two of us.'

'You don't understand. I wanted to say it when you first came into the office, but I had to stop. I have mixed-up feelings.' Maxime hangs his head.

'You and me both.' Imogen squeezes his fingers and releases Maxime's hand. So this is how it ends.

'Maybe I took you to Anton's vineyard for a reason.' Maxime lets breath slide from his mouth. 'He didn't have anything to do with Josh going missing, but I had to stand with Anton. He was in trouble and I stuck to him. I'm sorry. I should have said goodbye before we left Le Camping. I have regrets but I was too young and too stupid to do right.'

Imogen absorbs his words.

'I wanted to say these things for years,' he continues, 'but when the chance came, I was too slow.'

Imogen grips Maxime's shoulder and gives a shake. The corners of his mouth crease while frown lines pucker his forehead.

'Show me your dimple,' she says.

He smiles and the star springs onto his cheek. 'Like this?'

Imogen nods and slides a finger across her face to find the patch of scar tissue. 'Do you remember the mole I used to have?'

He squints. 'I knew there was something different.'

'I had surgery to remove it and now I'm left with a tiny white feather scar.'

'You had it cut?' His lips shape into an 'O'.

'There's no need to look shocked. It wasn't simply for

cosmetic reasons. I thought perhaps if the mole was removed, some of the responsibility I felt over losing Josh would also be sliced away. It worked for a while.'

Maxime cradles her chin. 'Now there's nothing to see.'

'There is,' she says. 'The scar is a mark of my cowardice.'

'Cowardice? That's not right. You are brave.'

She tilts her head, letting the idea settle. 'You think so?'

'You're the bravest person I know.'

She laughs and crashes her forehead against his. It's more than a bump but she continues to laugh from the shock of it. She holds her head as the pain throbs and tears drip. She wants to leap around as a distraction from the ache. Instead she sits, cupping her forehead and thinking herself an idiot. Maxime finds a handkerchief in his pocket and passes it to her. She dabs her eyes.

'See what I mean?' he says. 'You are brave.'

Maxime keeps his promise. At the library, Imogen and Maxime sit together. On the desk, the computer screen shows a photograph of Hector Pascal. Imogen grips the chair, squeezing the plastic frame. She knows his face from Internet searches, but this time his features appear life-size, as if he's sitting behind the glass, looking directly at Imogen. Once her heart would've bolted but this time she stares at him squarely. Her lips open a crack as her lungs fill and deflate.

His features have been imprinted on Imogen's mind. There's his nose that flares at the nostrils and the thick brows. On his head, springy curls take the shape of a widow's peak and are neatly trimmed. Imogen centres her gaze on his eyes. The hooded lids slice away dark irises. He could be the man who lives along the street, if he didn't wear a terrified expression. His mouth is open, jagged, like he's ready to shout. If he did, which words would he scream?

'You must have seen the photo before. It was in the newspapers,' says Maxime.

'Somehow he looks different.'

Maxime presses the link and columns of text appear beside a picture showing a brick building with razor wire wound on top of the perimeter walls.

'What does it say?' asks Imogen.

'Let me read to the end.' Maxime scans the text.

Imogen laces her fingers, trying to keep her anxieties in check. 'Have you finished yet?'

'It says he moved to a psychiatric hospital near Dijon. His punishment is there. He's too sick, too ill, to cope with anything.'

'Even prison? He needs to be put away for good,' says Imogen. 'Little children deserve safety.'

'Don't worry. He will not be free.'

'D'you think he's allowed visitors?'

'I don't know,' says Maxime.

'How far is Dijon?'

'Much too far,' says Maxime. 'You can't want to go there. It's not a good idea. He probably won't talk to you, anyway.'

'Maybe I could find out.'

'It will take weeks, maybe months, to get permission … if they let you.'

'I'm not sure I have the courage.' Imogen blows away a breath. 'But if I did see him, I could find out what was in his head. Understand why he took Josh. If he hurt or abused my brother.'

'I can tell you.' Maxime returns his gaze to the screen and points. 'Josh wanted a football shirt and followed the man. I read from here. They went to his home, a shack on the edge of town. Josh wore a football shirt and ate beans from a tin. When he cried to go home, Hector Pascal put his hand over Josh's mouth to stop the noise.'

'I know. I know that's what he said in his defence. Josh cried, wanting to be with his family, and that bastard smothered him.'

'It's horrible but there's nothing more. It says that he

didn't want to hurt Josh. Your brother died quickly, without damage.'

Imogen remembers the journey to France and the accident that was their first encounter with Hector Pascal. She sees Josh, the football shirt pressed against his chest, the hem falling below his knees. If only Mum had bought it. Instead, Josh helped to collect the other packages and stowed them in the broken cardboard box.

'He ruined everything for me and my family. I came to France with my mum, but went back with another sort of mother. She's never been able to talk about it. My dad managed better but now he's gone.' Imogen shrugs and swallows. 'He killed my whole family.'

Maxime drapes his arm around Imogen's shoulder. 'That is sad. I am sorry to hear but you will find a way through. You don't need to see Hector Pascal.'

Leaving the library, Imogen is despondent. She hasn't learned anything new. Air rushes as Imogen picks up the pace of walking. Beside her, Maxime matches her speed and the tail of his scarf swings as he strides. Imogen's disappointment dissipates with exercise but new niggles come to mind. This whole visit is pointless if she can't find anything to settle her thoughts. Help her to dispel the ideas that crowd out logic. They reach the hotel in fifteen minutes and Imogen is out of breath. She leans against the hotel wall.

'Why hurry?' asks Maxime.

'It's a way of coping. I walk fast to relieve the frustration. I wanted some new nugget of information.'

'You must try to accept what's happened and start over.'

'Absolutely. And if I knew how to do that, I would.'

'You will be okay.' Maxime tucks his hand around her waist. 'You are resilient.'

'I don't know about that.' She lets Maxime pull her into a hug.

'It's never easy.' Maxime talks into her neck.

'Let's go for a drink.'

'I can't.' Maxime steps away and checks his watch. 'I need to get back.'

'But you're not working, are you?'

'No, but I have things to do.'

Maxime takes Imogen's hand and traces the lines on her palm like he is going to read her future. She wonders what's so important that he has to leave her. She snatches her hand away. 'Go if you must.'

'Don't do that, Imogen.' Maxime tilts his head and catches her gaze. 'I have an idea. I'm not sure you will want this, but I tell you anyway. My neighbour helped at the homeless hostel where Hector Pascal went. I can talk to her. Ask if she will meet you. It will be a chance to find out more about him.'

'What does she remember?'

'I don't know exactly but he went to the hostel all the time. Let me talk to her. I'm not sure she will agree but if she has information, she can help.'

'I want to believe that he didn't hurt Josh, that he never intended to kill him. But at the moment, it's impossible. If I knew a little more, could trust what he says. That might make all the difference.'

'I will ask.' Maxime links arms with Imogen and they stand together. Tipping her head onto Maxime's shoulder, Imogen hopes for a proper embrace. She's fed up with the pecking routine but it's difficult to be together while the pity of losing Josh gets between them.

'Thanks for your help,' says Imogen. 'It's good to have you on my side.'

Maxime tightens his grip, drawing Imogen closer. She likes him near, enjoys the warmth from his body and allows a silence to rest between them. Maxime nuzzles her hair and breaks free.

'So what are you thinking now?' she asks.

'Only about you.' He smiles and holds her neck gently in his hands, sending a zing through Imogen's body. She angles her face, ready to receive the kiss, and her eyes close.

FORTY-SEVEN

Imogen recognises the road names and landmarks as she follows the directions sent in the text from Maxime. She's been invited to his house to meet his neighbour, who's agreed to talk about Hector Pascal. While she's there, she'll also have the chance to find out more about Maxime.

Imogen has time to squander, so she stops outside a brasserie. Her eyes flit across the menu but the thought of food makes her queasy. The pang in her stomach is a sign of nerves. She will be brave and have some answers.

With minutes to spare, Imogen stands at Maxime's front door. She notices a grab rail cemented into the bricks. She presses the doorbell, curiosity bubbling. Footsteps from behind the door announce Maxime's approach. Imogen raises her chin and commands her heart to stop jabbing. He cradles her neck and kisses Imogen's lips as a greeting. There's no mistaking the welcome.

'Come in.' Maxime kicks an empty two-litre tin of paint along the passageway. 'I'm decorating. I have to make the house nice so it will sell.'

'You're moving?' asks Imogen.

'My mother is leaving. She will live in Rouen with my sister.'

'You live with your mother?'

'Of course. She has a disability. La sclérose. She can't walk very far.'

Imogen is surprised and relieved at the admission. 'I'm sorry.'

Maxime shrugs. 'I made some changes but the house is no good. It is better in Rouen. My sister and her kids are there.'

'Where will you go? What will you do for accommodation?'

'I'm in the right business to find somewhere. But it's not easy to sell your childhood home.' Imogen walks with Maxime to a room at the back of the house. 'Fabienne is here.'

'She's the neighbour who knew Hector Pascal?'

'Yes. We have one hour.'

'What about your mother, is she here?'

'No. She's at the clinic. She will come later.'

In the salon, Fabienne sits in an armchair. She greets Imogen with a smile and approaches with her arms spread wide. They exchange kisses and the routine doesn't feel awkward, especially with someone Imogen wants to like. Fabienne brushes a permed curl from her forehead as she exchanges words with Maxime. When the talk is finished, he does a little bow.

'Let's sit.' Maxime takes the chair with wings and Fabienne returns to her place. Imogen chooses the chintz sofa rather than sitting on the wooden dining chair placed between Maxime and Fabienne. The matt lemon walls and the glossed woodwork make it a comfortable space.

'You've decorated this room beautifully,' says Imogen.

'Oui.' Fabienne appears to understand but says no more.

'You can ask questions, Imogen. I will say the words in French for Fabienne.'

'Perfect.' Imogen takes a notebook from her bag. She skims over the questions she's listed and finds the ones she most wants to ask. 'We'll start with an easy one. How did you meet Hector Pascal?'

When Maxime finishes translating, Imogen watches Fabienne's lips move as she speaks. Imogen clings to the words, trying to glean meaning from every utterance. An ache behind her eyes begins to throb. The only word she recognises is his name. Hector. Imprinted on Imogen's consciousness are his startled eyes captured in the photo.

Maxime nods his head as Fabienne's words keep coming.

'Okay.' Maxime holds his hand in the air signalling for Fabienne to slow down. He laughs a little. Although he turns his head and smiles at Imogen, she senses the seriousness. 'I will ask Fabienne to speak in short sentences. But first, let me explain what she said.'

'Thank you,' says Imogen.

'Fabienne helped at the homeless hostel for a long time. She stopped when her legs hurt from standing too much. Hector came every week. He washed his clothes and showered. She remembers he never liked to eat hot food. He watched his meal until it was cold then he ate everything. He had a lot of problems. She thinks he heard voices.'

Imogen's heart thumps and heat chases from her toes to her fingertips.

'Are you alright?' asks Maxime.

'I have another question,' says Imogen. 'What was he like, as a person?'

Maxime swivels to face Fabienne. The words come in

streams and Imogen imagines swimming like she did as a teenager. The water slapping her shoulders as she turns in the lane, the stretch of her arms and the twist of her head as she gulps a breath.

'Are you ready to listen?' asks Maxime.

Imogen phases back into the conversation. She grips the arm of the sofa. 'Yes, I'm ready.'

'She says Hector Pascal smoked too much. His fingers and teeth were yellow. When he had cigarettes, he gave them away until he had none. The others made fun, took his things, like his hat or his belt, and never returned them. He was …' Maxime rubs his chin. 'How do you say? Picked at.'

That's no excuse. Poor little Josh. Her thoughts fall away as Imogen constructs a picture of Hector. He sits on the wooden chair in the salon, wearing flip-flops in the winter. His trousers flap against his ankles, too short for his nearly six-foot height. Not that he appears tall. He's withered from the weight of living. Whittled by circumstances. His ankles are flexed like he's ready to run.

'What are you thinking?' asks Maxime.

'Nothing.' Imogen shakes her head. 'Please ask Fabienne what Hector did all day.'

Fabienne slants her head and moves her hands, opening and closing them like flower heads. 'What does she say?'

'A minute,' says Maxime.

Fabienne continues to talk, the words overlapping. Imogen focuses on the dining chair where Hector sits. He wears a grey shirt with food stains across the chest. He has a piece of string tied around his wrist and the ends are fraying.

'She says the same – like we read in the newspaper. He had a basket on wheels that he pulled. He walked around the streets. Sometimes he asked for money. Fabienne remembers he was always polite. He said thank you.'

'Ask about his health. Does she know anything?'

'Okay.' Maxime poses the question.

Fabienne thinks for a second, then speaks. Her language rises and falls. Imogen listens to the pattern of her words while she stares at the chair. This time Imogen sees Hector's face: sad eyes and drooped lids. His thin lips are open, making a gash across his face. The room becomes quiet.

'Let me think,' says Maxime. 'Fabienne doesn't know, but the trial said Hector Pascal had schizophrénie. He didn't take medicine. Sometimes he was quiet, sometimes he was afraid. One day he wanted to help Fabienne clean floors. He was too quick and he pushed the bucket. Water was everywhere. He went to the corner of the room and cried.'

'I see,' says Imogen.

In the silence of the room, Hector appears again. He holds his knees like this will anchor him to the chair. His eyes are wide, brown against the milky white. His lips move slowly. Imogen catches the whispered words: *I didn't mean to do it. Forgive me.*

'What else do you want to ask?' says Maxime.

'There's a question in my head but I can't pin it down.'

'Take your time,' says Maxime.

He turns to Fabienne and says a few words. Imogen settles her gaze on the wooden chair. Four stout legs against the floor and a fabric back. Hector has gone.

'I'd like Fabienne to know that what she's said has really helped. The way she's described him has turned

Hector into a real person, not a monster to fear.'

'What he did was terrible, but he was a sick man,' Maxime interjects.

Imogen concentrates as Maxime interprets. It's strange how the words make sense. When Maxime finishes, Fabienne gives a smile of encouragement and makes a final statement.

'That's it,' says Maxime. 'Fabienne read the newspapers like everyone. It's possible to believe a crying child would frighten him. It was a tragedy. No one could have predicted. To lose a child is terrible.'

Fabienne's explanation has finished. She stands to leave. The parting is one of smiles and tearful eyes. She clasps Imogen's hands and wishes her well. They stay linked together until Maxime escorts Fabienne to the door. Imogen goes to the window and stares at the garden. There's a swatch of grass and some fruit trees. She wonders what the view is like from Hector's window. Brick walls and razor wire, perhaps. It's the way it should be. There's satisfaction in knowing he's no danger to anyone else.

Maxime returns to the room and steals behind Imogen. He wraps his arms around her waist and sinks his chin onto her shoulder. 'How do you feel now the work is done?'

'I am fine.'

Maxime collects Imogen from her hotel in the Renault. He follows the road that leads to the top of the ridge in winding bends. The engine growls and the windscreen rattles, making the music on the player barely audible. Imogen turns the empty CD case and realises the soundtrack is from a film she's never seen. The photos are black and white, a silhouette of a cyclist pedalling through snow-covered fields.

'It's a good story,' says Maxime. 'They fall in love, they separate, they get back together.'

'A happy ending.'

'Of course,' says Maxime. 'All good stories end well.'

Maxime parks the car and they walk. The wind makes her jacket puff and she secures the belt to stop the whole thing from blowing away. Swinging his arms, Maxime strides across the dirt. He's wearing lace-up shoes again, this time suede in royal blue. It's coincidence that their footwear coordinates, she in her turquoise flats.

At the lookout, the ground falls away and far below is a foil of water that twists through the gap. It's the same water that fills the pool at la plage but here the river is insignificant. It's the sheer rock faces that dominate. Clumps of ferns cling to the cracks – snippets of colour on the cliffs. Over in the distance, there are other peaks, triangles in the drizzle. Maxime counts off the chateaux he knows are there, but Imogen can't see them through the clouds. When there's no longer a need to point, he drops his hand and his knuckles brush her thigh. A zing of excitement makes her burst into giggles.

'What's funny?' he asks.

Her eyes dance to the horizon and the timing is perfect. 'Look, there's a rainbow.'

'Do you wish when you see one?'

'There's no harm,' she says. 'I could wish for better weather. Those clouds are lead and fit to burst. If we don't take cover soon we'll get soaked.'

'Wait. We have time.'

Imogen stares at the bands of colour permeating the sky, delighted by the surprise. When she turns, she finds Maxime's more interested in examining her figure. From her pocket, she whips out her phone. 'Let's take a photo.'

Maxime packs his frame tight against Imogen and presses his face next to hers. His hair smells sweet, which distracts Imogen for a second. She angles her head and decides he uses fruity shampoo. She takes a couple of sensible shots then she can't resist pulling faces: showing her tongue, puckering her lips. He raises his eyebrows and winks. They stand together, examining the camera roll, laughing at the sight of them together.

A fat raindrop falls followed with others plinking the ground.

'Send me the pictures, Imogen. But now, we must find a dry place.' He reaches for Imogen's hand and her fingers fold into his. 'There's a bar. We can have an aperitif and watch the weather.'

Rain makes a polka-dot pattern on the ground. They

follow the path away from the gates of the chateau and towards a whitewashed building. The stable doors are closed but there are steps leading to the first floor. When the rain pelts, they dash for cover. At the entrance, water slides from Imogen's fringe and down her nose. Maxime's curls are flattened.

'It could be worse.' Imogen finds a paper tissue in her pocket and pats her face. Rain pummels the roof of the porch as if drumsticks are falling. 'We could be completely soaked.'

'See the way it falls in straight lines,' observes Maxime. They watch the earth turn to the colour of cocoa as it soaks up the rain. 'Let's go inside and get dry.'

In the restaurant, the walls are lumpy and decorated with redundant farm equipment; a scythe has been mounted above the tables that are laid ready for service. The place is empty because it's early for lunch in France. Imogen follows Maxime to the bar where a picture window gives a view over the car park. The Renault is parked alone.

'What do you ... pardon me ... what would you like to drink?' asks Maxime.

Imogen runs through the options. She usually drinks wine but that isn't an aperitif.

'Beer,' she says. 'A beer would be nice. Thank you.'

He orders two and they're served in narrow tumblers. While he chats in French to the man behind the bar, Imogen traces the line of condensation on the glass. If she concentrates, maybe she could understand the conversation. It's not as if they're talking about anything important, pleasantries she guesses, observations about the weather, perhaps. Or is it the English alone who do that? She recalls some vocabulary: la pluie, parapluie. The words hang together. She hated French lessons at school but maybe that had something to do with losing Josh. At secondary, most people thought she was an only child, as if Josh had never existed. A ribbon of sorrow ripples through her.

'Are you hungry?' Maxime hands her a menu.

'Starving,' she says. On cue, her stomach groans as if she's had no breakfast. She tightens her muscles to deaden the noise.

'You're a tiger.' He smiles. 'You sound like one.'

'Such a giveaway,' says Imogen.

'We've come to the right place. The food is very good here.'

At the table Maxime orders for them both, and although she's slightly worried about ragoût de porc et de moules nothing can go wrong with a salad to start. So long as the nuts are chopped, that is, not whole Brazils that might fly off the plate. She touches the cutlery. One prong on the fork is bent and she taps the end with the pad of her finger. When the plates arrive, there are toasted walnuts hidden among the leaves. Imogen can't resist stealing a nut from Maxime's plate. He watches her, a bundle of salad leaves speared on his fork. This is a performance more than a meal. Bring on a glass of chilled white wine and the next course. It's the second act in a stage play where she's not aware of the ending.

'Is there a restaurant where you work?' he asks.

Imogen's forgotten she's mentioned her job. Momentarily, an image of the fifth floor restaurant comes to mind. It's time to contact her manager and confirm she'll be back at work. Fiona's latest text needs a reply.

'It's very different from this place. Part of a hotel chain

on the South Bank. When I've finished my six-month placement, I'll be going to head office.'

'You're ambitious?' he asks.

'One day I'll be part of the management. But maybe not with Mezzo Hotels.'

'You've come a long way.'

'You mean I'm not the girl at the river.'

'But you are the same. She has to be inside.'

'I'm not sure.' Imogen wonders about the child, the Nim she used to be. Perhaps it's possible to become whole.

'I remember you on the scooter. You were strong. You knew what you wanted.'

'Was it that obvious – I wanted you!'

Maxime gives a slow blink, showing his straight lashes. 'You were my first kiss.'

'Mine, too.'

'Of course, it didn't happen without Anton.'

Imogen speeds back in time. Sunlight filters through the leaves, the brakes on a bicycle squeal. 'Anton was watching.'

'Yes. He wanted to be sure I kissed you.'

'It was a dare.' Imogen folds her arms. 'How could you?'

'Don't be sad,' Maxime teases. 'We were kids. Boys do things.'

'I have to be grateful to Anton?'

'No, but don't be angry. He had a hard time with the police – all the questions they asked about Josh. Afterwards he turned the bad life around. He went to school, stopped stealing whisky. It was a good thing to happen when everything about Josh was wrong.'

The waiter arrives with the stew, a plate in each hand. Imogen scrambles to rearrange the cutlery and make space for the main course. Maxime pushes the salt and pepper pots to one side. Imogen studies the plate of food. The mussels are orange boats bobbing around a hunk of meat. Maxime tears bread ready to soak up the juices and Imogen uses a spoon to take a mussel. It's slick in her mouth and oozes sweetness.

'Do you like it?' he asks.

'C'est magnifique.' Dee's phrase is a cloak around Imogen's shoulders.

After the main course, Imogen's too stuffed to consider a dessert, although she'd like crème brûlée. She hasn't had sufficient puddings, considering she's been in France for days. But, it is time to go home, return to work. Yet she isn't ready to say goodbye to Maxime.

'I must pay this time.' Imogen lays out some notes.

'Let me buy the drinks,' he says.

'No, it's done,' she says. 'You can leave a tip.'

Maxime takes a few one-euro coins and they clank as he counts them onto the tray. 'Let's meet again tomorrow.'

'That's a good idea, but there's still one thing I need to do before I go home.'

'What's that?'

'I have to find la plage. I can't leave without going there.'

'Don't do that alone, Imogen. It will make you too sad. Wait until the end of the week and I will go with you.'

'I'll be in London then.'

Maxime's eyes are large and round. 'That is not good.'

'I'm ready to go back because you've helped me. Now that I've learned about Hector Pascal, I can begin to remember Josh properly.' Imogen drums the table with her fingers, deciding what to say next. 'You're right about what happened at la plage. It was bad luck, a chance happening that Josh was taken. You've helped me to see that. I am freer, thanks to you.'

'Okay.' Maxime squeezes Imogen's hand.

Once they reach the ring road, the traffic becomes clogged and progress is slow. Imogen studies the words sprayed onto the shutters at the rear of a lorry from Eastern Europe. The language is full of s and z combinations. It's a mystery to an English girl who can't get to grips with French. When the brake lights on the lorry flash, Maxime slams down his foot and Imogen lurches forward. The seat belt catches her and a chinking noise from the boot echoes around the space.

'I hope the bottles haven't broken,' says Maxime. 'The wine from Anton's place is in the back.'

'Perhaps we should open a bottle when we get to the hotel,' says Imogen.

'The proprietor won't like it.'

'Let's drink in my room. There's a glass in the bathroom we can share.'

'Very romantic.' Maxime smiles, showing that dimple again.

Imogen thinks about putting her hand on his thigh, stroking his muscles. Instead she stares at the flecks of mud on the windscreen, waiting for her heart to stop thumping.

At the hotel, Maxime parks the Renault and tucks a bottle of wine under his arm. There is no one at the reception desk, so they charge up the stairs like naughty schoolchildren. Inside the room, Imogen closes the curtains.

'Why the dark?' he asks.

'It's better.' Shadows are comforting, safe.

'I have a corkscrew.' Maxime strips plastic from the neck of the bottle with the knife on his key ring.

'Let's not bother about the wine,' she says.

In the half-light, Maxime takes off his shirt without unbuttoning it, pulling the whole thing over his head. His fingers dance in an invitation to embrace. The kiss starts with her lips. His mouth moves along her jaw, smearing her skin, making excitement ignite. She breathes the salty smell of him and finds her place at the nape of his neck. He works the clasps on her top, releases her arms. Pressing his hand inside her jeans, his fingers are cold and make Imogen hold her breath. Loosening the zip he drops down and draws the denim over her knees. She steps out, joining him half-naked. They fall together on the bed, making the springs play a chord.

Ditching her underwear, Imogen dives under the covers and waits. She might've longed for Maxime when she was a girl but now's her chance to have him. Her thoughts surge then scatter. She stretches her neck. Her mouth is greedy and she licks his shoulder, tasting him. Their legs entwine, sharing skin.

'You have contraception?' he asks.

'Of course,' Imogen holds a finger to his lips. 'Shush now.'

Maxime understands and nuzzles Imogen's neck but her mouth is ready for him, slippery and warm. She closes her eyes, waiting to feel his weight. He leans against her and the colours behind her eyelids merge and spark. Breath surges hot as she guides him inside, her senses taut. They crack and open each other. She writhes and stiffens, full of him. Then, like an ammonite, she curls, her heart thundering.

'I'll get some water.' He goes to the bathroom and she

hears him filling the glass. He leaves the door open and his outline is smudged by shadows. Returning, he passes the tumbler.

'Thirsty work.' Imogen drinks the water and grins at him. Sex is better than any meal.

He goes to the armchair and collects his clothes. Turning his wrist, he reads the time on his watch, the one thing he didn't take off in the rush to get laid.

'I have to get home,' he says.

'Really?'

'You know about my mother. She needs help.'

'Of course.' Imogen can't argue but disappointment wells.

He finds the other sock. 'I can come round tomorrow lunchtime. Perhaps we can visit la plage then.' The shirt goes back over his head.

'I want to go alone.'

'You're crazy.' He shakes his head and the curls spring about. 'Take the Renault. You will find the place. There's a map in the car.'

'Okay.' Imogen feels the muscles of her forehead tightening. 'It'll be okay.'

'It will.' He drops the keys onto the bed. 'Let's have dinner tomorrow night. You can tell me about la plage.'

'How will you get home?'

'I can walk, it's not far. I need to make my head clear or my mother will guess.'

'Guess what?'

'That you are special.'

Want for Maxime flares and lacerates. She'd talk about love but it's too soon. 'Thank you,' she says.

FORTY-NINE

Imogen checks her mobile. Fiona from work wants an update, asking how Imogen's doing, whether she's feeling better. The reply comprises two words: *back soon*. Draining the last of her coffee from the breakfast cup, Imogen allows la plage to fill her mind. She sees the water lapping, feels heat in the air and the straps of her swimming costume digging. She is Nim, the girl at the river, and it's time to be brave.

Gravel in the courtyard pitches her feet onward as if the world is opening to her. Inside Maxime's Renault, an air-freshener hangs from the mirror, making the car smell fresh, masking the hint of damp and rust. Imogen sits in the driver's seat and becomes acquainted with the left-hand drive. She waggles the gear stick, getting used to its position near the dashboard. When she starts the engine, the wipers are activated. She searches for the switch to turn them off. There are challenges in driving a strange car along foreign roads, but Imogen is up to the task. She reverses in a neat manoeuvre, congratulates herself, and exits through the gate.

The road to la plage takes her over a bridge and she watches traffic speeding underneath. It's true what Maxime says: people ignore the town and charge past without a glance. As she goes downhill, land encircles her and the trees on the ridge bend. The colours are dull, not grimy. An

313

absence of pavement reminds Imogen of the moment Mum's car skidded. She remains calm as she passes a clump of trees and a rock the size of a dog's kennel. Soon after, Imogen notices a sign, so faded it's hard to make out the words, but the arrow shows where the entrance to Le Camping had been. Excitement and nerves rub together.

After taking the next turning, potholes in the dirt road make driving a struggle. She tugs the steering wheel and the car moves onto the tarmac where it rolls to a stop and Imogen yanks the handbrake into place. This is it. The café stands alone; its windows are blank with the blinds drawn, as if the building's hibernating. She tries to feel kindly towards the café, for the protection it offered. A wire fence marks the boundary, four foot high and taller than Josh ever was. He'd stick his nose through the mesh given half a chance, like he did at the airport the day Dee and Ella arrived. Imogen threads a finger through the links, remembering. The path leads to a line of trees that are silver in the winter light. The oak tree is taller than the others, its branches pricking the clouds. The wind makes the tree shake its limbs and plead no, no, no. It's a warning and Imogen hesitates. She waits for the truth of what happened to protect her. Dee was there with the little children, paddling, when Josh got bored. She watched him walk back to base camp, saw him tap Mum's shoulder, but she didn't wake. Standing on the rocks, Nim had the best view over la plage but she never looked around. If she had, she might have seen Hector Pascal trampling along the road with his box on wheels. She might have seen Josh wander over, noticed the two of them together. He offered Josh a football shirt, helped him climb into the box for a ride.

Imogen approaches some concrete steps that she doesn't

remember, ugly with a bent handrail and a pockmarked platform. Looking over, she sees the river sliding past the throng of trees. The water's grey like the clouds above and languid. She needs to get closer. This is nothing like la plage. It's an empty stretch of river on a winter's day.

Broken paving stones are scattered over the slushy mud. In one direction there's nothing but scrub, so she makes for the only thing that's familiar: the oak tree. Taking a meandering route, she finds firmer ground where rocks sprout. They're shrunken from the ones in her memory, more like boulders wedged together. The stone glistens and invites Imogen to touch it. The cold makes her fingers spasm as she tries to leave a palm print. She wants to show she's made it, but there's no mark left behind.

The lowest branch of the oak tree stretches parallel to the water, the bark smoothed away. There's a large stone positioned like a diving block where the water pools. So this is where she climbed. Above her, the branch is scored with lines where ropes have been tied over the years. There's a remnant from summer, a loop of cord like a tiny stalactite that's lost its tail. This is where she played, thinking herself daring when she launched into the water. Further along, the surface ripples as the river continues its path downstream. She cleaves the memories, noting the changes, and harnesses courage. Getting closer to the water, she absorbs her surroundings. With a bat of her eyelids, the picture is captured. It replaces the old and the unreliable.

Walking back to the car, Imogen stoops to pick up a twig. Turning it, she tests its strength. They have to be strong, not floppy or prickly, Josh's instructions echo. She gathers more and the bending makes her giddy. Her head is full of Nim

315

and Josh and what it was like to be happy with Mum and Dee and Ella. When Imogen gets to the concrete slab, she has a fistful of twigs. Taking a scrunchie from her handbag, she secures the bunch. It's perfect: a little broom to clear away the dust and make her past into something useable.

Imogen spends the afternoon in town. Time slips along. She walks and rests, reads and waits. Anticipation of seeing Maxime builds as darkness gathers. She takes time in dressing for dinner. From the wardrobe she chooses the silky skirt she's been saving. The folds ruffle as she secures the waistband. She breathes the scent from the heart-shaped rose-petal bag attached to a padded hanger. In the mirror, she checks her appearance, applies scarlet lipstick and darts her tongue between her lips as she smiles. She dabs perfume on her neck and notes of vanilla linger.

In the lounge, Maxime sits in a high-back chair, waiting. How long has he been staring like that, ready for her entrance? His gaze is steady and his lips turn into a smile. Those liquid eyes tempt her. She wants to run her fingers through his hair, chase the curls around his jaw, lick his skin. Checking herself, she pins her shoulders back and moves towards him. He's on his feet and ready with the kissing routine. Cheek against cheek, his skin's clean-shaven and he's wearing a freshly ironed shirt.

'You smell nice,' he says.

'So do you.'

Maxime moves to the sofa and they sit. Imogen stares at his shoes. She likes a man who uses polish, makes an effort to impress. Turning her head, she studies his face, the contours of his nose, the angle of his jaw. He pushes a glass towards her. It's brimming with bubbles and has a pinkish hue. 'Kir Royale.'

'Lovely.' She takes a sip, recognising the hint of blackcurrant. Josh never failed to acquire a purple moustache whenever he drank juice. Her lips twitch. She wants to grin as the picture of him develops.

'Are you okay?' asks Maxime.

'I'm fine.'

'And the visit to la plage?'

'Perfectly fine,' she says.

'Good.' Maxime tips his head and shows his dimple. 'And the Renault?'

'No dings or dints. The car's rather like me, in one piece.' Imogen reflects on the journey and a sense of triumph stirs. 'Thanks for the loan.'

They choose from the bar menu, nothing heavy. Imogen orders salad and he has a steak sandwich. She's hungry, working through the plate until the last tomato is gone. He gives Imogen a nudge and abandons the second half of the sandwich as they race for the bedroom. There, Imogen remains ravenous, kissing his neck, gnawing his skin, tasting him. They fumble to the bed, discarding clothes as they go. She lies on the covers, the throw slipping beneath her as she snakes her legs around his hips. Their bodies collide and she guides him inside where it is slippery and warm. When he stiffens, she arches her back and all is quiet. Imogen slides away, finding her space on the bed. She pulls at the cover and launches the sheet. It floats like a parachute then drapes over them while they rest.

Maxime stumbles in the half-light, collects his clothes and dresses. Under the covers, Imogen remains warm. The buckle on his belt clanks as he secures it, and coins in his pocket jangle as he swings on his jacket.

'I have to go,' he says.

'I know.' She can't begrudge Maxime the need to be there for his mother.

'I will see you again,' he says. 'When I come to London.'

'Of course.'

There isn't more to say. Maxime cradles his hands around her face and offers a final kiss. It's another good memory to pack in her bag and take home.

The flat is tidy. Thick cream emulsion frames the view into the garden where shrubs show their waxy leaves and buds are furled tight like pearls. Secured to the wall is a batten, ready to hang the new Roman blind. A smell of fresh paint lingers. Mum removes the rectangle of fabric from its wrapping; the geometric pattern will go with the room, dressing the window, a finishing touch. She hands Imogen a corner and together they stretch the blind taut, matching the lines of Velcro to secure it. The pull cords fly and stick to the fabric in swirls. Imogen gathers them into a tidy line.

'Here.' Mum passes Imogen a weight. The metal is cool in her palm. 'You can finish the job.'

Imogen feeds the strings through and ties a knot. Testing the blind, she draws up the folds but they bunch together at one side. She lets the blind drop, blocking out the daylight.

'Shall I do it?' asks Mum.

'No, thanks.' Loosening the knot, Imogen redraws the cords and makes sure they are completely even. This time the folds are level and she secures the cord around the cleat, turning the strings in a figure of eight. The action reminds her of the pattern her scooter made, racing over the tarmac as she turned in circles, scooting in France.

'That's everything done.' Mum goes to the kitchen and draws

water, filling the kettle to make tea. While she's busy, Imogen finds the page on her laptop that shows the cartoon image of a large woman with corkscrew curls. Dee's a freelance journalist now, living in the same place as she did thirteen years ago. Imogen wonders what Ella is up to, but she'll find out soon enough. Mum carries the mugs and places them on a low table. She sits beside Imogen on the bed and stares at the screen. A smile flutters around her lips.

'Are you ready to ring Dee?' asks Imogen.

'You dial the number,' she says.

So that's what Imogen does.

ACKNOWLEDGEMENTS

To those who supported my academic and creative journey, which resulted in *The String Games,* thanks to Philip Gross, Diana Wallace, Stephen Knight and my fellow students at the University of South Wales.

To those who have championed my creative writing, thanks to Carol McGrath, Sue Stephenson and Denise Barnes. Also thanks to members of the Wimborne Writing Group led by Sarah Barr.

I have enjoyed being part of online communities during the process of writing this novel. My thanks to #writingchat and #womenwritersnet plus many wonderful readers and book bloggers including Jessie Cahalin and Anne Williams.

Thank you, for your on-going support, to the Cerne Abbas Readers.

For professional help with editing, thank you to Helen Baggott and Charlotte Maddox. Also thank you to Nina Kilham, Elizabeth Reeder, and Ian Stephen for feedback on the novel.

Thank you to the lovely people at Victorina Press, who have given *The String Games* a good home.

Finally, thank you to my supportive family, who have understood my need to write when I could have been spending time with them.